Even as Chiara spoke, she wondered that the words slipped off her tongue so easily. Never in her life had she opened herself this way to another. Never in her life had she confessed a weakness to another.

"Of me?" Luca asked.

"Of you. Of myself. Of the confusion in my mind." She lowered her head into her hands. "Everything used to be so clear. I knew my path. I knew what I had to do." She pulled in an unsteady breath. "Now nothing is clear. Nothing."

That wasn't quite true, she thought. It was clear that there was something between them. Something deep and real, far beyond her fears, her visions.

Something she was afraid to look at more closely....

Dear Reader,

Next month, Harlequin Historicals® turns ten years old! But we have such a terrific lineup this month, we thought we'd start celebrating early. To begin, longtime historical author Nina Beaumont returns this month with *The Shadowed Heart*, set in eighteenth-century Europe. In this suspenseful story, our beautiful gypsy heroine seeks revenge against the man she believes harmed her sister. She finds him, only she senses that he can't be the one, especially when she finds herself falling in love with him....

Also out for revenge is Jesse Kincaid, of MONTANA MAVERICKS: RETURN TO WHITEHORN fame, when he kidnaps his enemy's mail-order bride in *Wild West Wife*, by bestselling Silhouette® author Susan Mallery. In *A Warrior's Honor*, the next medieval in Margaret Moore's popular WARRIOR SERIES, a knight is tricked by a fellow nobleman into abducting a beautiful lady, but, guided by honor—and love—vows to rescue her from his former friend.

Laurie Grant, who is known for her stirring Medievals and gritty Westerns, returns with a delightful new story, *The Duchess and the Desperado*. Here, a rancher turned fugitive inadvertently becomes a bodyguard to the very visible Duchess of Malvern when her life is threatened during a goodwill tour of the American West.

Whatever your tastes in reading, you'll be sure to find a romantic journey back to the past between the covers of a Harlequin Historical®.

Sincerely,

Tracy Farrell
Senior Editor

Please address questions and book requests to:
Harlequin Reader Service
U.S.: 3010 Walden Ave., P.O. Box 1325, Buffalo, NY 14269
Canadian: P.O. Box 609, Fort Erie, Ont. L2A 5X3

THE
SHADOWED
HEART

NINA BEAUMONT

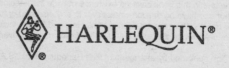
HARLEQUIN®

TORONTO • NEW YORK • LONDON
AMSTERDAM • PARIS • SYDNEY • HAMBURG
STOCKHOLM • ATHENS • TOKYO • MILAN • MADRID
PRAGUE • WARSAW • BUDAPEST • AUCKLAND

To Kathy Ketonen Clark, my "Dearest Roommate."
Thanks for making life in Room 423 easy
and for all the years of friendship since.

ISBN 0-373-29022-5

THE SHADOWED HEART

Books by Nina Beaumont

NINA BEAUMONT

is of Russian parentage and has a family tree that includes Count Stroganoff and a Mongolian Khan. A real cosmopolitan, she was born in Salzburg and grew up in Massachusetts before moving to Austria, where she lived for twenty-five years.

Although she has relocated to the Seattle area, her European ties are still strong, so she plans to stick with the exotic settings she has had the opportunity to get to know firsthand.

Books and music are her first loves, but she also enjoys painting watercolors and making pottery.

ACKNOWLEDGMENTS

My thanks to Karen David of Cleveland, OH,
Maria Lujan de Peralta and Phoenix of Seattle, WA, and
Rita Louise of Everett, WA, for the information they
shared with me regarding clairvoyance.

Chapter One

Venice, October 1767, the first day of Carnival

Chiara's hand stole toward the slim dagger concealed at her waist as the man who held her arm tightly turned her away from the brightly lit Piazza San Marco. Her breath quickened slightly as he steered her down a shadowy passageway, which was just wide enough for three people to walk abreast, but the handle of the weapon dug comfortingly into the palm of her hand and kept panic at bay.

If he noticed her apprehension, the man ignored it as he hurried her along. Finally he stopped in front of a door, the wood faded and cracked with age and moisture. Raising his hand, he knocked twice with his fist.

"We're here," he announced, giving her a fleeting look.

"You told me that you would take me to the house of a great lady." Chiara wrenched her arm out of his grasp and shifted away, prepared to run or to use her dagger, whichever seemed more expedient. "I do not believe that a great lady would go near such a miserable place.''

The man looked down at the girl. The flickering light of the single lantern that hung above the door gave her skin a sallow cast, but he had seen it in daylight and knew that it had the golden color of a ripe apricot. The eyes of a startling blue were wary but held no fear.

She had spirit, he thought. He would keep her for a while and she would make him a nice sum. And when he was done with her, there were plenty of back-alley pimps who would take her off his hands. He felt a small flash of guilt, but it was easy to suppress it with the image of his daughter, who lay still in her bed no matter what new and expensive treatments the doctor invented for her.

''It is as I told you. This is the *casino* of Signora Giulietta Baldini, the widow of Ser Luigi Baldini.'' He had no trouble injecting a smooth confidence into his voice, for—this time—he happened to be telling the truth.

''If you were from Venice,'' he continued, ''you would know that he was a very rich man. And you would know that Venetian ladies receive guests in their homes only on formal occasions. They have little houses like this one where their guests can enjoy themselves as they please in more intimate surroundings.'' His fleshy mouth curved in a mocking grin. ''But isn't that something you should know? If you truly have the sight, that is?'' He reached for her arm.

''I see what is given to me to see. Sometimes it is a great deal and sometimes it is nothing at all.'' Chiara evaded his grasp. ''Having the sight does not make me all-knowing.''

The man laughed, the sound echoing a little between the high buildings. ''You don't have to be all-knowing, little one.''

In fact, he thought, it was better for her that she was not. He leaned down toward her, his movement distracting her from the hand that snaked out from beneath his voluminous black cloak to curl tightly around her arm.

''All you have to do is tell a few fortunes like you did in the piazza this afternoon.'' She had wrapped a shabby black shawl tightly around her, but an expanse of pale skin remained visible above the small gathered ruffle of her blouse and his gaze skimmed approvingly over her. ''And be pleasant to Signora Giulietta's guests.''

The door opened with a creak and Chiara turned to see a footman in costly green-and-gold livery holding a large candelabra.

''You are late, Manelli. Signora Giulietta is getting impatient.'' The footman turned sharply and moved toward the narrow staircase.

Her fingers on the hilt of her dagger, Chiara allowed herself to be pulled into the small entry.

A small table with curved legs, chairs upholstered in rich, wine red velvet and expensive candles in gilt sconces on the walls gave some small reassurance that this house was indeed that of a great lady. Laughter and the sound of a mandolin drifted down the stairs, together with the scent of coffee, perfume and warm candle wax.

She thought of the coins she had earned today and tucked into the shabby purse she wore around her waist. She thought of the coins she had been promised for the evening's work and how they would enable her to pay for her sister's care at the small farm she had found near Padua. But, most of all, she thought of how it brought her one step closer to finding her father and getting the revenge that had been the focus of her life for more than two years.

She lifted her eyes to the florid face of the man the footman had called Manelli. "Let go of my arm," she said softly.

As Manelli looked into the girl's eyes, they lost all expression until they became as blank as glass.

She sensed greed and an almost casual brutishness, but the anxiety she sensed was stronger than either one so she looked at that more closely. An image rose of a young woman lying in a bed. She saw the woman sit up and hold out her hand. *"Babbo,"* the woman said and smiled.

Chiara blinked and focused on Manelli's face. He had grown a little pale beneath the ruddiness and she gave a satisfied little nod.

Manelli watched the strange light fade from the girl's eyes. He felt an icy chill along his back and told himself that it was only the October wind blowing in from the still-open door.

"Don't worry. Your daughter will be healthy again." Manelli was staring at her. Then she saw a desperate hope seep into his eyes and she smiled. "It is so," she said. "I have seen it."

Turning, she moved to follow the footman up the stairs toward the blazing lights.

Irritated by Giulietta's inane chatter, Luca Zeani turned away and slung one leg carelessly over the arm of his chair. Picking up a mandolin, he plucked its strings absently. He heard the tinkle of coins in the next room and briefly considered joining one of the games. Perhaps a few hands of *faraone* at high stakes would speed his pulse a bit and burn off the indolence that had crept into his blood since his return to Venice.

But the languor that seemed to infect all of Venice kept him in his chair, his long, slender fingers idly strumming the mandolin. His half-open eyes were fixed on a gilded stucco border near the ceiling, but what he saw was the sunlit blue of the open sea.

The ache of longing for the sharp, clean air of the sea drifted through him, but even that did not rouse him from the languidness. It was so easy to give oneself to pleasure in this city where no one seemed to think of anything else.

The atmosphere of temptation and sensuality gripped you like a fever, he mused, making the pleasures offered the only reality. More real than the fact that he was in Venice to speak to the Great Council in the name of Admiral Angelo Emo, demanding more men and ships to fight the Barbary pirates. More real than the masked man who had approached him to speak seductively of freedom and renewed vigor for the sickly Venetian Republic.

Luca saw Giulietta rise from her seat beside him, and he gave a small sigh of relief. She was very beautiful and in bed she was as accomplished as a high-priced courtesan, but she was a tiresome woman. The showy necklace of rubies and diamonds that he had thought to give her as a parting gift had been in a cabinet in his apartments for weeks, but somehow it always seemed simpler to allow things to go on as they were.

When he felt the touch on his shoulder, Luca

looked up in surprise, not having heard anyone approach him. But there was no one beside him.

Sitting up straight, he looked around him to see who could have touched him. Across from him, an elderly man dozed in his chair and, on his other side, a masked couple was engaged in such fervid flirtation that they seemed in imminent danger of forgetting that they were in public.

He looked across the room to where Giulietta stood speaking to a heavyset man and a tall young woman who was wearing a multicolored skirt that molded her hips—and again felt a touch. But this time he would have sworn that he felt the touch of a woman's hand against his skin just above his heart.

Putting the mandolin aside, he leaned forward, his hands propped on his ivory-colored silk breeches. Deliberately he met the young woman's gaze. She was staring at him with such undisguised animosity that he stiffened, his own eyes narrowing.

Intrigued, he rose and sauntered to where Giulietta stood, cupping his hand around her neck more by habit than desire.

"What have we here?" he asked, never taking his gaze away from the girl's eyes, which were the color of the Adriatic when the midday sun was upon it. Eyes that held hatred, more relentless and cold than he had ever encountered.

"A Gypsy fortune-teller. She will look into our guests' future and then—" she paused and gave a malicious little laugh "—entertain them. An amusing little diversion, don't you think, *caro?*" She looked up at Luca, leaning back to press her neck still more firmly against his fingers.

Giulietta's words passed Luca by unheard as he

stared into the girl's eyes. He had made his share of enemies in his twenty-seven years, but he had never seen such loathing, not even over the point of a sword.

For the first time in weeks he felt the prickle of real excitement. A riddle to solve, he thought. A riddle involving a woman whose face would have done justice to one of Titian's portraits. As he tore his gaze away from her eyes to allow it to drift over her, he felt an absurd pleasure in her lack of artifice.

Her curls fell beyond her shoulders in a tangled black mass and had obviously never seen the creams and lotions Venetian women used to bleach their hair to a fashionable blond color. Her lips, the color of strawberries, needed no rouge. Her golden skin was untouched by powder and, instead of a beauty patch, there was a smudge of dirt on her cheek.

He felt his body tighten with that first, pure, sweet rush of arousal, untainted by skillful tricks or stimulants. His gaze returned to her eyes.

They were still trained on him, but they were strangely unfocused now as if she were looking far beyond his face. Baffled by the sudden change, he found his interest piqued still further. This was definitely a puzzle he wanted to solve.

It was him. Chiara stared over the lady's shoulder, not quite believing what she was seeing. That hair the color of ripe wheat, unpowdered and uncurled in defiance of fashion, merely tied back carelessly with a dark ribbon. That chiseled, perfect profile.

No, she thought, shaking her head to clear it. She must be mistaken. She could not possibly have the good fortune to stumble across the man she hated so fiercely. Perhaps even more than she hated her father.

Then he turned to face her and she knew that she had not been mistaken. There could not be another mouth like that in the whole world, its sensuality promising both pleasure and cruelty. This is what Lucifer must have looked like, she thought. The fallen angel who had chosen to rule in hell rather than serve in heaven.

She watched him rise and come toward her and, despite her hatred, which was so real its bitter taste lay on her tongue, she found herself much too aware of the man's beauty.

He stood in front of her, close enough that she could have reached out and touched him. Beneath the cover of her shawl, her hand moved to the dagger hidden in the folds of her clothes and touched the hilt. This dagger had spilled his blood once before and it would spill his blood again.

She drew her hand away from the metal with an effort. Not today, she told herself. She would have her revenge, she swore, but not today.

As she stared at him, the hatred inside her was suddenly pushed aside as if by an invisible hand and she heard a voice within her. The voice of the spirit that sometimes called to her, telling her to dip down to that shadowy region of impressions and images and look inside the man who stood before her.

She saw light. A clear, pure light like the rays of the rising sun. She searched for the darkness, for the evil that she was certain would be there. But all she saw was the light. Surely this was some kind of trick, a clever ruse to blind her. It was then that she saw it.

Behind the figure wreathed in light, she saw the dark apparition. She recognized his perfect features, his fine form. Recognized, too, the evil aura that surrounded the dark figure. The aura that was almost palpable.

So he was versed in the secrets of the occult, she thought. He had wanted to blind her with his light so that she would not see his darkness. But he would not succeed, she thought triumphantly, for she had seen the evil.

She pulled herself back to reality and saw that he was still looking at her. There was more than curiosity in his eyes. He was looking at her in the way that men looked at women.

But it was not the devilish, naked lust that she had seen that night in the Gypsy camp on the outskirts of a small town in Tuscany. The lust that had been glittering in his dark eyes even after he had slaked it on the unwilling body of her sister.

This time it appeared in a different guise. It was a desire that was far more subtle and seductive. For a fraction of a moment it reached out to touch her before she was able to draw back and protect herself against it.

"Well, get on with it."

Giulietta's sharp voice intruded into Luca's sensual reverie. He watched the odd glow fade from the young Gypsy's eyes. For a fraction of a moment before the hatred returned, he saw a softening, as if he had touched a string within her that had resonated with a harmonious sound.

"But get rid of that ugly black shawl of hers."

The petulant tone of his mistress's voice had Luca

looking at her with irritation. It occurred to him that this was the strongest emotion that he had felt toward her in days. Perhaps it really was time to finally give her the ruby necklace and send her on her way.

"And you really could have cleaned her up a bit, Manelli." The ivory sticks of her fan of fine painted parchment clattered as she waved it in front of Chiara's face. "But I suppose some might find that wild, crude look appealing." She shrugged. "Oh, well, just make sure my guests are well pleased, Manelli. I'm counting on you."

Obediently Manelli plucked the shawl from Chiara's shoulders and pulled her toward the first group of guests, who were already tittering expectantly.

Giulietta hooked her hand through Luca's arm to take him away from the clutch of people who had drawn close together to hear what the young Gypsy had to say, but he resisted.

"You seem inordinately interested in her, *caro*." Her rouged mouth pursed in a pout and she leaned close, inviting his caress.

"Wasn't that what you wanted?" Luca raised an eyebrow. "To pique your guests' interest?"

"But you're not a guest, you are—"

He lifted a finger to her mouth to silence her and, extracting his arm from her grasp, shifted so that he could watch the young Gypsy's face.

The guests crowded around her, thrusting their palms toward her, their voices raised in a babble of questions.

"I do not read palms."

Luca straightened at the sound of her voice. It was low and husky for a girl so young. A voice that would go well with Gypsy fires.

"I cannot look at your whole life. You can ask me a question and if I am allowed to see the answer, I can tell you."

Murmurs greeted her statement, which had been made in a clear voice that carried no apology.

"What a sham," Giulietta hissed. "Manelli will not see a lira from me."

Absently Luca shushed her as someone wearing a *bautta,* a kind of domino that was the simplest and most popular carnival disguise, stepped forward. The molded white mask covered the upper two thirds of the face and a black lace hood fell to the shoulders, making it impossible to say if the person beneath the disguise was a man or a woman.

The figure briefly lifted the black tricorn hat in a mocking salute and sketched a bow, revealing the dark silk breeches beneath the floor-length black cloak.

"Tell me, will the woman I love finally surrender?" The question was asked in a scratchy whisper.

Luca watched the young Gypsy's eyes again grow unfocused, glassy. She went so completely still that she did not even seem to be breathing.

Minutes passed. Then Luca saw her chest move with a deep breath, saw her eyes lose that odd, empty expression.

"The woman you love will surrender many times," she said. "But she will never surrender her heart."

"Why not?" The scratchy whisper asked.

"Because her heart belongs only to herself."

The figure made a gesture of disbelief with a gloved hand.

Chiara looked directly into the eyes visible

through the slits of the mask. "No man will ever love you better than you love yourself, *signora*."

Gasps of surprise and flustered giggles greeted her words.

Manelli gripped her arm and leaned close to her ear. "In Venice, the mask is to be respected above all things."

Chiara wrenched her arm away and stepped away from the man's smell of onions and cheap wine. "Those who do not want to know the truth should not ask me questions."

"Leave the poor girl alone," the masked figure said, the voice undisguised now and obviously female. "She spoke only the truth."

The woman laughed, reached into a pocket and handed Chiara a gold coin. Then she turned sharply, her cloak belling out for a moment before it settled around her again, and strode toward the door.

There was a moment of stillness, for everyone had recognized the voice, although no one was impolite enough to acknowledge that openly. It was the fabulously wealthy and eccentric Signora Laura Paradini. Laura Paradini, who had broken every rule in an already permissive society. Laura Paradini, who had outlived three husbands while half the patrician women in Venice took the veil for lack of marriage-minded men.

Everyone in the room seemed to start talking simultaneously at this sign of approval and began to press closer to the Gypsy. Suddenly everyone was eager to have the Gypsy answer their questions.

But Chiara pushed her way past the people milling around her. She had to talk to the woman. For the few moments that she had looked inside this woman, she had felt the presence of her father. She had not seen him, but he had been there just the same.

She had to know if the woman knew him. Perhaps she was the key to finding him. Perhaps she was the key to her revenge.

"Signora!" Chiara reached the door to see that the woman was already halfway down the stairs. "Wait, please."

The woman turned, her mask ghostly in the dim light. "I must hasten to find that surrender you promised me." She raised her hand in a wave. "Perhaps we will meet again." She waved again and ran down the stairs, her cloak floating behind her.

"What do you think you're doing? Are you mad?" Manelli grabbed her, afraid that she would flee. He had already seen that Signora Giulietta was not pleased with him.

Chiara shook off his hands. She would find the woman, she swore to herself, and through her she would find her father—after she had wrought the vengeance that a kind fate had placed in her path. Her eyes searched out the blond man in the crowd.

Yes, she thought as she returned to where the crowd stood waiting for her. Today had brought her good fortune, and vengeance—more vengeance than she had ever hoped for—would be hers.

His arms folded across his chest, Luca leaned against the wall that was covered with fine leather stamped with a delicate gold pattern. He had not taken his eyes off the girl for the past hour. He had watched her as she had seemed to descend time after time into some secret place, her eyes becoming unfocused and blank, her body growing as still as if she were dead. And when she moved again, she had every time said something that impressed the questioner with its accuracy.

He had always considered himself an enlightened, pragmatic man. A man who did not believe in the supernatural—not in Gypsy fortune-tellers, not in divine deities—so he was certain that this had to be some kind of a trick. And he was determined to find out just what her trick was.

And why did she look at him with such hatred in her eyes? Perhaps he could change the hatred to something softer. He acknowledged the excitement she aroused in him. Acknowledged it and relished it. It had been a long time since he had felt anything so strong or real.

"No! That is untrue what you say there!" The voice rose hysterically over the hum of conversation. "I will have you turned over to the Inquisitors—"

Giulietta moved quickly toward the shouting man, her hooped skirts of oyster-shell colored satin making her look like a caravel in full sail.

"But, my dear Savini, how can you get so worked up about the words of a silly little Gypsy." She wound her arm around his and tugged him away, at the same time signaling Manelli with her eyes. "Would you expect her to speak Gospel?" She smiled up at him. "Now I have a little proposal for you on how we shall resolve this." Leaning closer, she began to whisper in his ear.

Luca watched how Giulietta skillfully soothed the disturbance. Within moments, she had poor Savini under her spell. The guests had dispersed around the room and were drinking coffee and brandy again, gossiping desultorily as if nothing unusual had hap-

pened. And Manelli had bundled the Gypsy girl off
to one of the small side rooms.

Luca pushed away from the wall and followed
them.

Chapter Two

"Are you insane?" Manelli shouted. "How can you speak of such things as alchemy?"

Luca stepped into the room and closed the door behind him so softly that neither Manelli nor the girl heard him.

"I know nothing of al-alchemy." Chiara stumbled over the unfamiliar word. "I only said what I saw. And I saw the man putting a black stone in a bowl of liquid and waiting for it to turn into gold."

"*Dio*, stop it." He pressed his hands to his ears. "Just listening to you would make me guilty in the eyes of the Inquisitors."

"Why did you bring me here, if you did not wish me to speak the truth?" Chiara demanded. She wanted to run, but something kept her standing there, as if her feet had been planted in the ground. "Now I want the coins you promised me." She held out her hand.

"*Sei pazza!* You're crazy!" Manelli tapped his hand against his forehead. "You may have called down the Inquisitors upon my head." He began to pace. "The bravest man trembles at the mere thought of the dungeons in the Doge's palace. And now you—'' he pointed a meaty finger at her ''—you dare to ask for money?''

''You promised you would pay me to use the sight.'' There was no petulance, no whining in her voice, only a resolute tenaciousness.

''Listen to me!'' He stopped in front of her. ''Be grateful if all I do is not pay you.''

Chiara stared up at him. Rage had lived within her since she was a child, watching her father treat her mother worse than he would treat a servant. Now it sprang to life, just as a smoldering fire springs into flame at a breath of air. Her arm brushed against the dagger at her waist, but it did not even occur to her to reach for it. She had a better weapon for this toad of a man.

''It would not go well for you to cheat me.'' Her voice lowering, she shifted closer to him. ''Do you know what Gypsies do to those who cheat them?''

Paling, Manelli retreated from her, making the sign against *il malocchio,* the evil eye, with forefinger and little finger of his right hand. ''I—if you promise to do what you are told, I will pay you.'' His gaze shifted away from her face.

Chiara's eyes narrowed. If he thought to cheat her, she thought, she would—

''Leave us, Manelli. I wish to speak to the girl.''

Like matching puppets, both whirled to face Luca.

''B-but, *signore,* Signora Giulietta—''

''Leave Signora Giulietta to me.'' Although he was not aware of it, Luca's chiseled features grew as cold as if they were carved from ice at the unaccustomed contradiction. ''Out.'' He tipped his head toward the door.

Manelli felt sweat begin to dribble down his back at the icy anger in Signor Luca Zeani's black eyes. But still he hesitated to obey, for he knew well what cruelties Signora Giulietta was capable of.

Luca heard the door behind him open and turned to see Giulietta with Savini in tow.

"What are you doing here, Luca?" Giulietta demanded.

"I could ask you the same question, *cara*." Even as he addressed her, his eyes skimmed over Savini. The man was staring at the Gypsy girl with undisguised lecherousness and Luca's eyes narrowed as he returned his gaze to his mistress. "Or have you brought Savini here to take his pound of flesh from the girl for telling the truth?"

Chiara's eyes widened as the terrible understanding of what was happening penetrated her mind, why she had been brought to this room. She understood that this scarecrow of a man with his protuberant eyes intended to take her body. And all these people standing around her intended to let him.

She suppressed the cry of protest and fear that rose in her throat. Like a wild animal circled by hunters, she remained perfectly still for one moment, her eyes darting from one to the other. Then she ran.

Luca had his back to the girl, but by some instinct he was aware of her intention before she ever moved. Spinning on his heel to face her, he blocked her way so that she slammed fully into his body. Capturing her in his arms, he held her relentlessly as she began to fight like a wild thing, twisting and turning within his harsh embrace.

Confident of his muscular body, toughened from

years of seafaring life, Luca curbed his strength, not wishing to hurt her.

Grimly determined, Chiara fought on. He was a soft fop, she assured herself, with his silks and brocades and lace. He was evil and brutal, but he was a coward. He had run from her once before, after all.

Twisting her body around its axis, she raised her bent arm as high as she could and then drove it back, plowing her elbow into his middle.

Luca swore as the girl's elbow struck his midriff, but he only tightened his grip. Still she fought him. Suddenly she bent like a poplar sapling in the wind and, before he realized what she intended, she had sunk her teeth into his wrist.

Dropping all pretense of civility, he grabbed a handful of her hair and jerked her head back. "Be still, damn it," he growled into her ear. "I mean you no harm."

"No!" Her voice rose. The memory of how his eyes had glittered so demonically that night almost two years ago enabled her to fight on even though her strength was flagging. "Let me go!" She managed to free one hand and, forming her fingers into claws, gouged deep scratches into his cheek before he captured her hand again.

His patience snapped and, unleashing his full power, Luca manacled her hands with his and twisted them behind her back, ignoring her cry of pain. Holding her wrists with one hand, he pressed his other arm against her throat, drawing her flush against him.

As he pinned her against him, Chiara stilled, the strength flowing out of her abruptly, as if he had severed some lifeline by pressing her against his body. The light surrounded her again. And warmth.

She shook her head in disbelief, as she looked for the dark apparition, but this time it eluded her.

As she surfaced, she found herself staring directly into his eyes. They were the color of the night sky at its darkest hour, but there were tiny specks of gold strewn throughout the blackness, like points of light. She waited for the malevolent glitter, but it did not come. Then she realized that the eyes were smiling at her.

"Well?" he asked, his smile coloring his voice. "Have you decided to surrender?"

Because her life had taught her that it was sometimes wise to give up to be able to fight another time, she lowered her eyes in a gesture that could be taken for assent.

"I do not surrender," she said softly. "But I cannot fight against your strength."

"A wise decision. Now if I release you, will you remain still and not try to maim me?"

She gave a jerky nod.

"Look at me."

Hesitating for a long moment, Chiara felt him push her chin upward with his arm. Reluctantly she lifted her lids. As their eyes met and held, she felt the hatred within her pall. Panicking, she tried to hold it, but all she could see was the light that rose from the recesses of her mind to surround the man who held her, until he seemed enclosed in a bubble of light.

Luca saw the panic in her eyes and felt something within himself soften.

"I won't hurt you." He lowered his arm slightly so that it lay just above her breasts. Cautiously he loosened the fingers that shackled her wrists.

When Chiara immediately tried to move away from him, his hands tightened again.

"Stay close until I'm sure that you're not going to run." His tone was mild, but the command there was unmistakable.

"You said you would release me." Her voice was low, furious.

"And so I will." He smiled. "Just humor me for a bit and stay close." He lowered his arm. It brushed her breasts and he felt his body stir. He curved his hand over her hip, to make certain that she did not run and because it pleased him to touch her.

"What a touching scene." Giulietta raised her hands and tapped her fingers against one another in a parody of applause. "If I had known you had a taste for violence, *caro*, I would have obliged you earlier. Now—" she struck her closed fan sharply against her palm "—I suggest that we return to business."

"And I suggest that it is time for Signor Savini to retire," Luca said smoothly. "I am told that the Great Council meets early in the morning."

"But you promised—" Savini began, his voice rising to a whine.

"I'm sure you misunderstood." Luca's mouth curved in a smile that would not have looked out of place on a wolf. "Signora Giulietta only meant she shall endeavor that nothing that transpired here tonight shall become common knowledge."

"The damage has been done and people will talk. You know that. Gossip is the favorite pastime in Venice." Savini's voice rose. "The least you can do is to—"

Luca felt the girl stiffen and he gave her a reassuring squeeze. *"Buona notte, signore."*

Savini opened his mouth to speak, but then he closed it with a snap. With a glare in Luca's direction, he whirled to leave. Giulietta reached out to stop him, but he shook off her hand and swept out of the room, slamming the door behind him.

"Now look at what you've done." Giulietta turned on Luca, her dark eyes snapping with displeasure. "What kind of game are you playing?"

"I dislike seeing those who cannot defend themselves coerced." Suddenly conscious of the warmth of the girl's body beneath his hand, the irony of his words occurred to him and he released her.

Chiara looked up sharply at him. What unspeakable gall, she thought, to speak like that when he was so good at coercion himself. She remembered only too well how she had come upon him holding her sister's hands pinned above her head much as he had held her own behind her back. And she remembered Donata's terrified eyes. The memory brought a comforting return of the hatred just as she felt his hand lift away from her hip, the tips of his fingers lingering for a moment before he released her completely.

"You've been reading too many philosophical treatises from France, *caro*. You seem to have begun to believe all that tripe about the purity of the savage and the rights of humanity." The melodiousness of Giulietta's voice could not hide the vibration of anger. "Now I suggest we let Manelli take her back to wherever it was he found her."

Taking his cue, Manelli hurried forward. "Thank you, *signora, signore*." He grabbed Chiara's arm so violently that a seam tore, leaving one sleeve of her

linen blouse barely hanging on by a few threads.
"Come, now. Come."

"Let me go." She tried to escape his grip, but his
meaty fingers dug into her flesh unmercifully.

As she twisted from side to side to escape Manelli,
her gaze met the night eyes. She hated Luca. Someday she would kill him. But he had been kind to her
a few moments ago. He had touched her briefly with
gentleness. All these thoughts came together in a
twisted kind of logic. And her eyes asked for his
help.

"Didn't you hear what she said, Manelli? Let her
go."

Manelli's fleshy mouth fell open as he stared at
Luca. "But, *signore,* she belongs to me."

"Are you saying she is your slave?"

"No!" Chiara cried, horrified at the word. "I am
no man's slave."

Manelli's eyes darted to Signora Giulietta and he
saw her almost imperceptible nod. "Yes, *signore,* my
slave."

Chiara struggled against Manelli's hands. This
couldn't be happening to her, she thought. Surely she
would wake up and discover it was all a bad dream.

"Good," Luca said. "Then I will buy her from
you."

Chiara spun her head to look at him. Going still
with shock and disbelief, she watched him dip his
hand into a pocket of his brocade waistcoat.

"That would appear to be too little for a good
female slave," he said matter-of-factly, looking at
the coins in his palm. "You will not deny me a loan,
my dear, will you?"

"Wh-what?" Giulietta sputtered as he turned toward her.

As if she had graciously consented, he reached out and undid the clasp of her necklace of large square-cut amethysts surrounded by small pearls. He jiggled the necklace in his hand as if testing its weight and then, without warning, tossed it in Manelli's direction.

Manelli let Chiara go and grabbed the necklace in both hands. Terror warred with greed in his eyes as his gaze swept around the room. Then, like a rat scurrying for cover when faced by two dangerous cats, he ran out of the room.

For a long moment, all three remained perfectly still, as if they were part of a tableau vivant, a living portrayal of a painting. Then, while Luca remained still, the women moved, Giulietta sweeping forward, all unsheathed claws and fury, Chiara stepping back.

"How dare you insult me like that." Giulietta's voice was high and ill-tempered. "Just what are you doing?"

"I will never be your slave. Never."

The Gypsy's voice was low and throaty. Luca found it as arousing as a caress, but he ignored her as if she hadn't spoken, and continued to look at his mistress.

"You have eyes and ears, my dear. I would think it was perfectly obvious what I am doing." His mouth curved in the glib smile of a man well skilled in pacifying troublesome women. "I've just bought myself a slave."

"Do what you wish in private, but how can you do this to my face?" Giulietta demanded.

"I have done nothing but purchase a slave." He emphasized his shrug by raising his hands slightly palm upward. "Do moderate your histrionics, my dear."

"Don't tell me you do not intend to take her to your bed." Her lips trembled. "You're my lover. How can you betray me thus?"

"Your lover, perhaps, but not your *cavaliere servente,* sworn to serve you in all ways." Luca expelled a sharp breath, no longer trying to hide his irritation. "You were eager enough to welcome me to your bed without any promises. And, I would remind you, I have never made you any."

Giulietta's mouth thinned as she fought for composure. "We will speak later. I must see to my guests now."

"We will speak another time, my dear." It was definitely time to send Giulietta on her way, Luca thought. He would send her the rubies tomorrow. "I find that I am not in the mood for more talk tonight."

Giulietta looked from Luca to the Gypsy, then back to her lover. "I see." Fisting her hands in the folds of her skirt, she managed to keep her tone light. "Amuse yourself well, *caro*. Just make sure you wash off her smell before you come to my bed again."

Sending a glance that was both contemptuous and furious in Chiara's direction, she flounced out of the room.

The room was so silent that all Chiara heard was her own breathing. He stood perfectly still, looking at her, his eyes intent.

She concentrated, trying to see what was inside his

mind. She *knew* there was evil within him. Why could she not see it? Why could she not even feel its presence? Yes, there was a darkness within him, but it was like the darkness of a shadow where there is much light.

"Come closer."

"No." She threw up her chin. "I am not your slave."

"Come closer, I said." A fine edge of steel crept into his mild voice. "If you knew me better, you would know that I am not known for my patience."

She could not feel his evil, but she felt his power. And still she defied him. It was her only chance.

"I am a free woman and I have no wish to know you better."

His face changed, so subtly that she could not have described it. It was Lucifer, she thought again, and he was displeased with what he saw in his kingdom. Fear rose so suddenly that she had no time to control it before her breath seemed to congeal in her throat.

"I'm free," she repeated. "You cannot force me to do anything." Her voice sounded winded and she took a moment to draw a deep breath. "Except by your superior strength."

"But you're wrong. I bought you from Manelli." Tucking the tips of his fingers into the pockets of his waistcoat, he spoke as lightly as if it were a matter of a basket of fruit. "And slavery is still quite legal in Venice, you know."

"I do not believe that it is legal to sell what you do not own." The brave words could not mask the sick feeling in her stomach. "Manelli did not own me."

"No? Why should I believe you?" Even as he

spoke the words, Luca asked himself if he had gone mad. Why was he tormenting her when it had been his intention to purchase her freedom and let her go? By all the saints, he had never owned a slave in his life. The thought alone was repugnant to him. Yet, within moments, the need to keep her had become an obsession.

"I do not lie." She straightened.

She was afraid. He could see the wild pulse fluttering at the base of her throat. But she stood there, defying him with a courage that few men would muster. He felt a flash of respect, but it was obscured by yet another flicker of arousal, stronger this time. More urgent.

"No? Are you not a woman?"

"A woman, yes. But you will hear no lies from my lips."

He began to move slowly toward her, the high heels of his buckled shoes clicking on the terrazzo floor.

The closer he came, the harder her heart began to beat. Chiara took a step back and found herself against the wall. Because she had no place to run, she met his eyes fully.

She was beautiful in an untamed, earthy way, Luca thought as he walked toward her. But there was more there besides her entrancing face, her seductive body. There was something about her—something heady and powerful. He felt a pull and, had he been honest with himself, he might have correctly identified it as need.

He stopped an arm's reach away from her, not because he did not want to frighten her further, but because he found himself wanting to touch her. And he knew just how dangerous it was to want anything so badly.

Crossing his arms across his chest, he leaned against the marble mantelpiece. "So," he said, helpless to stop himself from continuing this game of cat and mouse, "you are a woman without lies."

Chiara gave a choppy nod.

"What is your name?"

"Chiara."

Luca's tawny eyebrows rose. "How convenient."

"What do you mean?"

"You claim to have the sight, to be a clairvoyant, and your name signifies 'clear.'" He chuckled. "It's just too perfect."

"I cannot help the truth. And I cannot invent lies to please you." She tossed her hair over her shoulder. "That is the name my mother gave me."

"So, Chiara." He drew the name out so that it rolled off his tongue like a caress. "What do I do with you now?" Unable to resist, he stepped away from the mantel and reached out to touch her.

"Don't touch me." She pressed herself against the wall, as if she could make herself disappear into it. Just the thought of his hands on her filled her with panic so vast and absolute that it left no place for anything else. Her mind went blank but for the terror of being touched by this man.

Luca stilled, his hand hovering a palm's breadth away from her face.

"I don't want to hurt you." His voice was gentle.

Chiara fought back the terror that was rising within her like black, noxious smoke, but still it came. And came. Until she was choking with it.

Wanting to soothe the unreasonable fear in her eyes, Luca cupped her cheek.

She cried out and spun away from his touch.

Something snapped within him at her strangled cry. At the new wave of abject terror in her eyes. At the way she recoiled from him as she might have recoiled from a man repulsive with the French pox. The dark violence that he had worked so hard to control all his life burst forth as blood spurts from a deep wound.

Forgetting that he did not want to hurt or frighten her, forgetting everything but that he wanted her, a low sound of fury built in his throat.

Moving forward, he slapped his hands against the wall on either side of her head, effectively imprisoning her.

Chapter Three

Chiara shuddered as she heard the hideous slap of his palms against the wall on either side of her head.

For a moment she almost gave in to the terror. Almost gave in to the desire to close her eyes, slide down the wall and curl up like an animal playing dead. God, she prayed, don't let him touch me. Please don't let him touch me.

A breath away from surrender, hatred and pride, those old twin friends that had been with her for so long, came to her aid, slowly pushing back the terror. She turned her head and met his eyes.

The soothing darkness of a star-studded night, which she had seen there before, had disappeared. Instead, the opaque blackness of a sky roiling with storm clouds stared back at her. But the very violence in his eyes gave her something to focus on and she felt the fear recede further.

Luca saw that fear was still lurking in the depths of her eyes, but the hatred that he had seen there before was back in full force now. Hatred that, had it been a knife, would have been sharp enough to kill. Strangely enough it was that hatred, so real and basic, that soothed the wild fury riding him to a controllable anger. And when he spoke, his voice carried more puzzlement than anything else.

"Why do you hate me so?"

"You know," she spat. "Or, if you do not, you should."

Baffled, Luca stared at her, digging into the recesses of his mind. Had they met before? Had he done something to cause her enmity? He shook his head. What could he have done to inspire hatred so deep? He could not imagine it. Besides, he knew that if he had ever seen this woman before, he would not have forgotten her.

"For a woman with the sight, you have remarkably poor judgment."

She said nothing but stared back at him, her eyes like blue flames, provoking him with their fire.

"Manelli would have sold your body to the first comer," he snapped. "Don't you understand that?"

She had known that she was taking a risk, Chiara thought. But she had thought she could protect herself. And she had needed the money to pay for her sister's care.

"He *did* sell me to the first comer," she said tonelessly. She let her head fall back to the side so that her cheek lay against the wall, and she closed her eyes.

Luca's fingers curled as he fought the need to touch her, to cup her head and make her look at him again.

"I paid him, with every intention of letting you go." He had the uncomfortable feeling that he was apologizing. "I have never owned a slave in my life."

Slowly she turned back to face him fully. "But now you own one," she said. "And you have no intention of letting me go, do you?"

Some of the fire had returned to her low, smoky voice. The fire drew him, aroused him, and Luca shifted forward until his body was pressed against hers.

Chiara sucked in her breath as he pressed against her, pushing herself back further against the wall, but he moved closer still—so close that it seemed as if their bodies were one. He was pressed against her so tightly that she could feel the rise of his aroused sex against her belly. He was crushing her. She wanted to cry out, but she knew there would be no help for her here. And she had never been one to waste her energy on useless gestures.

He would move any second now, she thought. Every muscle turned to ice as she stiffened in expectation of his rough touch. He would push up her skirt. He would penetrate her body with his.

But he did none of those things. Instead he remained still, his eyes on hers, as if he thought to find her secrets there.

The dagger! How could she have forgotten it? Relief rushed through her. Chiara lifted her hand, but she could not reach for it without alerting him. Her mind raced. Before he tried to rape her, he would have to step away from her to free his body. Then she would be able to reach the dagger, she thought. Then she would kill him.

She felt a little flicker of regret that she would have to do it quickly, and not be able to tell him why she was planting her knife in his heart. But perhaps it was better to do it swiftly, before she had time to think about the light she had seen when she had looked inside him. Before she had time to question why her sight was showing her what her eyes knew was false.

The decision made, a small part of the tension seeped out of her even as she braced for his attack.

Luca felt the slight relaxing of her body against his and smiled. She had been hurt by some rough, careless man, he thought. He would show her what it could be like.

His hands still propped against the wall framing her head, he lowered his head toward her.

Chiara stilled when he touched his mouth to hers. Because she'd been expecting a brutal assault, the light, gentle touch took her breath away. She found herself incapable of movement as he rubbed his mouth back and forth over hers. When he slid the tip of his tongue along the seam of her lips, she trembled but still could not move.

With infinite patience he traced her lips again and again. When they parted, his mouth curved against hers.

"*Sì*," he murmured, "*così*. Yes, like this."

Desire was urgent in his blood, but even now he did not take what she offered. Instead, he leisurely dipped his tongue inside.

Chiara could see them together. They lay on a couch, surrounded by bright-colored cushions. Her shoulders were bare and pale against the coverlet of crimson silk. Somewhere there was the sound of water lapping against wood. The smell of sweet incense drifted through the room and mingled with the scent of arousal—his and hers. Then he moved over her so that she could see only her eyes—wide-open, smiling with welcome.

"No." The single word was directed at the vision, not at the kiss.

Luca withdrew far enough so that he could see her face. "No?" He smiled, his anger forgotten in the sensual pleasure of the moment. "Are you sure? That certainly felt like a yes." Without giving her time to reply, he took her mouth again.

Chiara wanted to fight him, but she found herself unable to move, as if her limbs had suddenly turned to water. He filled her mouth with his tongue, tasting her.

There was an answering heat within her, but she told herself that it was the heat of hatred. Desperate, she tried to hold on to that, but the heat merged and melded with the light, blinding her as if she were standing in the full sunlight.

His taste filled her. In a reflexive curiosity, she touched her tongue to his.

Luca felt that first tentative touch of her tongue go through him as if it were a bolt of lightning. Grasping her head, he gave in to the consuming need to plunder.

As he plunged into her mouth, possessing her with all the fever of a virile man's passion, Chiara jolted, as if shaken awake from a dream. Rational thought returned, reminding her of just who this man was. She began to struggle to free herself from his voracious kiss, just as she struggled against that unfamiliar ache in her belly.

Luca felt her move against him. Pleased, he slid his hands into her hair and delved more deeply into the pleasures of her mouth. Only gradually did he realize that her movements had nothing to do with passion.

Luca pulled back, trying to ignore the desire that was making his blood race, his body throb. The moment he freed her mouth, she went still.

Realizing that he had twisted his hands in her hair, Luca loosened his fingers and began to rub her scalp lightly.

"I did not mean to hurt you." He let his hands drift down slowly, caressingly until they lay on her shoulders. He brushed his mouth against hers and felt her stiffen.

"What's the matter?" Leaving his hands on her shoulders, he took a step away.

She waited for the malevolence to come into his eyes, but it did not. Traces of passion were there and questions, but none of the evil she had been waiting to see there ever since she had first laid eyes on him an hour ago. How long could he pretend? How long could he keep up this facade? Where did he get his power? Why could she not *see?* It was the last question that frightened her most of all.

"Did I frighten you?" He slid his thumbs beyond the neckline of her coarse linen blouse to stroke her skin. "Was I too rough?"

"I am not easily frightened." She swallowed and fought—unsuccessfully—to suppress the involuntary shiver of pleasure.

"Perhaps not." He smiled at both her evasive answer and the shudder of response that went through her. "Have you ever lain with a man before?"

His words reminded her of who he was. Reminded her of what she needed to do.

"What difference does it make to you?" As she

spoke, her hand crept upward, then across her middle. Her fingers closed around the hilt of the dagger, and she slid it out of the sheath.

Strike! Strike! The command thundered through her head, but her hand remained still, as if she could not force it to do her bidding.

"None." He laughed softly. "None at all." His fingers continued to stroke her skin. "I want you. That is all that matters."

The soft, lightly mocking laughter struck a chord in her memory and she lifted her hand and plunged it down toward his heart.

Ensnared in his arousal, Luca did not give heed to her movement. By the time the realization hit him that what she held was a weapon and he had flung his hand upward to ward off the blow, the momentum of her downward stroke was too strong, too fast to stop completely.

He felt—and ignored—the hot flash of pain as the tip of the dagger pierced his skin and sliced through his flesh a moment before he struck her hand.

The dagger clattered to the floor. His hands captured hers. For a moment, they remained still, as if frozen in a dance of violent beauty.

Luca's fury exploded like a volcano spewing forth hot lava. His fingers tightened around her wrists and he bore her back so brutally that her head hit the wall with a sharp crack.

"Damn you. I have killed men for less."

"I'm not afraid to die."

"Perhaps not." He ground his hips against hers. "But you are afraid of this."

Chiara could feel the cry growing in her throat,

but she battled the weakness, clamping her mouth shut until her teeth ground against each other.

Luca saw her fear, saw how she fought it, saw how she still defied him. And her desperate courage seemed to feed his fury.

"Why did you try to kill me?" he demanded. "Is it such a terrible fate to lie with me?" He gave a short laugh. "Some women might even envy you."

Chiara thought of her sister's blank eyes. She thought of the pitiful whimpering sounds Donata sometimes made in her sleep, and felt the fear recede before the hatred of this man.

"I hate you. And I despise you."

"Why?"

"I told you. If you do not know it, you should."

"My patience with your riddles is at an end," he snarled. "Tell me."

For a moment Chiara was tempted to tell him who she was. But only for a moment. He would find a way to use that knowledge against her. The less he knew about her the better it was. She would bide her time and someday she would tell him, right before she killed him.

She shook her head.

"Tell me." He tightened his grip on her wrist.

"No," she whispered.

"Do you know how easy it is to make someone talk?" The wildness was roiling within him like a storm-swept sea. He grappled for control, but it slipped away like water. "With just a small movement I could snap your wrist."

She could feel his hot breath on her face. "What good would a slave with a broken wrist be?"

His mouth curved in a hard smile. "You don't need your hands for what I want from you."

"And you will take what you want no matter what I do or say."

"Perhaps." He shifted his fingers a fraction of an inch to increase the pressure on her wrist. "Try me."

Chiara understood then that she had exhausted all her possibilities.

"You are a Venetian patrician," she said, trying desperately to keep her voice steady. "That is why I hate you."

It was surprise more than anything else that had him easing his hold on her wrist. The wildness within him eased as well, as if it had been a seizure that was now passing.

"Why?"

She hesitated, but feeling his hand tighten again, she decided to give him part of the truth. "Because my father is one."

"Your father?" His eyes narrowed, but he did not dismiss her words. "What is his name?"

"I don't know," she lied. "I came to Venice to find out."

Luca caught the tiny flicker in her eyes that told him she was lying, but he kept the knowledge to himself.

"So…" His voice held a touch of humor. "Did you come here planning to kill all Venetian aristocrats?"

Chiara gave a shake of her head. Understanding that the greatest danger had passed for the moment, she allowed disdain to color her words. "Only those who try to rape me."

"I don't intend to rape you."

She said nothing, but the contempt that darkened her eyes made it quite clear to Luca that she thought he was lying.

"You don't believe me, I see." He did not release her hands, but he moved a step back.

Chiara flinched at his movement and despised herself for it. When she saw that he was stepping back, relief and a new wave of bravado flowed through her.

"I have no reason to lie," he said.

"And I have no reason to believe you."

He stared at her for a moment. Then he laughed richly. "It's a pity that you're not a man. With audacity like yours we could whip the Barbary pirates in a few weeks." He paused. "And then again—" his gaze drifted down to her breasts "—I'm very glad that you are not a man."

A whisper of hope drifted through her. "If it is true that you do not intend to rape me, will you let me go then?"

His smile died and his gaze returned to her face. "No."

Hope grew cold. "Why not?"

"I want you. But then I told you that, didn't I?"

The accusation returned to her eyes, stronger than before. "So, rape after all."

"No, not rape." His grip loosened and his thumbs began to rub the inside of her wrists. "I trust that I shall be able to persuade you that it is not such an ugly fate to lie with me."

"Persuade a slave?" She made a sound that might have been a harsh laugh. "Do you really expect me to believe that?"

"Believe what you wish. But you can believe me when I tell you that I do not find the thought of rape arousing. I, for my part, have always preferred persuasion.''

Chiara's eyes narrowed at his lie, yet just the fact that he had gone to the trouble to tell it had her relaxing a little.

"And when you have *persuaded* me," she asked, "will you let me go then?"

"Let you go?" He shrugged. "I don't know. I think that is a question for another day."

Chiara was used to taking risks. After all, she had been living on the edge for so long that she had almost forgotten what it was like to know what the next hour would bring. Perhaps, she calculated quickly, perhaps it would be worth it to give him her body. He would be careless in the throes of passion and then she would k—

"Enough talk now." He released one of her hands but, keeping the other firmly in his, he turned. "Come."

"Where are you taking me?"

"Home." He moved toward the door.

Tears, unexpected, unwanted, shot into Chiara's eyes as the single word struck a long-forgotten chord deep within her soul. Once, long ago, she had thought to have a home. She almost lost her balance as he pulled her along. Swallowing the tears, she stumbled after him.

Chapter Four

Downstairs in the entry Luca barked an order that had the lackey scurrying to get his things.

Emotions—anger, horror, disgust at the violence he had displayed—rushed through him like a roaring river. A candle flickered on the opposite wall and he concentrated on that point of light as he fought to deal with them.

He had always believed that uncontrolled violence was his brother's province. From the time when they had been small boys he had seen it. He had seen Matteo strike out at servants and torment playmates. He had stopped it when he could, knowing all too well that Matteo would again do the same thing. And he'd done it because, despite everything, he had loved Matteo. He'd done it because he had always known that some of the same violence, the same cruelty lived within him.

But Luca had always believed that he had the violence under control, like a dangerous criminal locked in a secure dungeon. Instead, he had found tonight that all it took was the right moment—and the right woman—for it to escape its cage and spread its poison.

Was this urgency that drove him like a whip when he looked at the Gypsy girl the same madness that had overtaken Matteo when he had raped and killed Antonia? Had Matteo merely taken the same passion, the same compulsion that he himself felt for this black-haired seductress one step further? Oh, God, he thought as he scrubbed his hands over his face, was he like his twin brother after all?

Luca remembered how he had found Matteo, standing over Antonia's bruised and broken body. He had sworn then that he would never give in to the evil that lived within him. Not even to avenge the girl he had loved so tenderly. But, he thought, he had given in to the evil now. And the bitter knowledge shamed him.

He had put his hands on this girl until she had cried out in pain. He had been within a breath of taking her where they had stood, with no care, no tenderness. Cursing silently, he told himself that he had to let her go. He could not force an unwilling woman to go with him just because he found himself wanting her beyond all reason.

Had he gone mad? he asked himself. And if he had, would the madness pass? Was it only the madness of an instant, born of his violent fury, or would it stay with him like a witch's curse?

Even as his blood grew calm, he found that the venom had unfurled within him like a pernicious flower. He was unable to forswear his own wickedness. Unable to undo what madness had wrought. Unable to follow his conscience and let Chiara go.

It did not occur to him that he had thought of her by name for the first time.

Chiara watched him. He had released her hand and he was ignoring her as they waited in the small entry for the footman to return. Perhaps, she thought, he was already losing interest. A small shoot of hope burgeoned within her. Perhaps he was already regretting the trouble he was putting himself to.

She eyed the door. There was no key in the lock and the bolt was open. If she was quick enough, she could slip past him and out the door before he noticed her. Or should she wait and try to escape once they were outside in the narrow, dark alley?

Carefully Chiara took a small step. He was staring at the candle in the gilt sconce on the opposite wall and gave no sign of having observed her movement. Slowly, her gaze never leaving his scowling face, she began to edge toward the door.

The sound of footsteps jolted her. The footman! She gauged the distance to the door. Three steps, perhaps four. Taking a deep breath, she prepared to run.

Luca knew the moment she took the first step. He would let her go, he told himself. Perhaps then he would be able to look himself in the eye again. She was almost behind him when she paused. If she stayed now, he bargained with himself with shameless sophistry, it meant that she was staying of her own free will. If she tried to escape, he would let her go.

As she leaped toward the door, he swung around, blocking her way, forswearing the promise he had made to himself.

"Going somewhere?"

Chiara dragged in a breath that was almost a sob. He would never let her go now, she thought. She was his property and this was a man who guarded his possessions. She looked up at him.

"I was going to let you escape." He lifted his hand to her face, but when she flinched, he let it fall back to his side. "But I find that I can't."

"Won't."

"Can't." He shrugged. "And won't."

"Your *tabarro*, Don Luca."

Not taking his eyes off Chiara, Luca let the long, black cloak settle on his shoulders and clapped the black tricorn hat on his head. Letting the molded white mask, which the footman handed him, dangle from his fingers by its laces, he took her arm and stepped out into the alley.

As they turned onto the Piazza San Marco, the blast of wind met them head-on. Chiara shivered in her torn blouse but said nothing.

Even at this late hour, the piazza was full of life. The cafés and even some of the shops were brightly lit. A violin began to play a melody from a popular opera and was joined by the high, pure voice of a castrato tenor. A couple had linked arms and was whirling in a dizzying dance that needed no music, save that in their heads.

Chiara glanced at the groups of people that dotted the square, wondering if there was someone among them who would help her. Some were garbed in colorful costumes as Moors or harlequins or Chinamen, but most looked like ghosts in their long, black cloaks, their heads covered with the black *bautta* topped by tricorn hats, their faces disguised with white, beaked masks. Laughter and chattering voices drifted over and she understood just how alone she was.

Luca hurried them past the cathedral, with its Byzantine facade that seemed to glow even at night, past the Doge's palace, to the quay, where the black gondolas bobbed on the dark water silvered by moonlight.

"*Olà*, Tommaso," he called out toward the group of gondoliers who were huddled together at the base of one of the Egyptian columns. Immediately one of the men detached himself from the group and came toward them.

"You are early tonight, Don Luca." He slid a sly glance toward the girl at his master's side. "Do you wish to go—"

"Home, Tommaso."

The gondolier acknowledged the command with a small bow, but his eyebrows shot up in surprise. In silence he herded his passengers around the column, in obeisance to the long-standing superstition that to pass between the columns, where on occasion the scaffold or a gibbet stood, would bring misfortune.

Luca stepped down from the dock onto the stern of the gondola, balancing his body against the gentle pitching of the craft with the ease of long practice. He turned and held out his arms.

"Come, I will lift you down."

Her gaze darting around, hoping to find yet another way to escape, Chiara shrank back and bumped into the gondolier's stocky body.

"Don't be timid," the gondolier whispered on a laugh. "He's generous and, from what I hear, well skilled." He gave her a push.

She stumbled forward. Before she could brace herself against his touch, he had lifted her into the gondola and released her.

"Sit down in the *felze*." Luca pointed to the cabin in the center of the gondola.

When she hesitated, he jerked the door open. "Get in," he growled. When she still did not move, he grasped her arm to maneuver her inside.

"*Dio,* you're freezing." Her gaze skittered up to his as he stroked his hand up her arm. He wanted to put his arms around her and warm her. Giving in to the desire, he pulled her closer only to see her eyes widen with alarm. Swearing, he pushed her away and toward the cabin so that she tumbled onto the cushioned bench.

Unhooking the clasp of his cloak, he shrugged it off and tossed it at her. Damn her, he thought, as he leaned his elbows on the roof of the *felze*. When she looked at him like that, her huge eyes full of loathing, she made him feel like a beast. Glancing up, he caught Tommaso's cheeky grin. Swearing again, he ducked into the cabin and sat down beside her.

Although he could feel her shivering, she had not touched the cloak, but sat staring at it. With an impatient sound, he picked it up and slung it quickly around her, forcing himself not to allow his hands to linger. Then he leaned back into the corner and closed his eyes.

Gradually Chiara stopped shivering beneath the soft woolen fabric of the cloak. Letting her head fall back against the cushioned back of the bench, she closed her eyes. Why did this evil, cruel man show her compassion, generosity? Those small flashes of kindness made her doubt what her eyes told her was true.

Again she gathered all her power and probed. But it was as if a black curtain had descended before her sight. She was exhausted, she comforted herself. She had exhausted herself in body and spirit tonight. Surely when she had rested, her sight would be clear and true again.

Since her sight could not help her, she opened her eyes and slanted a look toward him. A thin band of light from the lantern on the stern crept in through the narrow window on the back of the cabin, illuminating his profile.

Again her heart jolted against her rib cage. She had not been mistaken. It *was* him. It could be no other. Maybe his hair was longer now and the cruelty in his eyes hidden under his charm, but the face was the same. The horror, the revulsion flooded over her anew, almost obliterating the pull of his beauty.

Luca felt her eyes on his as he might have felt a touch of her hand. Turning his head, he looked at her.

"Why do you look at me as if I were the very devil?" It hurt him, he realized with surprise and displeasure. Deep inside him was a place she could touch at will. A place she could ease as effortlessly as she could hurt it. But she said nothing and only stared back at him.

"Ah, yes. You've told me that I am supposed to know why." He laughed mirthlessly. "Well, perhaps I will learn it by and by."

The gondola bumped gently against wood and Chiara started.

"We're here."

There was the scrape of a key in a lock and the grating sound of rusty hinges. The gondola slid into a vaulted, shadowy entry, lit by a single torch, the smell of burning pitch mingling with the smells of dampness and decay.

Within moments Chiara was standing on the slippery stones, watching the gondola glide back out onto the dark canal. A silent servant closed the water gate, the hollow clank of metal on metal sounding like a final judgment.

It was done, she thought, as she looked through the gate's intricate wrought iron design that allowed a teasing glimpse of the dark canal and freedom. Now she was truly his prisoner.

Despair welled up within her, but she fought it. It was fate, she told herself, and for a purpose that this man had been put in her path. She could not believe that she was here only to be used by him. Perhaps it was a bounty given her by fate. An opportunity for a revenge she had not hoped for.

Yes, she thought. She would defer the revenge she would take upon her father. But this revenge that fate was putting into her hands would be hers. And soon.

"Welcome to the Ca' Zeani, Chiara."

She stiffened at the soft, mocking words but refused to look at him. Even as he took her arm and led her up a stone staircase, she kept her eyes stubbornly averted from his face.

Luca closed the door to his apartments and leaned back against it.

"Don Luca!" The servant who had looked after his needs since he was a boy, jumped up from the chair where he had been dozing and came running up to him.

"*Santa Madonna!* What has happened to you?" he demanded. "Were you set upon?" His gaze slid over to the girl who stood next to his master then back to Luca.

"A minor scuffle." He pushed away from the door. "Now listen."

Chiara watched him give his orders to his servant. Watched him give the man a familiar, friendly clap on the shoulder. It occurred to her that he treated his servant with more courtesy than her father had accorded her mother.

"*Signore,* let me care for your wounds."

"Later, Rico. Go now."

When the door had closed behind the servant, Luca walked to a round table inlaid with alabaster and serpentine that he had brought back from Constantinople and poured himself a glass of wine. As he raised it to his lips, he felt Chiara's gaze upon him and remembered how cold her skin had been to his touch.

Turning around he walked to where she stood, still wrapped awkwardly in his cloak.

"Here." He thrust the goblet at her.

She reached for it before she remembered that she wanted no more kindnesses from this man. Pulling her hand back, she shook her head.

"Have it your way." Lifting the wineglass, Luca drank deeply without taking his eyes off her face.

Chiara felt herself grow warm under his gaze. She wanted to look away, but pride would not allow it.

"Where do you come from?"

"Gypsies come from everywhere." She shrugged. "And nowhere."

He acknowledged the evasion with a nod. "But you're only half a Gypsy."

"In my heart I am pure Gypsy." Even as she spoke the words, she knew she was lying. She remembered too well how it had been for the short time they had traveled with the Gypsy caravan. She had been almost as much an outsider as the *gadjé,* the pale-skinned men and women, who had come to have their fortunes told. It galled her to see the faint amusement in his eyes that told her he knew it, too.

"But your eyes are not Gypsy eyes," he said softly. "They are the color of the sea when the sun is upon it." He tipped his glass toward her. "To your eyes, Chiara."

His words, the mellow sound of his voice touched her, no matter how she tried to deny it. She watched him put the goblet of cobalt blue glass to his lips again, watched his throat move as he swallowed the wine and she felt something flicker to life within her. She had never felt it before, but she knew instinctively that this was the heat a woman felt for a man.

As the horror washed over her, she spun her head away from him. How could she feel this for him? What kind of monster was she? No wonder her sight had deserted her.

Luca saw the spark and, eager to see it again, he lifted a hand to her face to turn it back toward him. Just as he was about to touch her, the door opened to admit a procession of servants carrying buckets of water and bed linens.

Luca stepped back from her and gestured his manservant over. "Rico will take you to your room now."

She turned to look at him then, but her gaze was as cold as yesterday's ashes. He wondered if he had imagined that one flare of heat.

"Rico, this is Chiara. She's my—"

She looked at the manservant, her chin lifted in defiance of the hated word.

"My guest."

Her eyes widened in surprise. She looked back at Luca, but he had turned away. Silently she followed the servant.

Luca stood in front of the mirror in its ornate gilt frame that stretched from the mantel of the fireplace almost to the ceiling, watching her progress until the door had closed behind her. As he turned away, he caught sight of his reflection. *Dio,* she had managed to carve him up nicely, he thought. He touched the scratches on his face, then the sticky, scarlet stain on the shredded silver lace at his throat. He laughed with something like admiration. He need feel no guilt, he assured himself. She would be a worthy adversary.

"I left the women with her," Rico said. "May I tend to your wounds now?"

Luca nodded and began to shrug out of his coat.

A fire burned brightly in the fireplace that was edged with pale yellow marble, but a chilly edge still remained in the room. Chiara pulled a coverlet of sapphire-colored silk off the bed and, hugging it around her, walked over to the window.

Below her the canal wound like a wide black ribbon. Moonlight and the flickering torches that were fastened to the walls of some of the houses made reflections of gold and silver on its surface. She tried the bar that closed the window. To her surprise it opened easily and she pulled the casements open and leaned out.

Somewhere there was the echo of music and voices and faint laughter. She looked down to where the water was lapping gently against stone and wood. The water came flush up to the foundations so that the house seemed to be growing out of the canal. A narrow wooden dock surrounded by striped mooring posts was built out over the water. Tied to one of the posts, a lone gondola, coffinlike under its cover of dark canvas, rocked gently.

"It's a long way down. If you're contemplating jumping, I wouldn't advise it."

Chiara started at the sound of his voice. Slowly she straightened and turned to face him.

They stared at each other in silence as his man-servant placed a tray on the table and unloaded platters of food and dishes before scurrying out of the room.

Without taking his eyes off her, Luca reached behind him and turned the key in the lock. Then he tucked it into the pocket of his robe of dark blue silk.

Understanding the message well, Chiara stiffened as she waited for him to come toward her, but he remained where he was and merely looked at her.

"Well?" she finally demanded, unnerved by his stillness, his silence. "Am I clean enough for you now?" When he gave her no answer, she tilted up her chin. "I would not have thought that a thing like that mattered for a man like you."

He still did not speak, but he began to walk toward

her then. When he stopped in front of her, he looked at her for a long moment before he spoke.

"And how is a man like me?"

His face was calm, his eyes seeming to carry only a faint interest in whatever she had to say, but she could feel the edgy anger within him.

She shrugged. "As I have seen him this evening."

"Seen with your sight?"

Her eyes narrowed a little as she wondered if he somehow knew that what her sight told her was in discord with what she saw with her eyes.

"My sight? No." She shook her head. "I need only my eyes to know what manner of man would mark a woman's skin like this." She pulled back the sleeves of her nightgown and held out her hands.

The bruises that marred the skin at her wrists had Luca's stomach turning over in disgust with himself. Perhaps he was not a murderer like Matteo, but the same mad, wicked blood flowed in his veins. Slowly he reached up and cradled her hands in his.

"I'm sorry," he said softly as he raised his gaze. Then, his eyes on hers, he lifted her hand and pressed his lips against the marks he had made.

A treacherous pleasure drifted through her. She jerked her hands, but to her annoyance found herself too weak to pull them out of his grasp.

"Stop it." Her breath hitched. "What are you doing?"

"Soothing a hurt. Apologizing. Making amends. Doing penance." He shifted his head and stroked his lips over her other wrist. "Take your pick."

"Stop touching me."

He smiled. "That wasn't one of the choices." His eyes still on hers, he touched his tongue to her skin.

"Don't."

"Don't what? Touch you? Kiss you? Taste you?"

His warm breath flowed over her skin like a caress. Her body was betraying her, she thought. How could she feel pleasure and excitement from this man's touch when it was horror and revulsion that he roused within her?

"Don't do anything," she said. "Let me go."

"I'm touching you, but I'm not holding you." He pressed his mouth against the pulse point of her wrist and was rewarded by the pounding of her blood against his lips. "All you have to do is step away."

She wasn't held captive, Chiara realized. She was captivated. Captivated by his touch, by the warmth in his eyes that promised every earthly delight. She felt the pleasure race through her in tandem with the loathing as if they were two halves of the same whole. Panic licked at her as flames lick at parchment.

He must be truly evil, she thought. He must have sold his soul to the devil to be given this power to enchant, to seduce, although she knew him to be capable of the vilest abomination.

She closed her eyes, gathered all her strength and lifted her hands from his.

Luca watched her, felt her tremble as she might under a heavy weight. And he smiled, although his own desire was so sharp that it slashed at him as fiercely as her dagger had slashed at him an hour before. It would not be easy, he thought. But it would be worth it.

He took a step back from her and then another.

"Come," he said softly. "Rico has brought us some food."

Chiara felt the warmth from his body recede and she opened her eyes, hating herself for her own weakness.

"Come," he repeated. "You must be hungry." He smiled. "I know I am."

The merest hint of sensual suggestion tinged his smile. Forcing herself to look away from him, she crossed the room toward the table.

Luca picked up the silk coverlet that had slipped from her shoulders and followed her.

Chapter Five

As the delicious scents rose toward Chiara, she twisted her hands in the folds of her nightgown to prevent herself from rushing toward the table and stuffing handfuls of food into her mouth. She'd eaten nothing for the past three days but some bread and cheese the man on the *burchiello,* the barge that had brought her to Venice, had given her and an apple she had stolen that afternoon from a street vendor's basket.

Because the enormity of her hunger was like a beast within her, she sat down and took a deep breath before she reached for a piece of bread. She began to eat, forcing herself to break off small pieces of the bread.

Luca watched her eat with a steadiness that indicated both extreme hunger and extreme control.

"Here." He stopped behind her and slid the coverlet around her shoulders. This time he allowed his hands to linger for a moment. "It's still chilly in here. This room hasn't been used for a long time."

Chiara pulled it around her closely and tied it in a loose, large knot.

"You mean, you don't bring women here every night?" She glanced at him over her shoulder.

"No." He sat down and, in an attempt to keep his hands to himself, picked up a slice of cheese. "But if you truly had the sight, you would not need to ask that."

Her hand paused an inch from her mouth. "I do not waste my sight on what has no importance."

"I see." He leaned back with a mocking smile. "And I suppose it was important for you to use your sight to peer into the lives of a few indolent patricians?"

"I needed the money," she said simply.

"What for?"

For my sister. For Donata, whom you raped and turned into a lunatic. The words were on the tip of her tongue, but she swallowed them and merely shrugged.

"So tell me," he drawled. "What else do you do for money?"

Chiara heard the mocking insinuation in his voice and her fingers tightened on her fork. Resolutely she kept her eyes on her plate, knowing that if she looked at him now, she would not be able to control herself.

"I do what I must," she said quietly. "But I have never lain with a man for money."

"There's always the first time."

She raised her eyes now and met his. "But that time is not going to be with you."

The moment the words were said, she stilled, remembering that snatch of a vision she had had when he had kissed her. If the vision was true, she thought with horror, it would not be for money that she lay with him. Nor for revenge.

Fighting against the memory of the vision and her own words, she sent him a cool look and returned to her food.

Damn her, Luca thought. Damn her pride and the way she cleverly mimicked aloofness when he knew she was anything but indifferent to him. He had felt her respond to him, damn it. He had *felt* it.

He splashed wine into two goblets of indigo-colored glass, lifted one, emptied it and filled it again.

"I will have you, money or no. And you will be willing," he said, his voice soft and urgent. "Here." He pushed a goblet toward her. "Let us drink to that."

"No, thank you."

"Drink."

His voice had hardened and Chiara looked up at him. Traces of the fury she had seen earlier were in his eyes. Even as she took stock of it, she sensed the struggle within him. Sensed how he fought to harness the wildness within himself that was flaring like fire in a forest of dry pines.

Slowly she picked up the goblet. Not because he had ordered her to do so, but because she needed the time to come to terms with what she had sensed.

She took a stingy sip and then another one before she set down the goblet.

"Is the wine not to your taste?"

"It's fine."

"Then why do you not drink as much as you would like?" he demanded. "Are you trying to keep your head clear?" As if in defiance, he lifted his goblet to his lips and drank deeply.

"Yes," she said cautiously, and edged her chair back. "Yes, I am."

"Why?" He leaned a little closer and picked up the ends of the coverlet around her shoulders to toy with the silk fringe. "Do you think you can escape?"

She would not even try to escape, she thought. Fate had put her here. And fate would give her her revenge. And the price? What will be the price of revenge? a voice within her whispered. But she knew that whatever the price, she would pay it.

"No, I know I cannot escape." she said.

"That's very wise of you." He wound a length of blue silk around his hand. "Then why do you want to keep a clear head?" He gave the coverlet a tug, bringing her to the edge of her chair. "Are you afraid the wine will make you willing?"

"Wine can make me weak, but it can never make me willing." She closed her hands over the soft linen of her nightgown. "Nothing can make me willing."

"You're wrong. I can make you willing and we both know it."

He had leaned close enough so that she could feel the warmth of his breath on her lips. Already she could feel her body softening. He could do it, she thought desperately. He could make her body willing. But surely never her spirit. Never her mind. Never her soul.

As if he could read her mind, he smiled. "And you *do* feel. No matter how you lie about it, I make you feel." Rising, he twisted yet another length of silk around his hand, pulling her onto her feet so that she stood flush against him.

As her body made contact with his, Chiara felt a jolt of fear so strong that for a moment she lost all awareness, as if she had slipped into a faint or a trance. But as the fear faded, she felt the waves of Luca's emotions breaking against her like waves break upon the beach.

It did not occur to her that she had thought of him by name for the first time.

The violence she had felt earlier was still there, but it only hovered at the edge like a banished spectator. Desire was there, strong and hot, and need, deep and powerful. The need of a man for a woman. The need of one human being for another.

Confused, she shook her head. How could he hide his evil so smoothly? She had no doubt that he could feel desire, but how could there be such true, deep need within a man such as this?

Against the back of his hand, Luca felt the soft give of her breasts, the pounding of her heart. He saw how fear flashed into her eyes, but only for a moment. Then he saw confusion there and surprise. And something softer that was gone before he could identify it.

Dio, he wanted her. Desire swept through him. Had he ever wanted, had he ever needed a woman so badly? Unable to resist, he lowered his mouth to hers.

He was holding her so close, so tightly that she could not move away. Unable to do more, Chiara turned her head aside so that his mouth missed her lips and brushed her cheek instead. She felt his fingers cup her chin and she tensed.

But his fingers did not tighten. Nor did he try to turn her mouth back to his. Instead, his thumb stroked her skin while his lips drifted to her ear. Nudging her still-damp hair aside, he kissed his way along the contours of her ear. Chiara heard herself sigh.

Again he traced the contours of her ear, this time with his tongue. When Chiara heard herself make a sound like a hungry kitten, she remembered where she was. And just who it was that was touching her.

How could she respond to him like this? She knew what brutality, what cruelty he was capable of committing. She had heard his mocking laughter as Donata had screamed in terror. She had seen the gleam of evil in his eyes. No matter how well he hid it now behind a mask of gentleness, she knew what manner of man he was.

"Let me go."

He let her go so swiftly that her legs gave way. Biting back a cry, she managed to grasp the edge of the table for support. Relief and surprise warred with anger. Anger at him. But most of all, anger at herself and at her own weakness.

"As you wish, my dear."

Chiara straightened, hoping that her legs would hold her up. The fact that they did had some of her audacity returning. "I thank you for your generosity." She inclined her head in a mocking little bow.

"And so you should. Believe me, it would have been quite easy to ignore your plea—" he laughed "—and concentrate instead on those tempting female noises you made."

His eyebrows lifted in a mocking curve, giving him the aspect of a fallen angel. Chiara said nothing, but she could feel heat flooding into her face. Heat from the way his closeness stirred her senses. Heat from his soft laugh that seemed to make tender promises. Heat from the shame that filled her because he could make her feel this way.

"You see it as a weakness. Perhaps I should not tell you this, but it is a great strength." His voice softened, lowered. "Do you know how much power it gives you over a man, when you respond to him like that? Even when it is against your will. Especially when it is against your will."

Reaching out, he drew a single finger down her throat and let it rest in the hollow at its base. "Do you have any idea how it makes a man feel to know he can make your pulse beat like a drum, even though you would rather take a knife to him."

His last words had Chiara's gaze skittering down to his chest where the deep V-shaped neck of his robe exposed the wound she had made with her knife.

"You should put a poultice on that so it doesn't become inflamed." The words were out before she could stop them and she bit her lip.

"I'm touched by your care."

She tried to counteract her incautious words with an insolent shrug. Her movement had his finger shifting in the hollow of her throat and she tensed against her involuntary shiver of pleasure.

Luca felt her tremble. Because he wanted badly to cup her neck and draw her toward him, he let his hand fall to his side and took a step back.

"Ah, Chiara, what am I going to do with you?" He looked at her for a long moment. "No suggestions? No requests?"

Chiara met his gaze. There was a sort of tired amusement in his eyes and a kindness that she found herself responding to, even as she had responded to his touch, his kiss. God help her, she thought. How could she fight against him, when he could make her forget who he was so easily?

"Well?"

She shook her head. "No suggestions."

"Then I will wish you a good-night." He paused. "Don't get any ideas about making a ladder of your sheets. Your window will be guarded."

"Don't worry. I will not try to escape." The minute the words were out of her mouth, she saw his eyes narrow with suspicion and knew she had made a mistake.

"At least not tonight," she corrected quickly, looking away from his sharp gaze.

"What plan are you hatching in that sly Gypsy head of yours?" he demanded. "Look at me."

Sullenly she obeyed him but said nothing.

"I'll find out by and by."

Yes, Chiara swore silently, *you will find out. No matter how you can make me feel, you will find out and you will pay.*

His eyes still on hers, he picked up her hand and pressed his mouth against the bruises he had left on her wrist.

"It is not my way to touch a woman's skin with so heavy a hand as to mark it." Pleased, he felt her pulse jump. "This *you* will find out by and by."

Chiara stood very still and watched him leave the room without once looking back.

He had to be in league with the Supreme Evil to be so powerful, she thought. Her body still warm, her blood still pounding, she sank down where she stood and prayed incoherently, desperately for the strength to resist him.

* * *

She awoke to the clatter of dishes and the sinfully tempting fragrance of rich chocolate. Remembering where she was, she sat up quickly.

"Good morning."

"Good morning." Chiara returned the serving girl's smile.

"Come and eat your breakfast. The dressmaker is coming in an hour."

"The dressmaker?" Chiara slid down from the bed and padded over to the table. "Whatever for?" Greedily she broke off a piece of the fresh, crusty bread.

"Don Luca has ordered that a dressmaker come to fit you with new clothes."

"I don't want any new clothes. I have my own clothes." She looked around the room. "Where are they?"

"They're gone. Don Luca said they should be burned." She made a vague gesture toward the door.

Chiara jumped up, ready to storm, but then she saw the girl take a step back. There was no sense in raging at this poor girl, she thought, and there was no sense bewailing something she could not do anything about.

Slowly she sat back down and picked up the bread she had tossed down onto the plate.

"Do you need anything else?" the girl asked in a cautious voice.

She shook her head and, when the girl turned to leave, she grasped her arm. "What is your name?"

"Zanetta."

"Sit down, Zanetta, and tell me about—" her tongue almost tripped over the polite address "—Don Luca."

The girl darted a glance over to the door and sat down on the very edge of a chair. "Don't you know him?" she asked, her eyes curious. "The whole house is talking about you," she added.

"I can imagine." Chiara took another bite of bread spread with butter and honey and almost closed her eyes with the sheer pleasure of it.

"Rico, Don Luca's manservant, says you are his guest. Some whisper you must be his mistress. One of the footmen heard Don Luca arguing with Don Alvise and Signora Emilia." The words came out in a rush.

"Who are they?"

"Don Luca's older brother and his wife. He is a good master, but strict." She paused, as if considering her next words. "He said he would not allow a loose woman under his roof."

Chiara felt a flash of pain as she remembered how her father had cast her mother out into the street with those same words.

"And you, Zanetta?" she asked. "What do you think?"

"I don't know." The girl twisted her fingers nervously at her waist. "But if you are his mistress—" Her mouth curved in a mischievous smile "—then you have chosen a beautiful man. Not like—"

There was the sound of footsteps outside the door and the girl jumped up.

"I must go now." Curtsying quickly, she moved toward a door that Chiara had not noticed the night before. As the girl opened the door, Chiara caught a glimpse of a corridor. Thinking to explore, she rose, but immediately heard the key turn in the lock.

So everyone was locking her in, she thought, even the servants.

She had barely finished breakfast when the corridor door opened and Zanetta returned, followed by a plain woman wearing a severe brown gown. Several maids carrying gowns, hoops and bolts of fabric trailed after them.

The woman immediately marched up to Chiara, briefly mustered her up and said, "Take off your nightgown so that we can measure you."

She snapped her fingers and one of the maids came running up carrying a shift. "Put this on." She fluttered her fingers, first at the flimsy undergarment, then at Chiara. "Quickly now. I don't have all day."

Chiara began to protest but thought better of it. After all, if her own clothes had really been burned, she would need something to wear. She quickly exchanged the nightgown for the thin shift and the maids swarmed around her to take her measurements.

"The yellow gown." The dressmaker gestured at the maids behind her and they came running like well-trained soldiers, carrying the gown and the necessary accoutrements.

Chiara took one look at the gown of yellow silk, the hoop and corset and stepped back. "No."

"You're right." The dressmaker gave her an approving nod. "Yellow makes you look sallow. The blue one."

The yellow silk was exchanged for pale blue satin.

"No," Chiara said.

"Why not?" The dressmaker frowned. "The blue suits you to perfection." She held up the gown to Chiara.

"I will not wear a contraption like that."

"What do you mean?" the woman demanded. "Don Luca is paying me a goodly sum to see you properly outfitted."

"And I've said that I will not wear anything like that."

"I don't have time for this. I have customers all over Venice waiting for my services." The dressmaker's voice rose. "These are clothes of the highest quality and the latest fashion. What more do you want?"

Thrusting the gown at one of the maids, she turned away and muttered, "Gypsy tramp."

Chiara moved after her and gripped her arm. "Would you care to repeat that?"

"What?" The dressmaker jumped as if she had been burned, her hand lifting to the lace fichu at her throat. "I—I did not say anything."

One of the maids tittered and, just as the dressmaker whirled around and boxed her ears, the door that led to the adjoining room opened and Luca stepped across the threshold.

Chapter Six

There was a collective gasp and all the women dropped into curtsies. All but Chiara. She stood very straight in the thin shift, her shoulders bare, and met Luca's eyes over the heads of the curtsying women.

"Well, what's all the commotion about?" Luca felt a jolt of possessive pleasure. She was staring at him, pride in her stance, her fabulously colored eyes full of scorn that was already edging into the hate he had seen there the evening before. He'd wanted her last night, but now, in the hazy morning sunlight that streamed in through the windows, he found himself wanting her with an unreasonable sharpness that was closer to pain than to pleasure.

Because her pride shamed him, he averted his eyes. "Don't just stand there," he snapped at a servant girl. "Bring the *signorina* something to cover herself with."

The girl scurried to the bed, brought one of the silk coverlets and slung it around Chiara's shoulders like a shawl.

She had expected to stand there like a half-naked slave, his avid eyes upon her for all to see, and she was taken aback by his consideration. Chiara felt something within her soften toward him, but when his gaze returned to meet hers, she determinedly recalled the belligerence.

"It must be a long time since you have had guests in your house, *signore*," she said, modulating her voice to such exquisitely barbed politeness that the insult could not be overheard. "Otherwise you would surely remember that a gentleman does not enter a lady's bedchamber unannounced."

Luca's eyes narrowed. He had noticed last night that there was a trace of the soft, sibilant dialect of Venice in her speech, so he had no reason to disbelieve that her father was a Venetian, although he had thought her story about being the daughter of a patrician a lie. But now, as he heard her tone, which was such an exquisite combination of politeness and insolence, he wondered if she had told the truth after all.

"My apologies, *signorina*." He sketched a bow. "But what can one expect from a man who has spent one third of his life at sea." He lifted a shoulder in a self-deprecating shrug. "We are naught but rough seamen, only a cut above the pirates we fight."

A seaman? Chiara frowned. If he was really a seaman, then what had he been doing on the outskirts of a hill town in Tuscany two years ago? And if he was a seaman, used to fighting pirates, then why had he cried out and defended himself against her knife like a coward, his hands shielding his pretty face?

Doubts crept in again, but she pushed them away. It had to be him. She could not be mistaken. There could not possibly be another face such as his in all of Christendom.

Luca watched the play of emotions on her face. He saw the same cold hate he had seen last night come into her eyes. Then he saw doubt, but only briefly, before hatred returned to sweep it away.

"What seems to be the problem?" he asked.

"I will not wear clothes like that." She flung the words at him like a gauntlet.

"Like what?" he inquired politely, only the tension around his mouth hinting at what it cost him to keep his tone light.

"I will not wear clothes that are as comfortable as an instrument of torture. Besides, those—" she pointed at the gowns "—would make me look like a beached fish."

Her indignant tone and her choice of words had the tightness around his mouth easing into a grin. "And just what kind of clothes would you suggest then?" he asked. Against his better judgment, he let his gaze drift over her.

Chiara felt the anger well up in her again and she fought to keep it out of her voice. "A simple Gypsy skirt and blouse such as I was wearing when I came here would be quite sufficient, thank you."

Amused at her haughty tone, Luca smiled. "I bow to your wishes, my dear." He gestured to the dressmaker to approach. "You will make the young lady the type of clothing she wishes."

"I make gowns for the finest ladies in Venice." The dressmaker sniffed. "I would not wish to ruin my reputation by making Gypsy rags."

"You will make, let's say, five or six outfits to begin with." His tone was mild, but the look in his eyes had the dressmaker taking a step back.

"I don't need—"

He continued as if Chiara had not spoken. "You will make her a full wardrobe—undergarments, nightgowns, shawls, cloaks, whatever is needed." His mouth curved suddenly, the brilliant smile lighting his face as if the stormy look in his eyes of a moment ago had never been. "Do we understand each other?"

"O-of course, Don Luca." The dressmaker rose from her deep curtsy and gestured jerkily at the maids. "The work will be done as soon as possible."

"I shall count on it. We will require one outfit today, by the way."

"Yes, *signore*."

The women filed out of the room in a rustle of fabric like flustered hens, but neither Chiara nor Luca paid them any attention.

"I don't want your charity," she snapped when the door had closed behind the women.

"Charity?" His eyebrows, shades darker than his hair, rose. "This has nothing to do with charity. Here is my pledge on it."

Smiling, he dipped into his pocket and took out a Venetian millefiori necklace, so named for the thousands of finely painted, tiny flowers that decorated the blue glass beads, and slipped it around her neck.

The beads carried the warmth of his body, which threatened to steal into her like an insidious drug. Chiara raised her hand to throw them off, but he was already reaching behind her, lifting her hair so that the necklace lay fully against her skin.

"There." He smiled. "You might construe food as charity, perhaps even clothing, but surely not this."

"What is it then? Payment?" She met his eyes. "You've already paid for me, *signore.*"

Because he understood pride very well, his eyes softened. "It is a gift."

"I don't want your gift, either." She reached for the anger that lived within her. "I don't need it."

"Perhaps not. But I needed to give it to you," he said softly.

"Why would you need to give a slave a gift?"

"I don't know." He shrugged. "Perhaps because it gave me pleasure to do so."

His eyes were serious as they rested on her face. The turbulence, the desire she had seen there the night before was gone and in their place was something else entirely. If it had been anyone else but him, she might have believed it to be longing. But not with him.

"If you wish to give me a gift, all you need to do is to let me go."

"I thought we had settled that question." He reached out and began to play with the fringe of the coverlet, much as he had the night before.

"*We* did not settle anything," Chiara said sharply even as she edged back. "Besides, there is no 'we.'"

"No?" Noticing her movement, Luca began to wind the silk fringe around his fingers. His mouth curving, he tugged her closer and closer still until they were almost mouth to mouth. "Are you quite sure?"

The hatred was still within her, hot and alive. Yet as she felt his warm breath feather over her mouth, she felt herself soften as the wax of a burning candle softens from the flame. This was temptation, she thought desperately. This was precisely how the devil tempted his victims.

"Yes," she said, fighting against the temptation, and against herself. "Yes, I'm sure."

Frantically she called on her sight again. She had to know now, in the light of day, what was truly within this man. She gathered herself and as she did, she trembled, finding that for the first time in her life she was terrified of what she would or would not see.

Looking straight at him, Chiara willed her sight to look inside this man and confirm what her eyes knew. Confirm his evil.

But again it was light that she saw, not darkness. Light that reached out and curled around her like an embrace. Light that made her want to yield to its warmth, its promise. Light that slipped into her heart to flower there.

Looking into her eyes, just inches away from his, Luca watched as they lost focus.

Then he felt something, not unlike what he had felt yesterday. It was as if she had reached inside him and was touching him where no one had ever touched him before. He had the absurd vision of her slim hands cupping his heart.

Then he saw her eyes focus again, and watched them grow puzzled—and afraid.

"Don't be afraid." Touched more than he would have liked to admit, he spoke softly. "Don't be afraid of me."

Chiara surfaced, made doubly vulnerable by opening herself to her sight and by what the vision had shown her. Yes, she thought, she *was* afraid of him. She was terrified of the needs he woke within her. And of her own weakness. The weakness that seemed to have frozen her in this spot and made it impossible to move away from him.

"It's all right," he whispered as he shifted closer.

Angling his head to the side, Luca brushed his mouth over hers. Just that brief taste had desire gathering in his belly, urging him to take—and take swiftly—what he wanted so badly. Tightening the reins on himself as he would have tightened the reins on a stallion eager to mate, he again stroked her mouth with his.

He felt her lips part beneath his, felt her breath flow to meet his. The need to plunge into that artlessly offered sweetness was strong, yet he held himself back, not taking the invitation.

He would show her, he thought. He would show her that she had nothing to be afraid of. That his roughness of the night before had been an aberration and would not be repeated. So he nibbled lightly at her mouth, first with his lips only, then slowly with his teeth and tongue.

Her taste had his blood pounding so heavily that his head began to spin. Still he kept the touch of his mouth light.

Chiara fought for the strength to step away, but she was unable to deprive herself of the touch of his mouth upon hers. She heard herself moan, powerless to stop herself.

He might have been able to control himself, but the low moan and the almost imperceptible softening of her body were more temptation than Luca could stand. The reins of control slipped from his fingers and his tongue slid inside her mouth.

He tried to keep his mouth gentle. Even when her taste heated his blood still further, he did no more than tease her tongue with his. But when she swayed toward him, her body brushing against his arousal, his kiss grew greedier.

The tide of passion rose. He wanted to touch her. He burned to run his hands over the hollows and valleys of her body, and yet when he lifted his hands, they cupped only her face.

Neither one of them heard the door open.

"What a touching scene."

Giulietta's peevish voice had them stilling, although their mouths remained linked. Luca watched the glaze of passion slowly disappear from Chiara's eyes and be replaced by ice. He felt her pliancy turn to stiffness. Before he could reach out to hold her, she had stepped away.

"I trust that you have sufficiently satisfied your curiosity." With a twist of her hips, Giulietta flounced farther into the room, the extravagantly wide skirt of her satin gown swaying.

"I am charmed that you have come to inquire after my well-being." Luca channeled his fury into sarcasm.

"Well, *caro,* are you cured or do you intend to keep her?" Giulietta reached up and untied the black half mask she wore. "Because if you do, perhaps I should warn you that I was never one to share gladly." Dangling the ties of the mask from her fingers, she sent him a flirtatious smile.

"I'm not asking you to. Nor her."

"What do you mean?" Her smile wobbled.

He turned to Chiara and saw that she was again looking at him as if he were the devil incarnate. Before he could say anything, she spun away. Swearing silently, he moved toward Giulietta.

"If you will grant me a moment of your time, I will explain it to you." He opened the door that led to his salon and gestured her through.

Stunned and confused, Chiara stood very still long after the door had closed behind Luca. How could her sight be telling her that he was a man of the light? How could she react so strongly to his kiss? How could she have felt that unreasoning flash of jealousy at the sight of Giulietta?

Gradually the numbness receded, making room for the panic. She had to find a way to get out of here, she thought, her thoughts darting around. He had already bewitched her. If she stayed, he would finish the work of seduction by means of that power he could only have gotten from the devil himself.

And how would she bear it, she thought as she buried her face in her hands, if she allowed herself to be seduced by the man who had raped her sister and reduced her to a lunatic, unable to speak or care for herself?

Yesterday she had thought that she could do it. She had believed she could stay and sacrifice her body for the sake of her revenge. And if it could have been no more than that, she could have done it, she told herself.

But now she understood that he could make her a willing participant of her own seduction. She understood that if he took her, he would take not only her body, he would take her heart, her very soul. And how could she survive that?

She would get her revenge some other way. Somehow she would find a way to make him pay for what he had done. But she could not stay here.

But how could she escape wearing a shift or a nightgown with only a silk counterpane as covering? No matter, she told herself. She would do what she had to.

Picking up the shoes that had fortuitously escaped the fate of her clothes, she grabbed her threadbare purse and ran toward the door that opened onto the corridor.

As quietly as she could, she pressed down the door handle. On bare feet she crept out into the corridor. The only sound she heard over the hammering of her own heart were angry voices in the next room. Just as she drew breath to make a run for it, the sound of the door opening sent her scurrying back into her room.

Her heart pounding, unshed tears stinging her eyes, she leaned against the wall.

"You will pay for this." She heard Giulietta's tear-filled voice clearly.

"I already have paid." Luca's voice held more than a hint of impatience. "As evidenced by the necklace which is now around your neck."

Chiara heard the rustle of satin, the sound of heels on the terrazzo floor and a woman's cry of pain.

"Don't try that again. I was never one to turn the other cheek." The fury was now clearly audible in Luca's voice. "Now try and act like the woman of the world you pretend to be. *Buona fortuna*, my dear, good luck."

Chiara heard the clack of heels running down the corridor, heard the door slam shut, heard quick footsteps in the adjoining room and knew that her opportunity had flown.

Luca reentered, his gaze going from her to the door, which she had not had time to close.

"You were planning to run away, weren't you?"

Chiara shook her head.

"Weren't you?" Already annoyed from his conversation with Giulietta, he felt the fatal fury rise within him, as one is aware of an incipient pain without being able to stop it.

Already familiar with the signs of anger in his eyes, around his mouth, she took a step back even as she denied his accusation.

"You're lying." He closed the distance between them and gripped her shoulders so that the hands she had hidden behind her back swung forward, releasing the shoes and purse she still held. They fell to the floor with a dull thud.

She should be frightened, she thought as his strong fingers bit into her flesh. But she was not afraid of this man. This man might leave marks on her skin, but he would not take her soul. It was the man with the gentle hands, the tender mouth, the kind eyes who was dangerous. He was the one she was terrified of.

"So are you," she said, calmly meeting his furious eyes.

"What?"

"You said that I need not be frightened of you. That you would not hurt me." She paused. "You lied."

He lifted his hands from her shoulders and looked from one to the other with disgust.

"I'm sorry. It would seem that you bring out the worst in me."

"How convenient to have a slave to blame for

your cruelty." Now that he was no longer touching her, her boldness returned.

Luca stared at her for a long moment before he spoke. "You know, I'm starting to believe that your father is a Venetian patrician. Your insolence is quite extraordinary. As is your courage," he added ruefully.

"If I have courage, it does not come from my father." She tossed her hair back.

"I thought you said you did not know who he was."

"I said I did not know his name." Because she knew that she did not lie well, she turned away to face the windows. "I do know his actions." Her hands balled into fists, although she was not aware of it. "Better than I would like to."

"All right. I'm not going to argue with you. I don't care who your father is. And I don't care whether or not you know his name."

"Then let me go so that I can look for him."

"I can't let you go. But then I've already told you that."

"Then rape me and be done with it." In defiance of the jolt of fear she felt at her own words, she let the silk coverlet drop to the floor, leaving her dressed only in the thin, almost transparent shift.

If he took her now, violently, in anger, she would be safe, she thought. Her soul would be safe. And when he lost himself in passion, she would find a way to kill him.

Luca felt his body tighten even as he distanced himself from the heat. "I do not deny that I want you, Chiara," he said softly. "But I've told you before that the thought of rape does not arouse me."

He watched confusion come into her eyes.

"I know that there is violence in my blood and although you may not believe it, I work very hard to keep it at bay." The old memories rose to haunt him.

She stared at him, her silence as insolent as the boldest words.

"I will have you, Chiara." He returned her stare. "And when I take you, you shall be willing." He paused. "When I take you, it will be anything but rape."

His mellow voice flowed over her as if he were touching her and her hands fisted.

"Never."

"A dangerous word, 'never.' But no matter." He smiled. "Now that I no longer have a mistress, I will have plenty of time to devote to your seduction."

"So that was why she was upset." Chiara felt a flash of pity for Giulietta. "It's abominably easy for a man to discard an unwanted woman."

"Is that what happened to your mother?" he asked gently. "Is that why you hate your father so?" It unnerved him to see how easily she could touch his emotions. No one, and certainly not a woman, had touched him this way since those long-ago days when he had shared that youthful, innocent love with Antonia. Poor, doomed Antonia, who had paid for their love with her life because Matteo had, from their earliest childhood, coveted everything Luca had—to possess if he could, to destroy if he could not.

She shrugged jerkily, unwilling to discuss her mother with him. Unwilling to feel that ache at the sound of his gentle voice. How long had it been, she wondered briefly, since anyone had cared about her?

"Shall I help you find him?"

"What?"

"Shall I help you find your father?"

"I don't want anything from you."

He shrugged. "As you wish. I will not offer you my help again."

"I just want you to let me go."

"That was not one of the choices." Striding toward the still-open door, he closed and locked it. "I thought you said last night that you weren't going to try to escape." He flipped up the key and caught it again.

"I changed my mind."

"Then I will leave you to ponder the fickleness of a woman's mind."

The sullen look she threw him over her shoulder grew still sulkier when she saw his grin.

He was laughing when he closed and locked the door behind him.

Chapter Seven

The blue glass beads still twined around her fingers, Chiara jumped up at the sound of the key turning in the lock. She had been locked in for three days, seeing only silent servants who had brought her food and her new clothes, having nothing to do all day but count off the minutes on the blue beads and look down at the canal and the boats, which taunted her with their freedom. If he thought to make her submissive this way, she would—

The furious words were already forming on her lips as the door opened and Zanetta appeared, a large tray in her hands. Chiara replaced the fierce look on her face with a smile of welcome.

"I'm glad to see you, Zanetta."

As she moved to close the door behind the serving girl, the key in the lock drew her gaze. Itching to take it, her fingers flexed so that the beads she held slipped to the floor. The key would not do her any good now, she thought with a sigh as she bent to pick up the necklace.

The beads slid out easily from under the door. Chiara rose, the key catching her eye again. She smothered a small gasp. Sending a guilty glance over her shoulder, she saw that Zanetta was busy setting the dishes she had brought on the table.

Quickly she crouched down and slid her fingers under the door. Plenty of space, she thought and felt her heart leap. Plenty of space to accommodate the key. If only, she squeezed her eyes shut, if only Zanetta left the key in the lock.

"Where have you been these past days?" She rose, fingering the necklace to hide her unsteady fingers.

"Signora Emilia had me helping in the room where the medicinal herbs are dried. We do that every fall." Finished, Zanetta stepped back.

"Can you stay a little while?" Chiara asked quickly, as much to distract the girl as because she wanted the company. "Tell them I needed help stitching something. Please." She put her hand on the serving girl's arm. "I'm going mad being locked in like this with nothing to do."

Zanetta sent her the uncomprehending look of someone who would have welcomed a little idleness. "All right." Gingerly she sat down on the edge of a chair.

Chiara felt her mouth begin to water as she uncovered the dishes. She was chafing against her imprisonment, but she had been hungry for too long to take three delicious meals a day for granted.

She put a generous helping of tortellini on her plate and pushed the bowl toward Zanetta. "Here, help yourself."

"Oh, I couldn't." Zanetta slid back in the chair and sent a guilty look toward the door.

"Don't worry. No one will see you or punish

you." She bit into the combination of pasta, cheese and the subtly spicy sauce and almost whimpered with the pleasure of it.

"Tell me, how long have you worked in this house?" Chiara asked, pushing the bowl a little closer to Zanetta.

"Since I was ten. Almost seven years now." Her hand hesitated over a spoon, then lost the battle and picked it up. "They've been good to me. They even kept me on when I got sick with the fever two summers ago."

"Who are they?" Chiara asked between bites. "Are they this Don Alvise and Signora Emilia you spoke of?"

Zanetta nodded.

"What about Don Luca?"

The serving girl sent her the kind of look a sparrow might have for a bird of prey. "He—he's not here very often. He is second-in-command to Admiral Angelo Emo and he's usually at sea."

Chiara frowned. "At sea? Does he ever travel by land? To Tuscany for example?"

"I don't know." She looked toward the door again. "I have to get back to the kitchen," she said, but remained seated when Chiara again touched her arm.

"So do Don Alvise and his wife still think that I am Don Luca's mistress?"

"I don't know." Zanetta sent her a curious look. "Are you?"

"No."

"Why does he keep you here then? And buy you clothes?"

"Because he wants me to be his mistress." Her appetite suddenly gone, she pushed her plate away.

"And you don't want to?" The girl shook her head. "I don't understand."

"I will be no man's mistress!" She sprang up and began to pace.

"But he's beautiful. And kind."

"Kind?"

Zanetta nodded. "Not like his brother."

"I thought you said his brother had been good to you."

Zanetta bit her lip and looked down, remembering that she was not supposed to talk about Don Matteo. "I have to go now." She rose and bobbed a curtsy. "When shall I come back for the dishes?"

"You can take them away now." She lowered her gaze, afraid that her plan would be legible in her eyes. "I don't want any more."

From beneath her lashes, she watched the girl gather up dishes, then put the tray down to open the door. Zanetta pushed the tray through with her foot. When she had put her hand on the door handle to close it, Chiara ran toward her, hoping to confuse her into forgetting to take the key with her.

"Zanetta?"

"Yes?"

Chiara watched the girl's eyes widen in apprehension and she almost smiled.

"On second thought, I will keep something here. Perhaps I shall get hungry during the night." She plucked a dish at random from the tray and picked up a fork. "I hope that you will bring me my breakfast tomorrow. Then we can talk more." She did smile now. "Good night," she said, and closed the door.

She heard the sound of metal against metal as the girl turned the key. Holding her breath, she waited. When she heard Zanetta's steps move quickly down the hall, she almost wept in relief. The key was still in the lock. Maybe, she thought. Maybe tonight she would have her chance.

He'd left her alone for three days and Luca sincerely doubted that she had suffered half as much as he had. He wasn't quite sure what he had wanted to accomplish. He doubted very much that this confinement would frighten her. But perhaps it would bore her into submission.

He couldn't count the number of times he had been on the verge of barging into her room during the past three days. And then what? he asked himself. Demand that she submit to him because he could no longer stand the waiting? Because he had fed and clothed her? Because he had *bought* her? What then of his fine words about not taking her unless she was willing?

Staring at his reflection in the mirror above the fireplace, he ran a hand over his face. What had happened to him? For years he had led a life circumscribed by the demands of duty—to family, to country. A life barren of all but a few stingily doled out pleasures, as if that could atone for the foolishness of his youth and for the violence, the cruelty that ran in the Zeani blood.

Now, within the space of a few days, everything had changed. Everything. It was as if the pendulum were swinging back, as if those wild years of his youth, when he had joined his twin brother for escapades and rebellions, had returned to reclaim him.

Chiara. She ignited needs he could not deny and could barely control. Needs that went beyond the merely physical to border on obsession. Her image, as she had stood before him, daring him, taunting him to take her, rose.

For a moment he wondered if the power she had over him had in some strange way propelled him into this secret undertaking. If she had not already pushed him beyond the boundaries of his disciplined life, would he have listened, truly listened, to the masked man who had sought him out a second time?

And he had more than listened. He had *heard* the man's compelling whispers of a fight for freedom, for glory. He had *seen* the images the masked man had conjured up of a life that offered the bright colors of power. And those images had sparked something within him that had been too long denied.

He had dressed simply tonight. Then, as he had been told to do, he covered his clothes with the typical black *bautta* and white mask, cloak and tricorn that would guarantee his anonymity. No one questioned a mask. And since thousands of men and women would be dressed in precisely the same way tonight—and every other night—it would not be a costume anyone would remember.

Quickly he left his apartment and ran downstairs to the gondola, which waited at the water gate. The gondola glided smoothly onto the canal where the ribbons of a misty fog were already floating above the dark water.

She was watching him. He recognized the warmth that seemed to wind through him whenever she looked at him. Tensing, he forced himself not to look up to her window. Instead, he remained standing, his fingers drumming an edgy beat on the roof of the cabin.

Relieved, Chiara watched from her window as the gondola emerged from the entry of the palazzo. There was no need to dip inside herself and ask who the man was. The knowledge rose of its own accord the moment her eyes settled on the masked figure. He was troubled. That knowledge, too, pushed itself into her awareness.

Doubts and self-reproach were troubling him. And a deep loneliness. No, she thought, it was more than that. They were paining him. How could something so insignificant weigh so heavily on a man like him? she asked herself.

Her eyes unfocused. Again she saw light instead of the expected darkness, but today the light was surrounded by black ribbons that seemed to wind around it like threatening serpents.

He was on his way to meet danger and deception and evil, she realized. And he would not see it because he was distracted. Because the razor-sharp edge of his instincts had been dulled by needs and desires.

As she surfaced, she found herself rubbing her arms to warm skin that had turned to ice. She wanted to push away what she had seen, what she had sensed. That was not something that needed to concern her, she reminded herself. What did she care if something was troubling him? What did she care if danger awaited him?

The gondola was still visible. Tongues of fog

swirled around it, reminding her of the black ribbons she had seen winding around the light.

This time it was not quite so easy to discount the vision. The other times *he* had been there to influence her, to color her perception. Because this time he was not, the vision stayed with her, like a thorn in her flesh.

As she watched the gondola be swallowed up by the fog, the knowledge flashed through her like a streak of lightning.

The hazards awaiting would cost him his life. Unless she warned him, they would cost him his life.

She sprang up, pressing her hands to her temples. Had she gone mad? Had he so bewitched her with his power that she gave even a passing thought to warning him?

But if his power was so great, then why was his soul burdened so heavily? a voice within her asked. Why, in fact, did he have a soul at all, if he had bartered it to the devil? The questions battered her, but there was no answer.

Chiara closed her eyes, trying desperately to reach the peaceful place within herself that had always waited to welcome her, like a candle burning steadily in a window. Always, no matter what had happened to her, this haven, where she could find rest and solace, had been there. But even that was gone now. And all that remained were visions that taunted her.

She had to escape, she thought wildly. If she had not yet gone mad, she would. If he had not yet bewitched her, then he would cast his spell upon her. If she did not flee, then that vision she had had of herself welcoming him into her body, into her soul would come true.

Forcing herself to move, she quickly donned a dark cloak and covered her head with a black lace shawl. Then she crept to the door and, pressing her ear against the richly carved wood, waited for the household to go to sleep.

"Take me to the canal that runs alongside the Ca' Foscari, Tommaso."

"I thought you were going to San Samuele to try your luck at cards tonight."

"Maybe later."

The gondolier kept on rowing and Luca found that the steady splash of the oar as it hit the water soothed his edginess. Skillfully Tommaso maneuvered the corner and slid into the narrow canal.

"You can stop at the bridge."

When Tommaso reached the designated place, he steadied the craft with a hand against the granite blocks that edged the canal.

There were no steps here, but Luca merely braced his hands against the edge of the quay and lithely vaulted up from the gondola.

"I won't be needing you tonight, Tommaso."

"Are you sure you don't want me to light your way?" He felt proprietary about Don Luca, who paid him well and treated him kindly. "The Campo San Barnaba is close by and those ragged *barnabotti* are as likely to steal your purse as look at you." He spat in the water to emphasize his words. The disdain for the impoverished, troublemaking patricians who lived there, in housing provided by the Republic, ran through all classes.

Luca laughed. Now that he had taken the first step, now that he was here, excitement was humming through his blood. He was on the brink of something important and, yes, he admitted it freely, on the brink of an adventure.

"Don't worry, Tommaso. Go home to your plump wife."

"But—"

Raising his hand in a silent salute, Luca turned away and soon he had disappeared in the warren of narrow streets that would lead him toward the meeting place.

From his hiding place Matteo Zeani watched the men gather. They came one by one in their masks and black cloaks. They came stealthily. Some kept glancing over their shoulders. Some were careful that their heels did not make too much noise on the pavement. As they gathered at the appointed place, they shuffled uncomfortably but did not speak.

The sound of brisk footsteps had him pressing closer to the chink in the door. Although the man wore the same disguise as all the others, he knew that his brother had come. The relief that flooded through him was so great that he almost wept.

He watched the figure cross the *campo* with a loose, confident stride, the black cloak belling behind him. As his hands pressed against the damp, crumbling wall, all the hatred he had carried inside him for so long burst forth, as putrid as discharge from an old, festering wound. He remembered that everyone had loved Luca—their father, their friends and, of course, pretty little Antonia. Remembered how Luca had always stopped him when he was doing those things that gave him so much pleasure. Except that one time, when Luca had been too late.

When he let himself out into an alley just around the corner from the *campo,* he was smiling beneath his mask.

The time for revenge had come.

Chapter Eight

Luca turned at the sound of footsteps. The man approaching was dressed as they all were but for his mask, which was an elaborate affair that covered his whole face. The openings for eyes and mouth were rimmed with black and gold, giving the mask a faintly Oriental, exotic look.

He stopped a few feet away from the group. "*Siamo qui per il leone.* We are here for the lion," he said softly, giving the first half of the night's password.

Every man in the group straightened and one by one they approached him to whisper their half of the password.

Luca watched as one by one the men filed by the man in the black-and-gold mask to say the password they had been given. They all looked like supplicants, he thought with a faint disdain, as they whispered the words, their shoulders hunched over, their heads bowed. He had learned to take orders, but it was not something that came easily to him.

When his turn came, Luca stepped up to him and met the man's eyes. They were exactly level with his and as dark as his own. In the shadow of the mask, they glowed like live coals. He felt a shiver flicker down his spine. There was something about those eyes that touched him on some deep, elemental level.

Had he seen those eyes before? he wondered. But even as he asked himself the question, he rejected it. It was the passion there that he was reacting to, he told himself. The fire that had so long been lacking in his life.

"*Il leone risorgerà*. The lion will rise again." The last of the group, he spoke the password from where he stood, keeping his head up, his gaze on the eyes that looked at him from behind the mask.

Their gazes remained locked for a long moment. Then the man in the black-and-gold mask gave a brief nod, acknowledging the challenge that the gesture implied.

"I am glad that you are with us," he said, his voice hollow and muffled behind the heavy mask. "With men like you on our side, the lion of Venice will truly rise again."

"How do you know who I am?" Luca demanded. "Or what manner of man I am?"

"I know you well."

There was something like amusement in the man's voice. Luca tensed, not because the amused tone offended him, but because, for a moment, there was something very familiar about it. But the thought slipped away as the man spoke again.

"Let us begin." He strode toward the group that waited like a small herd of cattle. "We—all of us here tonight—love Venice. And we hate what she has become. The Queen of the Mediterranean is now a tired, tawdry whore." The voice did not carry beyond the ears it was meant for, but it vibrated with emotion.

"The docks are idle. The warehouses grow empty. Venice has grown feeble, so unable, so unwilling to vanquish her enemies that a few pirates hold *La Serenissima,* the Most Serene Republic, in check."

The man did not look at him as he spoke, but Luca felt his words as keenly as if they had been whiplashes aimed at his bare back.

It was not his fault, he reminded himself. What could they do but play a game of cat and mouse with the Barbary pirates when the Republic did not give them enough ships, enough men to do more? Wasn't that why Admiral Emo had sent him to Venice? To persuade the senate to give them the men and ships they needed?

But logical excuses and explanations are small comfort when a man takes a direct hit upon his honor.

"If Venice had a leader willing to use the Republic's riches to fight for what is rightfully hers instead of squandering it on idle pleasures, it could be done. Even the patricians grown fat and comfortable would rally around such a man." He paused. "And with such a leader Venice could be powerful again."

Men nodded, murmuring their assent.

"Are you saying that we, as we stand here, a dozen men, should depose the Doge, the whole government?" Luca asked. The idea was insane, he thought. And yet its very madness appealed to him, for surely only a reckless, daring scheme such as this could rescue Venice from its slow, painful death.

"Pare it down to the essentials, eh? I've always admired that," the man said. "Do not fear. When the time comes, each one of you will be asked to bring a few trustworthy men who can wield a sword.''

There was something subtly familiar about his soft, amused chuckle and Luca's eyes narrowed. But then the man continued, confidence coloring his words, and the moment was lost.

''Thousands of workers at the arsenal are idle because powdered wigs and silks and satins have become far more important than ships. The *arsenalotti* will follow us and they will fight better than any army. And I will show you that cleverness and the element of surprise are stronger than weapons.''

''And who will be the new leader, the new Doge? You?''

''Perhaps,'' the man said. ''Or perhaps you? We will choose him when the time comes.''

Luca frowned. The man's arrogance was tremendous and yet there was something compelling about it. ''And should it turn out that you are not clever enough, we will all meet at dawn on a scaffold between the columns of justice.''

''You were not always this way.''

''What do you know of how I was?'' Luca took a step forward.

''If fear for your life has become so strong, my friend, perhaps you should not be here.''

Unbidden, the old memories rose, still sharp and clear enough to draw blood. ''A little fear can be a useful thing,'' Luca defended himself both against the man's words and his own memories. ''It guards us from taking stupid risks. How do we know that one of us is not a spy for the Council of Ten? Or that a spy will not slip into our group under the guise of the mask.'' He paused to let the words sink in.

"It would be safer to keep our masks."

"Safer?" Luca met his eyes again. "Did you not just scorn fear?"

"I meant, safer for our common cause."

"Perhaps," Luca said, "But if I am to risk my hide, I, for one, would look into the faces of the men with whom I throw in my lot. I would know their names."

Luca loosened the ties of his mask and lifted it away. "Luca Zeani."

Matteo felt his knees go weak. He had planned for many things, but he had not foreseen this. He had not foreseen that any of the men he had selected would choose to forsake the safety of the mask.

He should have remembered his brother's penchant for honesty. It had cost him dearly many times before. He should have known, he thought, as hatred boiled up within him, that his twin would bring his carefully laid plans into disarray. Had it ever been any other way?

Because he knew that he had to go through with this revenge or go mad, he controlled the trembling in his legs. As one by one, the other men removed their masks and spoke their names, his mind worked desperately to find words, reasons. By the time when, as one, they all turned toward him, he was ready.

"If we are to succeed, I can only work in secret." He spoke slowly, measuring his words to keep the slight breathlessness, which his racing heartbeat brought, out of his voice. "I must be able to go anywhere, speak with anyone with no danger of recognition." He paused. "If any of you betray me, by so much as an involuntary glance, you will betray all that we wish to accomplish.''

''He's right.''

''That's true enough.''

Luca heard the other men's words of agreement and still he questioned. ''How do we know that you work for our goals and not for the Doge or the Council of Ten? How do we know that our names will not find their way into the *bocca del leone,* the mouth of the lion?''

There were uneasy murmurs from the men at this mention of the one instrument everyone feared. There was no Venetian who did not quake at the mention of the fierce lion's head whose mouth was the opening to the box used to collect denunciations. All of which found their way to the Inquisitors. All of which were acted upon swiftly and mercilessly.

''Every accusation requires three signatures.'' The man shrugged. ''And I am but one man.''

''And each one of us knows how easily a signature can be bought—with gold or with a dagger.''

Matteo heard the men's mutters. He couldn't lose them now. Not now when he was so close. So close.

He gestured for silence. ''I will not betray you. I swear it.'' He stretched out his hand, palm downward, as if he were swearing on a holy relic. ''I swear it upon the graves of my parents. I swear it upon the heads of my brothers.''

Still skeptical, Luca listened to the man's oath and wondered if perhaps it was true that he had lost the boldness of his youth. In his zeal to expiate the sins of the Zeani blood, to do his duty, had he become a man of caution, of fear instead of a man of courage?

''Well, Luca Zeani?'' the man said. ''Is what is

good enough for these men, good enough for you? Do you accept my mask and my oath, or do you still hesitate?''

Luca heard the undertone of mockery and was stung by it. If there was a voice within him that still questioned and cautioned, he quashed it. He did not want to be like the Venice they all wanted to change—cautious, unwilling to take a true risk.

"Yes," Luca said. "I accept it."

Matteo exhaled slowly beneath his mask, pure relief almost masking the flash of triumph. "We will meet again when I have news."

"How will we know that it is you beneath your mask and not another man?" A slight young man who stood at the edge of the group questioned in a wavering voice.

"By this you will know me." The man stripped off his left glove and, turning slightly, held his hand palm upward so that a band of yellowish light from the single lantern that illuminated the *campo* fell across it.

Luca stiffened. The scar that slashed across the man's palm was the twin of the scar on his own left hand, a memento of an attempt at peacemaking a few years ago, when he had stepped between two brawling sailors.

Perhaps it was an omen, he thought. A good omen. He smiled, the excitement he had felt earlier returning. It would be all right.

Slowly the men dispersed until the only ones left standing in the square were Luca and the man in the black-and-gold mask.

"So, Luca Zeani, are you truly with us or will the men here tonight be called before the Inquisitors?"

"How dare you ask me that?" Luca's voice was low, furious. "If you truly know the manner of man I am, you would know that I have many faults, but betrayal is not one of them."

"True," the man agreed. "Unless you are convinced that you are not betraying someone, but delivering them to the punishment they deserve." He paused. "Is that not so?"

Again Luca felt ice creep up his spine as all the old painful memories surfaced. He had never forgotten what it had felt like to find his beloved Antonia dead at Matteo's hand. Nor what it had felt like to deliver his twin brother to the *signori di notte* to await their justice. He had not forgotten how something within him had rejoiced when Matteo had escaped from the dungeons in the Doge's palace. Nor how he had mourned when he learned that Matteo lay dead, killed by a robber on some deserted road.

"Who are you?" he whispered, as suspicion insinuated itself into his mind. Could it be possible that Matteo lived? Luca took a step closer. He could not deny the resemblance of the man's figure, his voice to Matteo, but surely he would feel a true kinship if his suspicion were true. Surely some emotions were never erased, not even by crime, hatred or betrayal.

"I am the man who will make you famous in the annals of Venetian history." Matteo's mouth curved in a cruel smile beneath his mask. "Come now, my friend." He gestured toward the canal, where a slender gondola bobbed gently in the water. "I will bring you home."

Chiara was not sure how much time had passed, but she had heard not a single sound for what seemed like forever.

Deciding that she could wait no longer, she took the fork and worked the tines, which she had pressed as close together as possible, into the keyhole. Carefully she moved it forward, inch by inch.

She sucked in her breath as the key gave and fell out of the lock, the sound of metal against the terrazzo floor seeming as loud as a pistol shot. Falling to her knees, she slid the fork under the door but found nothing.

Moving it farther out, so that she was just able to guide it with the tip of one finger, she began again. When she heard the tinkle of metal upon metal, she was sure that she had never heard such a sweet sound in her life.

Slowly, painstakingly, she maneuvered the key under the door. By the time she finally unlocked the door and stepped out into the corridor, she was covered with sweat.

She put the key back into the outside lock and turned it. If anyone thought to check, she thought, it would look as if she were safely locked in for the night.

Picking up her shoes, she ran toward the stairs.

As she reached the ground floor, she recognized the *andron,* the large hall through which Luca had led her. The dim lighting illuminated the hall just enough that she could see the door at the far end. She knew that the water gate lay beyond it. There was no way out of there but the water. She had to look for another door, she thought, remembering her father saying that every Venetian house had at least one entry on land.

Almost afraid to breathe, she opened a door behind the staircase. The huge dark chamber smelled strongly of cinnamon and cloves and she groped her way the length of the room, keeping as close to the wall as possible. Gradually her eyes became accustomed to the darkness and she quickened her steps when she saw the outline of a door.

Without much hope, she tested the handle. When the door opened, bringing in a gust of damp, cold air, she almost wept with joy.

Quickly she put on her shoes and stepped out into a walled courtyard that was illuminated by moonlight filtered through fog. Ignoring the ghostly shapes of bushes and shrubs, she moved along the wall looking for a way out.

A rustling sound had her stopping, her heart in her throat. It was only the wind in the leaves of a shrub, she comforted herself, and continued.

She found the heavy wooden door tucked in the farthest corner of the courtyard. Her heart beating in her throat, she willed it to be open, but the wrought-iron handle did not give. She ran her hands around the door and over the ground. Surely she would find a key. She could not have gotten this far to be thwarted now.

But she found nothing.

Desperate, furious, she gripped the handle with both hands and rattled it. But the door still did not budge.

"Did you hear that noise?"

"Shh."

The whispers had her flattening herself against the

wall, her eyes wide with fear. She stayed perfectly still for so long that the chill dampness began to creep through her cloak. Then she heard a soft laugh.

"You see, it was nothing."

Again there was a rustling sound, followed by a giggle.

Her eyes filling with tears of disappointment and rage, she crept back to the house.

Chiara retraced her steps to the *andron*. There was no help for it. She would have to find some way to escape through the water gate. And she would, she swore to herself, if she had to swim her way to freedom. She would do anything to get away from Luca. And, she reminded herself, she needed to find her father.

The door to the water portico opened without making a sound. She edged through it into the arched entry. If she had not heard the snore, she might not have seen the servant curled up on a pallet, covered by a blanket.

Slowly, step by step, she inched along the wall, away from the sleeping servant, away from stairs that led up from the water, until she had reached the farthest shadowy recess of the entry.

She pulled the black lace shawl over her face and, leaning back against the damp wall, she settled down to wait.

The damp cold had long seeped through her clothing and Chiara started to shiver. She tried to ignore it, but then her teeth began to chatter so loudly that she was sure that the servant must surely awaken from the sound.

As she had done earlier that evening, she closed her eyes and tried to reach her haven, where she would be warm and safe and at peace. But again it remained beyond her reach.

All she saw was Luca, standing straight and beautiful in the light. Luca, serpents of darkness floating around him, closer and closer, like ropes that would bind him.

A sound jolted her out of her vision.

Her heart racing, she peered through the shawl that covered her face, the lacework allowing her to see only silhouettes. The gate swinging open. The gondola gliding up to the stairs. The two men standing in the center of the craft.

The servant took the pitch torch down from the wall and descended the steps.

In the light she saw one man extend his hand and grip the other man's arm.

Suddenly the vision rose again. Darkness was twining around the light, binding it as surely as chains bind a prisoner. Soon it would be too late. Too late.

Then she saw a slender hand, the hand of a woman, reach out and touch the streamers of darkness. Immediately they began to dissipate, but the hand hesitated, drew back, and they returned, dark and strong.

As she surfaced from the vision, a sense of evil engulfed her in a wave so intense that it was almost physical. She lifted her hand to her mouth to stop herself from crying out.

Luca stepped onto the stairs and the gondola slid back out into the canal, taking the stench of evil with it.

As she watched him mount the steps, the images of her vision stayed with her and she saw him, surrounded by light, the ribbons of darkness clinging to the brightness like leeches.

Chiara lifted her hands and pressed them against her eyes as if that could stop the images floating through her mind, tormenting her. But it did not.

Was he doing it again? she asked herself. Was his presence bewitching her? Was he conjuring up images to confuse her? Images to unhinge her mind? Had her sight deserted her and become his tool to do with as he pleased?

Even if the images were true, could they not be *his* own evil? But then she remembered that the evil had dissipated as the gondola had slid out of the gate.

Could it be, she asked herself frantically, that Luca was not the man she sought? Could it be that her memory was mistaken? What of the legend that every person on earth had a double, a ghostly counterpart alike in face and figure? But, she reminded herself, it had not been a ghost who had violated Donata.

"Go to your bed, Aldo. I will lock the gate."

The sound of Luca's voice had the images receding and she lowered her hands.

"*Buona notte*, Don Luca." The old servant shuffled off.

Again Chiara heard the sound of metal locking her in. But she was not a prisoner this time, she reminded herself. This time she could slip into the water and dive under the gate. And she would be free. Free from confusion and bewitchment and all those bewildering, alarming feelings he awoke within her.

He untied the mask and turned, his gaze going to where she stood pressed against the wall.

She could feel the need within him. It was great and she knew, for the space of a single moment, that she was the only one who could fill it. And she knew that same need was echoed within her heart.

For the space of that single moment she forgot who he was and what he had done. She forgot how much she hated him. She forgot what she had seen that night two years ago. She even forgot her visions.

There was only the reality of the man now. The man who had touched her heart. And she knew that she would not be going anywhere this night.

Pulling the lace away to expose her face, she stepped out of the shadows and into the circle of light.

Chapter Nine

Slowly Luca walked toward Chiara, stopping an arm's length away from her. Close enough to touch, but not close enough to crowd her.

Silently he stood looking down at her. She was so pale that the only color in her face was her eyes. Eyes that this time held neither fear nor hatred. Instead they mirrored distress and something more, something that edged toward desperation.

She stood straight and looked at him gravely. Something moved within him—something beyond desire, even beyond need. He found that he wanted badly to reach out and stroke his hand over her cheek. But, he thought, she would shrink away from him and he had already learned how sharply she could hurt him with her rejection. So his hands stayed at his sides.

"I knew you were there," he said softly. "I could not see you, but I could feel your presence." His mouth curved in a crooked little smile. "It was as if you had touched me. Like this." Giving in to the desire to touch her, he experimentally brushed his fingers over her shoulder.

Yes, she thought, her mind spinning. She had touched him. And he had touched her, as well, in ways that had nothing to do with the physical.

What was happening to her? What had she done? What had possessed her to make a conscious decision to remain in the cage? The questions whirled around in her head. And the answers were there, no matter how much she denied them.

There was more between them than the hatred that made her heart a dark, grim place. He had a need within him, a need that called to her heart and was echoed there. And he was in danger.

With more than a little desperation, she told herself that she would use his need to fulfill her desire for revenge. She had only stayed to save him from the danger, she assured herself. Save him so that he would not be snatched away from her avenging hand.

Have you not seen the light? a secret voice deep within her whispered. *Why do you seek revenge when you know Luca is innocent? Look and believe.*

But Chiara pushed the voice away in desperation. If she accepted what it told her, it would deprive her of her only support, her only weapon against Luca, against her own needs. But in her heart she knew.

"Would you have let me go?" she asked, testing him. "Would you have gone into the house and left me here, knowing that I would escape?"

"It would be easy to tell you yes." He shrugged. "Lies are always easier to tell than the truth. But I will not insult you by lying to you." For a long moment, he looked at her without saying anything.

"No, Chiara," he finally said, keeping his eyes squarely on hers. "I would not have let you go."

Expecting some fancy lie, her mouth was already

curved into a mocking twist. "How unusual to find a man who speaks the truth," she said, unwilling to relinquish the opportunity for a gibe.

"And you?" he asked. "Why did you not stay in the shadows?"

Chiara bit her lip. "I don't know."

"Who's lying now?" He laughed softly.

"No," she retorted. But even as she denied it, she remembered what she had felt. She remembered what the secret voice had whispered. She knew that she *was* lying and she lifted her hands in a helpless gesture as if to ward off the truth.

"Can't you admit it, Chiara? Can't you admit there is something between us?"

"Yes," she cried, her voice rising dangerously, "there is. I hate you."

She balled her hands into fists because she was starting to tremble. Because the hatred was shifting and slipping away. She willed herself to feel it as clearly, as hotly, as she had felt it in that first moment when she had seen him in Giulietta's *casino,* but she found that it had become hardly more than an empty word.

"Do you?" he asked. "Do you really?"

"Yes. I hate you, I despise you—" Her voice caught in a sob and she covered her face with her hands.

"Chiara—" Unable to resist, he ran his hands from her elbows up to her wrists. "You're trembling." Curling his hands around her wrists, he gently pried her hands away from her face so that she had no choice but to look at him. "Are you afraid?"

"No," she said, not quite truthfully. "I'm cold."

He swept her up into his arms and carried her inside, taking the stairs two at a time.

Luca set Chiara down next to her bed. "Your clothes are damp. You need to take them off," he said over his shoulder as he unlocked the connecting door to his rooms and called for his manservant.

"Have spiced wine brought, Rico, and make certain that it's hot." He shrugged off cape, *bautta* and tricorn into the servant's hands.

Turning, he saw that Chiara had not moved, and returned to where she stood.

"Do you really think that I would make love to a woman who is trembling like a leaf? What kind of a monster do you think I am?" he demanded, his hands itching to shake her. "You will become ill if you do not take off your damp clothes and warm yourself."

Now that she was far away from that shadowy, arched entry, where the emotions had flowed between them, overwhelming her, she could tell herself that it had been just an absurd, irrational moment. Or perhaps another trick he had played on her.

Feeling her strength and her bravado returning, she said, "And what good is a harem slave with a lung ailment. Is that not so?"

Moving so quickly that she did not have time to shift away, he gripped the front of her cloak with both hands, almost lifting her off the floor.

"If you were a harem slave, you would have lain with me in that bed three nights ago." Because he wanted to drag her still closer and press her against his awakening body, he released her so suddenly that she stumbled back and sprawled onto the bed.

"Now do as I said." Not sure of his control, he spun away and thrust his hands into his pockets.

For a moment Chiara lay breathless. Then, realizing that she had no choice, she rose and began to remove her clothing.

Fabric rustled against fabric, linen slid against skin and every muscle in Luca's body tensed as the sounds seemed to scrape over his own raw nerves. When he heard Chiara slip under the covers, he was relieved that those seductive sounds were over and he almost turned around. But then the image of her in the large white bed, wearing only a nightgown insinuated itself into his mind and his blood began to run even hotter.

There was a knock at the door and Rico entered with a pitcher of steaming spiced wine and two pewter cups. Grateful for the interruption, Luca relieved the manservant of his burden.

"I won't be needing anything more tonight."

Luca saw Rico's gaze slide past him to the bed.

"I wish you a pleasant night, Don Luca," he murmured, and closed the door behind him.

Luca said nothing as he approached the bed. Nor did he speak as he filled the cups and handed one to Chiara. Silently he watched her curl her fingers around the warm cup and drink deeply. She stared into the cup as if she could see something in its depths. Then she put it to her lips again, tipped her head back and emptied it.

As she brought her head forward, their eyes met. Picking up the pitcher, Luca gestured with it toward her cup. When she shook her head, he replaced the pitcher on the table and plucked the cup from her unresisting fingers.

"Better?" he asked, as he lowered himself to the bed.

"Warmer."

He lifted his own cup to his lips to hide his smile. "A fine distinction."

She said nothing, but the way she tilted up her chin spoke as clearly as words would have.

Slowly he sipped his wine until his cup, too, was empty. He watched her as he leaned forward to set the cup aside and, although she remained perfectly still, he could fairly see her skin tighten with tension.

"So you think that your grace period has come to an end?" he asked. "Is that why you drank the wine? A little to blunt the pain, but not too much so you could still fight me, if you saw a chance?"

He caught the flash of surprise in her eyes before she lowered her eyelids and he knew that he had hit upon the truth.

"Well?" he questioned softly.

"Yes." Her eyes blazed. "You will take me, if only to punish me for trying to escape."

"Your sight has shown you this?"

"I have not looked." Her chin lifted. "My thoughts are my own and I do not seek to prove or disprove each one with my sight."

"Then look now," he demanded, his voice urgent. "Look inside me and tell me what you see."

She shook her head and remained stubbornly silent.

"Look, Chiara, and see a man who wants you. A man who wants you more than it is wise to want anything." He leaned closer. "As a man starving wants a piece of bread. As a man dying of thirst wants a drink of clear water." His voice was low and urgent. "You've been hungry and thirsty. Can you measure just how badly I want you?"

Something flashed in her eyes, but it was gone before he could identify it. It occurred to him that it wasn't particularly shrewd of him to hand her such a weapon against him.

How did a man seduce a woman like this? he asked himself. A woman so untamed and wild. She would not be susceptible to blandishments, to sweet words. Nor to trinkets like so many other women. When the answer came to him, he almost laughed aloud.

A man did not seduce a woman like this. A man won her after he had gradually gentled her to his hand, as one gentled a wild mare who has never felt a bridle or the weight of a man.

It would be a trial for his body, already on the brink of arousal, but he was going to enjoy this. Yes, he thought, he was going to enjoy it very much.

Chiara felt her breath freeze in her throat as, suddenly, without warning, he shrugged off his coat and toed off his buckled shoes. Her instinct was to run or to fight, but she knew that she had nowhere to go, so she remained still. Only her eyes darted quickly back and forth, following his every movement.

When he removed the sheathed dagger from the waistband of his breeches at the small of his back, she tensed in anticipation. If he put it under the pillow or on the chest that stood next to the bed, she would have a chance.

But he tossed it on the floor and gave it a kick so that it skittered across the room.

"I remember too well your skill with a knife," he said over his shoulder with a smile. Then he swung his legs up on the bed and pushed himself back so that he lay against the pillows beside her.

"So what happens now, Chiara? Are you going to fight me?"

She shook her head, numb from that surge of hope so quickly thwarted.

"Good."

She jolted as he slid an arm behind her shoulders.

Schooling himself to patience, Luca lay very still, waiting for her to begin to relax. When his patience had been rewarded, he turned toward her, tucking her closer against him. Again she stiffened.

"What reason have I given you to mistrust me like this?" he asked, surprised and dismayed to find how much a small thing like that could hurt.

"I may be young—" Chiara looked up at him and met his eyes "—but I have seen enough to have plenty of reasons to trust no man."

"I won't force you to tell me why." He reached up and, with his fingers, combed back a few strands of black curls that had fallen across her cheek. "Besides, God knows, you have reason enough to mistrust me, when the bruises I put on your skin haven't faded yet."

She didn't understand him, she thought. He was like a chameleon, rough one moment, gentle the next. Surrendering to her exhaustion, she let her eyes fall closed.

Stray thoughts began to drift through her mind like smoke.

Perhaps it was not him at all whom she had dragged away from her sister's limp body. Perhaps her memory, her eyes, were betraying her. Perhaps another man walked the earth with Luca's features.

An evil man. But could there be another man in the world who resembled him so closely? Another man with that beautiful face of a fallen angel? She found herself wanting to believe it.

The man who had raped Donata had been a monster. If Luca was that man, after all, then she must be as monstrous, as vile as he to allow him to hold her like this. To take pleasure in how his hand was combing through her hair. To wish for a yet more intimate touch.

She shivered at the thought and felt his hand drop to her shoulder to stroke soothingly down her arm before returning to play with her hair.

Luca watched Chiara as she lay against him and wondered what thoughts were going through her mind, what she was feeling. Why did he feel so compelled to know her thoughts, her emotions? he asked himself.

Women had rarely been more than a means to assuage his hunger. At best they had been a pleasure, at worst an inconvenience. And while he had loved Antonia in her innocence, she had never filled his thoughts as completely as this girl did. He wondered if she had bewitched him with some Gypsy spell.

His thought found its way to his lips.

Her eyes flew open at his question and as he felt her brace herself against him, his hand, which was still caught in her hair, began to trace small, soothing circles on her scalp.

"Don't be afraid," he whispered.

She turned her face aside, but he grasped her chin with thumb and forefinger and brought her back to face him.

"Tonight you don't have to be afraid of anything." He rubbed his thumb back and forth beneath her lower lip. "Not me and—" he smiled "—not yourself."

She drew a sharp breath to speak, but his thumb slid up to lie against her lips.

"Shh. Someday you will tell me everything and we will both laugh about it." He cupped her face and turned it so that it lay against his chest. "Sleep now."

As she settled against him, Chiara's gaze fell on Luca's hand that lay palm upward on his thigh. She stiffened and sat up, pushing away from him.

"Where did you get the scar on your hand?" She remembered all too clearly how his high, girlish scream had echoed through the night when her knife had sliced through the palm of his hand.

"I tried to stop two drunken sailors from killing each other." He chuckled softly. "I really should know better than to get too close to people with knives." He touched his chest, where her knife had cut him.

The image of him stepping between two brawling sailors flashed through her mind. She saw the silver glint of a knife, the scarlet blood.

Her pounding heartbeat quieted. If this image was true, she thought, then he was truly innocent of Donata's rape.

Was it all a test? she wondered as she covered her eyes with her hands. Was she being asked to be true to her name and see clearly? See with her mind and her heart, apart from what her sight chose to show her?

Putting the images, the visions, the memories out of her mind, Chiara lowered her hands and focused her eyes on Luca's. She looked into the star-kissed blackness of his eyes, felt the warmth and the pull.

Shifting closer, she did not resist when he tucked her against him again.

The heat from his body crept through the covers that were wrapped around her. The steady beat of his heart against her cheek lulled her.

Chiara forgot to think of him as her enemy and she slept.

Luca watched Chiara awaken. He watched how she shifted and stretched as layer after layer of sleep fell away. Someday he would watch her awaken like this after a night of love. Anticipating that day, he brushed his mouth over hers.

Chiara surfaced from sleep slowly. Awareness of the physical came first—the soft bed, the warmth. Then some floodgate of her mind opened, bringing with it all the old fears. As her eyes flew open, her world filled with his face and she felt his lips against hers.

"Good morning." He pulled back slightly but remained bent over her, his hands pressing into the pillow on either side of her head. "You slept well?"

She moved her head in a choppy nod, her mind scurrying to remember what had happened the night before.

Luca saw the questions, the sudden terror in her eyes, and he felt as if he had taken a fist to his middle.

"Don't worry," he said, and pushed away from her. "You are none the worse for wear. Even depraved creatures like myself draw the line at taking women in their sleep." He slipped into his shoes and strode across the room to pick up the dagger.

"I wish you a pleasant day." He picked up his coat and moved toward the door to his rooms.

There had been a flash of pain in his eyes, Chiara thought, before he had masked it. She scrambled up from under the covers.

"Wait!"

"What is it?" His face impatient, he turned back.

Her fingers twisted on the coverlet she still held. "Thank you."

"For what?" he demanded, fighting to keep his voice casual. "For saving you from taking a chill? For not whipping you for trying to escape? For not raping you in your sleep?"

"No." She swallowed. "For being kind to me. It's been—"

"It would fascinate me to hear more," he interrupted her, "but I fear I have an appointment."

He closed the door behind him with more force than necessary. He should stay away from her, he thought as he crossed the room toward his bedroom. Her ability to arouse him, to touch him and, yes, to hurt him was truly frightening. He could not afford to give anyone such power over him.

He would send her away, he told himself. When he returned later that day, he would send her away.

Chapter Ten

On his way out of his apartments, Luca glanced at the reflection of the stranger in the mirror.

The curled, powdered wig, its queue neatly tied back with a black silk bow, itched a little, but he supposed that it was preferable to having his own hair covered with a pomade of lard and then powdered. The *velada*, a coat of pale blue satin, the embroidered brocade waistcoat, the lace, the breeches of ivory silk he wore were covered by the uniform of a patrician who held no particular office, a floor-length gown of fur-lined black silk.

It was only the eyes that he recognized as his own. The eyes of a man determined to fulfill a duty he no longer quite believed in.

For a moment, he paused outside Chiara's door. Temptation licked at him and his hand went to the key in his pocket. And what of the promise he had made to himself not an hour ago to send her away? he asked himself with a mirthless laugh. Empty words.

There was something between him and the Gypsy. Something far beyond his desire, far beyond her ha-

tred and her fear and her mistrust. There was a sea
of emotion between them. A roiling, stormy sea, full
of unimagined perils. And he knew that he would
not let her go until he had plumbed the very depths
of that sea.

Somewhere in the house a clock struck. Remembering that he had a duty to fulfill, he strode toward
the stairs.

Crossing the *andron,* he looked into the water portico, where Tommaso was chatting with a footman.

"Wait for me at San Marco, Tommaso. I'm going
to walk."

He needed to move, he thought as he passed
through the warehouse where workmen were busy
measuring out spices from the pungent-smelling
crates and barrels. Perhaps that would clear his head,
soothe his edgy nerves. Last evening's meeting, the
odd encounter with Chiara in the water portico, the
night spent holding her, all made him feel as if he
were walking on coals.

He let himself out of the door in the corner of the
cortile and walked briskly down the narrow alleyway, oblivious to the eyes that watched him from a
nearby doorway.

Matteo suppressed a pleased chuckle as he
watched Luca walk briskly down the alleyway. All
his life he had made it his business to gauge just how
Luca would react and he had not miscalculated more
than a handful of times, but his last miscalculation
had cost him bitterly, he thought. He had not believed that Luca would betray him and turn him over
to the constables. Oh, he'd known that Luca had had
feelings for little Antonia. That's why he'd done

what he'd done, after all. But he had never thought that it would weigh heavier than the bond between them. And for that Luca would pay.

What a pleasant discovery that Luca was still as predictable as he had been in his youth. He had known just how to maneuver Luca into a prank or challenge him into some act of rebellion, even on one or two occasions a petty crime. And today, he had known that Luca would not take the gondola. He had known that after last night, Luca would need to walk to the council meeting.

It only took two attempts to open the courtyard door. Tucking the ring of keys into his pocket, he slipped inside.

The simple molded white mask that he had worn today disappeared under his cloak as soon as he had passed through the warehouse. In the *andron*, a servant who had just come downstairs with an armful of fresh tapers for the wall sconces bowed as he passed. On the stairs a servant maid moved aside with a curtsy and a smiling invitation in her eyes.

Quickly he passed the *piano nobile*, the floor where the rooms used for entertaining were, and climbed the stairs leading up to the family's private rooms. The corridor was just as he remembered it, graced by ancestral portraits and the potted oleander bushes Emilia had always been partial to.

He had missed this house. No matter how he had chafed against the restraints of his life here, no matter that Luca had always eclipsed him with his easy charm, it had been his home. The home birth had entitled him to. And now he would never have a real home again. His mouth curved in a cruel smile. And soon neither would Luca.

He should go now, he thought. He had proved he could do it. There was no more reason to linger and perhaps be discovered by Luca's manservant. Old Rico had been the only one who had always been able to tell them apart.

Still, something prompted him to continue on. He listened for a moment at the door, then entered Luca's chambers.

The table was strewn with maps and books. A discarded shirt hung over a chair, the fine lace trailing on the floor. A heavy gold ring, the twin of the one he wore, lay in an enameled bowl. Only his ring was an imitation, fashioned by a goldsmith in Florence, because he had had to use the original to bribe his way out of the dungeons beneath the Doge's palace seven years ago.

The black hatred that had lived within him as long as he could remember welled up. He welcomed it, for it was that very hatred that had given his life purpose for the past seven years. But instead of giving him that familiar jolt of energy, it rose and rose, swelling until it was a roar within him, so great it robbed him of all awareness but that of the thundering black hatred in his heart.

He staggered as a dark curtain seemed to descend in front of his eyes, half blinding him. His hands flexing with the need for violence, he lurched forward and collided with a table. Struggling for purchase, his sweat-slickened palms slid over the smooth surface until one hand came to rest against something cool and solid.

His fingers closed around it and he lifted the object and sent it flying across the room. He did not know it, but his mouth opened in a hoarse cry.

The crash had the roar in his head fading. He shook his head to clear it and found himself trembling. Across the room, a three-pronged candelabra lay, one of its arms grotesquely bent, the candles broken. He drew a deep breath and then another and the trembling eased.

A sound in the next room had him tensing. His hand went to the hilt of the dagger at his waist and he moved toward the door, as quickly and silently as life on the edge had taught him. Drawing the dagger out of its sheath, he held it ready. Whoever came through that door, all he had to do was push the head back to expose the throat and then make that one quick slice that would send the blood gushing. He almost smiled in anticipation.

"Are you all right?"

The voice on the other side of the door was female, and he found his body responding to its huskiness.

As he watched, the handle of the door was pressed down, but nothing else moved. A pity that the door was locked, he thought. The tension of an animal ready to leap at his prey drained out of him and, exhausted, he rested his head against the wood.

He had been looking forward to it. There was something so basically satisfying about slitting a person's throat. It must have something to do with his sense of aesthetics—all that lovely scarlet blood.

"Luca? Is something wrong?"

The voice intrigued him. Who could Luca be keeping in there? he wondered. Surely not a mistress, for staid, proper Alvise would never allow a mistress under the sacred Zeani roof. And he would certainly have heard, if Alvise had finally conceded that his

Emilia was barren and Luca had been allowed to take a wife.

He returned the dagger to its sheath. Curiosity getting the best of him, he turned the key and opened the door.

The girl who stood there, staring at him with eyes of an incredible blue, was stunning. A vague feeling of recognition moved through him. He wondered if he had seen her before, but the thought was discarded as he felt desire move through his blood. Desire and an odd need.

"Now tell me," Matteo said, a smile curving his beautiful mouth, "why should anything be wrong?"

Chiara jumped up from her seat at the window when she heard the crash, followed by that almost inhuman cry. Even as she asked herself why she should care, she was already moving toward the door.

"Are you all right?" she asked. Reflexively she tried the door although she knew that it was locked.

The room remained so silent that for a moment she almost believed that she had imagined the sounds. But then she thought she heard the rustle of movement near the door.

A sense of anxiety drifted through her even as she told herself that she should be feeling nothing. She owed him nothing. But then she remembered that he had held her throughout the night.

"Luca? Is something wrong?" she asked.

Again the silence next door was complete.

Just as she shrugged and took a step back, the key turned and the door opened to reveal Luca's smiling face.

Within the space of a breath she was surrounded by evil. She tried to move, but she could not, as if a treacherous quicksand were sucking at her feet.

She saw his lips move. She knew he was speaking. But his words were lost in the sudden buzzing in her head.

Finally, she thought. Finally she was seeing the truth of this man. But even as her mind welcomed the truth, her heart wept.

He took a step toward her and she felt the panic swirling up within her. He said something, she knew not what, and reached out his hand toward her. Smiling, he spoke again. His outstretched hand, a heavy gold ring glittering on his middle finger, came closer. He must not touch her, she thought. If he touched her with the same tender touch as he had last night, she might forget the evil.

She shook her head. No, how could she forget? The evil was all around her, a noxious, pernicious perfume. What was wrong with her? Was she going mad?

Dipping inside herself, she sought the voice of her guiding spirit.

Look, the voice whispered. *Look and believe.*

He was dark, draped with still more darkness that surrounded him like a shroud. But behind him was a glimmer of light. A light that was pure and white, tinged at the edges with gold as if lit by the sun.

A mirror image. It was the mirror image of what she had seen when she had first looked at him. Even as the thought occurred to her, he gripped her shoulders, his fingers biting into her flesh.

She surfaced from the vision to see him, his beautiful face twisted with rage and fear. He made a sound, not unlike the sound she had heard in the adjoining room minutes ago. Then he pushed her back violently and she tumbled to the floor, bumping her head.

Raising herself onto her elbows, she opened her mouth to scream, but he had already turned away. For a moment the flowing black cape fluttered in the doorway like a bird of prey. Then it, too, disappeared.

Chiara stared at the empty doorway for a long moment. Then her vision began to blur and she crumpled into oblivion.

He watched her as she stared at him, her eyes dark and huge with panic. Why was she looking at him as if he were the very devil? he asked himself. He had done nothing but smile and say a friendly word. The rage within him that was never far from the boiling point began to simmer.

Then it occurred to him that it was not him she was afraid of. It was Luca.

Well, well, he thought. What had the good, honorable, righteous Luca done to this girl to make her react this way?

"Don't worry, my sweet, I am not Luca," he said, and reached out, wanting to stroke his hand down her luxurious black curls.

But she still stared at him with the eyes of a wild animal confronted by a hunter.

He curved his mouth in his most seductive smile. "Come here, little one. You're very lovely. Let me show you how lovely I find you." His fingertips tingled with the desire to touch and he brought his hand closer to her face.

She shook her head and, although his mouth was still smiling, his eyes narrowed. He would have to teach her a lesson, he thought. All his life, he had had to teach women lessons, painful ones. But women could only learn through pain.

His hands were almost around her neck when he saw her eyes grow blank and glassy. What kind of trick was she playing? His hands fell to her shoulders and he gripped the firm, young flesh.

"Damn you," he cried. "What are you doing?"

But she was still and silent as she stared at him, her eyes unfocused.

Rage and fear rose, bitter as bile.

"Answer me!" His fingers bit into her and he shook her limp body violently enough to make her head snap back and forth.

And still she gave no answer, but stared at him with those blank eyes that seemed to reach inside him. Rage warred with fear, but the latter won. His hands tightened, then shoved her away from him.

He whirled and ran.

The first thing Chiara became aware of was pain. There was a dull ache at the back of her head and her shoulders and upper arms felt as if they had been mangled.

The memory of what had happened hovered just beyond the edges of her mind. She did not try to reach it now. She simply lay there and gathered the strength to move. Finally she shifted and, although every movement had her body protesting violently, she decided that there was no permanent damage. Cautiously she sat up.

The movement changed the ache in her head to a

pulsing throb. She moaned softly. The sound of her voice echoed in her head, pushing the pain up another notch. Suddenly the protective veil lifted and the memory came flooding back.

She tried to rise as horror and panic surged through her, but she fell back to her knees. The throbbing in her head intensified and she began to retch. When her stomach was empty, she fell back, so weak that she was unable to hold herself upright.

She lay there, unable to move, eyes closed, breathing shallow. Was it minutes? Was it hours? She did not know. And all the while her body lay so still, her mind did not stop spinning, tormenting her with the memory of the evil she had sensed, the darkness she had seen.

Her eyes filled with tears and overflowed. Why was she weeping? she asked herself. Because she was terrified. Because she was too weak to move to save herself. Because she was at the mercy of this evil.

But how had he hidden this evil from her? How could he have held her throughout the night, pretending tenderness when there was only evil and greed and lust? How could she not have seen it, felt it?

She remembered the image of how she had seen him wrapped in light. Why could this image not have been the true one? And she remembered that one moment in the dark entry last night when her heart had connected with his.

Other memories imposed themselves upon the terrible memory of how she had last seen him, his face twisted with rage and fear.

She remembered how he had kissed the bruised

skin of her wrists where he had held her. How her blood had pounded at his touch. How he had tasted her mouth as if it had been an exquisite sweetmeat. She had tasted his mouth in return, and his aroused body had lit fires within her.

She felt the rivers of silent tears run into her hair. How much evil was there in her? she asked herself with despair so deep that it touched every fiber of her being.

How much evil was there in her, if she could long for what she had felt with him, for him, even for a moment? Despite the hatred, the fear, she had felt something beyond the physical passion he stirred within her.

It would be a just punishment for her to stay here, she thought. Stay here until she found the means and the strength to kill him. *If* she found it, an insidious voice mocked.

No. She could not stay. She had to escape. Perhaps the window was no longer guarded. Perhaps she could escape tonight. She felt her heart began to pound. She could not wait. He could return. He could touch her. The pounding intensified the throbbing in her head and she thought that she was going to be sick again.

Opening her eyes, she cautiously tipped her head to the side. And saw the gaping door to the other room.

Hope was fragile, but it sustained her as she, still unable to stand, crawled toward it. The sight of the second open door on the other side of the room had her fighting her way to her feet.

She managed to stumble halfway across the chamber before she collapsed onto a chair, breathing as if she had run a mile, and gave in to the weakness.

But her head shot up as if she had been stung by a scorpion and she stared at the shirt that hung over the chair as if it were a dangerous, living thing. On the fine linen his scent mingled with her own and reminded her of how he had cradled her through the night. She scrambled up, barely managing to hold herself upright by gripping the edge of the table. Determined, she kept her eyes on the open door and concentrated on taking a step. And then another one.

She had almost reached the door when she remembered one of the spells her mother had taught her. She had never set much stock in her mother's spells. She had seen her make too many potions, none of which had brought her a fraction of the love and respect she wanted. But she was desperate enough to try anything.

She needed something of his. Something personal. A strand of hair would have been perfect, but she would have to look for something else.

An ornate chest of drawers stood against one wall. She pulled a drawer open when her gaze fell on the heavy gold ring that lay in an enameled bowl. She picked it up and curled her fingers around it.

She saw him clearly and she staggered back, for a moment believing that she had conjured him bodily into the room. He was looking at her, his mouth curved, his night-sky eyes soft. Even as she willed herself to see his darkness, she saw the light envelop him. Then the image was gone.

Her fingers trembling, her breath heaving, she tore the purse from behind the waistband of her skirt and dropped the ring inside. As quickly as she could, she moved toward the door.

She did not know it, but as she crept down the stairs, her face was wet with tears.

Chapter Eleven

From his place in the speaker's box on the podium, Luca looked around the chamber as he spoke. The senators, in their brown robes, sat in double rows of wide, wooden seats around the circumference of the room. Most were listening attentively, with that exquisite politeness that had always been the mark of a Venetian patrician. Only a few of the older men were nodding, seemingly on the verge of sleep.

"*La Serenissima* was once a great power. Once." He saw how some of the senators shifted in their seats at his words. Some exchanged glances or discreet hand signals that he could not interpret.

"Once Turks trembled at the sight of vessels flying the flag with the lion of San Marco. And now? Now the pirates of Algiers and Tunis and Tripoli rejoice as they await yet another delegation come to pay a ransom of good Venetian gold. Ransom for safe passage of the *Serenissima*'s vessels. And they know that their profit is doubled. First the ransom, then the rich booty from the vessels that they will take no matter what they had promised."

"The *Serenissima* has signed treaties." The Doge's voice was thin and reedy.

Luca met Alvise Mocenigo IV's tired, old eyes straight on and hardened his heart against pity.

"Treaties that it would have been ashamed to even consider in the past."

Murmurs rose, but the Doge lifted a long, bony hand from where it lay on the armrest of gleaming reddish wood and the murmurs quieted.

"The *Serenissima* now pays sixty thousand ducats a year so that her ships may sail unmolested through the seas where she was once queen. And do they remain unmolested? You who have wares on the ships know the answer as well as I.

"And why does the Venetian fleet not step in, you ask. The Venetian fleet that was once victorious in Morea and Constantinople and Lepanto. I will tell you why. The fleet is a handful of ships, old and outdated. The whole fleet would have been judged a squadron at the battle of Lepanto.

"I am here as emissary of Admiral Angelo Emo, whom you all know as an honorable man and a skillful seaman. He asks for ships and ten thousand men to man them. Then Venice will stand a chance of regaining the power that was once hers.

"The noble Angelo Emo has a motto—'If I fall, it shall not be on my knees.' The *Serenissima* could do far worse than to heed it and take it as her own."

He bent his head in a salute.

For long moments the chamber remained so silent that Luca could hear his own breathing. Then it erupted into exclamations, shouts, angry gestures.

"*Silenzio.*" The Doge's voice was shaky, but the office commanded respect and the tumult quieted.

"Luca Zeani, we thank you for your eloquent words. We will discuss what you have said and our decision will be made known to you."

"When, Your Excellency?" Gripping the sides of the speaker's box, Luca leaned forward.

"In due time." The Doge lifted his hand in a gesture made to soothe. "In due time."

"With all *due* respect, Your Excellency, time is a commodity we do not have."

"At my age, I could say that." The Doge smiled thinly. "You have more than enough time."

"I speak of Venice, Your Excellency." Luca paused. "I have no wish to be a pallbearer at the *Serenissima*'s funeral."

Gasps greeted his words and the Doge again raised his hand. "You go too far." He gestured toward the helmeted guards who stood at the far end of the chamber to open the ornate doors. "You may leave us now to our deliberations."

Luca stepped down from the speaker's box and made his way across the podium. As he moved slowly through the room, he looked around at the men who had listened to him. The men who would make the decisions. Some men returned his gaze, others shied away. But nowhere did he see agreement or approval.

At least he knew now for certain, he thought. He knew that what the masked man wanted to do was the only way Venice would survive. This was not betrayal, nor treason, he told himself. It was a last effort to save Venice from crumbling. And he could do no less.

Luca took a deep breath as he stepped out into the piazza, glad of the breeze that was blowing in from the lagoon. Closing his eyes for a moment, he let the cool air, the scent of salt water clear his mind.

He had always found the atmosphere in the Doge's palace oppressive. The official chambers with their showy ceilings of monumental paintings and gilt that contrasted so sharply with the paneling of dark wood and, behind it, the tunnels that led to the torture chambers. And above and below the luxury were the dungeons. The *Piombi,* the Leads, the cells under the lead roof where prisoners froze in the winter and baked in the summer. The *Pozzi,* the Cisterns, at the level of the canal, dank and damp, where prisoners had been known to drown at flood tide.

The October sunlight had burned off most of the morning fog and the air had warmed. He had almost reached the quay where Tommaso was waiting when he felt the touch like a hand on his skin just above his heart.

Chiara. He looked around, almost expecting her to be standing somewhere near. What would he see in her eyes now, he wondered—hatred, or that reluctant attraction he found so arousing? But she was nowhere to be seen.

Suddenly the spot where he had felt the touch turned ice-cold and he broke into a run, almost tripping over the hem of the black gown.

"*Avanti,* Tommaso," he shouted. The gondola plunged dangerously as he jumped down. "Home, and quickly."

Tommaso took one look at his master and rowed with quick, choppy strokes, like a galley slave threatened with a whip.

As they approached the palazzo, Luca discarded

the gown and tossed the wig aside, sending up a cloud of powder. The moment the gondola slipped into the water gate, he vaulted up onto the damp stones and ran.

Chiara felt her legs slip out from under her and fell back against the top stair, breaking her fall with her elbows. A moment, she thought. She would rest just for a moment until she was strong enough to get up again. Rolling onto her side, she lay with her cheek against the cold marble.

The sound of footsteps did not register until it was too late. She struggled up onto her feet, but he was already there. As his hands gripped her shoulders, she screamed and tried to twist out of his grasp.

"What is going on?" Luca shouted, shaking her. "Where do you think you're going?"

"Let me go!" With the strength of desperation, she fought him.

The screams and shouts brought everyone running. Chambermaids and liveried footmen and the mistress of the house stood above and below them, staring at the spectacle with frightened fascination.

"Chiara!" Luca saw the wild look in her eyes and understood that something was terribly wrong. This was utter panic. This was hysteria, pure and simple. "Listen to me."

"No!" Chiara screamed, closing her eyes. But no matter how tightly she squeezed her eyes shut, she saw him, wrapped in light. "No!" Her desperate cry was as much for the image in her head as for the man who was holding her.

Bending like a sapling in the wind, she freed her shoulders from his grip. For a moment she teetered on the edge of a step. Then she tumbled headfirst down the long marble staircase.

Luca sat on the edge of Chiara's bed, where he had spent much of the past week, and held her limp hand. He ran his thumb absently over her knuckles. She looked so peaceful, as if she were just sleeping. But she had not moved, had not opened her eyes since they had brought her up here from where she had lain at the bottom of the staircase.

Physicians had come and gone, all shaking their heads, unable to do anything for her. She had no broken bones. Nothing but a few bruises. But she had lain here for a week, so still that her chest barely seemed to move with her shallow breathing.

She'd gone to some shadowy place to escape him, he thought, closing his eyes. Her utter stillness was a reproach, and looking at her magnified the guilt that ravaged his soul like acid. But he opened his eyes again, needing to look upon her face, no matter the pain.

Why? he demanded, the despairing question almost a prayer. What had happened that she had fought him with the last of her strength? What had put the wild, desperate fear in her eyes?

Luca had always been a man of action. But now the feeling of utter helplessness was overwhelming. And to sit here now and wait was torture.

It had been wrong to keep her against her will. It had been like caging a wild bird that was meant to fly into the sky. Perhaps she had gone a little mad with her imprisonment. Perhaps this is what had caused her to fight him with such frenzy.

If this was so, then he had killed her as surely as

if he had thrown her down those stairs. The guilt returned, stronger than before.

This was his punishment. He had had no right to keep her imprisoned like this. He should have let her go that very first evening. But, he thought, he had wanted her so badly. And even now, although she hovered in a state that was closer to death than to life, he found himself desiring her.

But it was more than desire. He had desired women before. But he had never truly needed one, like he needed her. And he knew that if he let her go there would always be something missing from his life.

But he *would* let her go, he vowed. *I promise,* he swore silently, sliding her hand between both of his. *I promise that I will let you go. As soon as you are well, you will be free to go wherever you please.*

"Luca, I would speak to you."

Luca suppressed the brief flash of impatience that he always seemed to feel when he heard Alvise's lugubrious voice, which was as measured and careful as the entries into his books.

"Go ahead." He turned his head to look at his brother. "I'm listening."

"I would speak to you in private."

"How private do you want to be?" he demanded. "She can't hear us."

Alvise's mouth tightened and he tugged at the front of his brown gown.

"As you wish." He cleared his throat. "It is this— this female I wish to speak to you about." His gaze brushed the girl on the bed, but skittered away. How like Luca, he thought sourly, to insist on such impropriety.

"Her name is Chiara."

"She cannot stay here."

"What do you suggest? That we throw her into the canal along with the garbage?"

Alvise sniffed. "You always were extravagant in your speech, even as a boy. That appears not to have changed."

"Just what is it that you are suggesting?" Luca made no attempt to disguise the impatience now.

"I am simply saying that she cannot stay here. And it is not a suggestion," he added. "The story of your wrestling match with her and the outcome is all over Venice. You know how the servants spread gossip."

Luca remained silent.

"I want her removed. Venice is not a city of barbarians, there are enough places where she can be taken care of." He gestured vaguely. "The charity hospitals, one of the convents."

"You can remove her from here over my dead body, Alvise." Luca's voice was quiet as his eyes were not. "And if you remove her when I am not here, then I will *really* give the Venetian gossips something to talk about." Turning his back to his brother, he went back to watching Chiara in her deathlike sleep.

"You cannot do this." Alvise bristled. "You cannot defy me this way. Our father made me the head of the Zeani family and it is my right and my duty to make all decisions." His thin mouth thinned still further until it was no more than just another line in his gaunt face. "Especially on what reflects upon the family honor."

"Indeed, we have always differed on what defines

the honor of the Zeanis." He glanced at Alvise over his shoulder. "Have we not?"

Alvise had the grace to drop his gaze, remembering all too clearly how he had tried to bargain with Luca not to turn Matteo over to the constables. He still thought he was in the right, he thought stubbornly. After all, what was the life of the daughter of a rich tradesman worth against the blot that would forever be on the Zeani name.

"I will arrange to have her taken away."

Luca felt his muscles tighten. With the sheer force of will, he relaxed. Carefully he lay Chiara's hand down on the coverlet and rose.

"You do that," he said so softly that he saw Alvise automatically crane his thin neck forward to catch his words. "You do that and you will learn just how great my capacity for violence is. Then you can finally stop wondering just how like Matteo I am."

Alvise opened his mouth to speak, but Luca shook his head. "Go now, Alvise."

The older man stared at his brother and saw how his hands flexed at his sides. His throat worked as he swallowed past the fear that was suddenly lodged there. He turned and fled.

Luca felt himself step back from the dangerous threshold. *Dio,* he thought, another moment and he would have wrapped his hands around his brother's throat. A thin line of sweat trickled down his spine.

For years he had believed that he had the violence that lived inside him under control. Then Chiara had come into his life, and all of a sudden he had found that he had lived a lie all these years. So much of the same violence, the same cruelty that had driven

Matteo to commit unspeakable crimes, was within him. But he had stepped back from the threshold, he reminded himself. This time and the other times.

He should leave the city and go back to sea, he thought. But he could not. He had made promises to the masked man, to the girl who lay unconscious because of him.

The touch came lightly, subtly, the merest brush of fingers over his skin. Then it settled against his heart like a warm caress. Afraid to move, almost afraid to breathe, he waited for it to turn to ice as it had a week ago.

"Will you really let me go?"

The barely audible, halting whisper touched him with the power of a lightning bolt. He wanted to spin around, to let his eyes confirm what his ears had heard, but his body refused to obey him.

Unable to move, he remained still but for the light trembling that ran through his body. A long moment passed and then another. When she did not speak again, he was sure that he had imagined that whispered question and he felt his heart contract with grief.

Then he heard the rustle of fabric and he knew that he had not been mistaken.

Slowly he turned and met Chiara's eyes.

Chapter Twelve

They looked at each other in silence.

Her breath frozen in her throat, Chiara waited for the horror, the panic to roll over her. She waited for the stench of evil to rise and choke her, for his beautiful face to twist with anger and fear. She waited for him to reach for her with hands intent on causing pain.

But a moment passed and everything within her remained calm as the surface of a clear mountain lake. No evil rose to choke her. And Luca's face mirrored neither anger nor fear. Instead there was something there that she could not quite grasp.

"I heard you promise," she finally said, her voice hoarse from disuse. "Or did you lie?"

When he did not answer right away, she dipped inside herself, cautiously, afraid of what she would see. The light was bright and she closed her eyes against it.

Why had she seen the darkness, the evil so clearly last time, she asked herself, when the light was so clear and bright now? Again the thought came that she was being tested. She wanted to look for reasons, explanations, but she found she was too weak and tired to think now.

All she knew was that she felt relief so great that her eyes filled with tears.

Luca saw tears seep out from beneath her eyelids. More than her pallor, more even than the fact that she had just woken from a deathlike sleep, the thin trickle that made its way down her cheek made him see how fragile she was.

He had seen her so strong, so defiant. Even when she had succumbed to his kiss, there had been far more power in her than surrender. But now he saw how vulnerable she was. And, perhaps for the first time in his life, he felt a need to protect, to cherish. A need to give her what he had given no other woman.

Moving closer, he sat down on the bed. He wanted to touch her, to take her into his arms, but, wary of frightening her, he only brushed his fingers over the back of her hand.

"I saw you look inside people and see their truth. Why can't you see mine?" He waited for her answer, but she gave him none. "No," he continued softly, "I did not lie."

He would let her go, he thought, the grief already spreading through him like a bloodstain on a piece of white linen. It would be the most difficult thing he had ever done, but he would keep his promise. Slowly he lowered his hand until it covered hers.

She lay still and, for a moment, he thought she had left him again, but then he felt her hand shift beneath his.

It occurred to him then, that perhaps she *had* seen his truth. That she *had* looked inside him and read his thought, his promise. But even as he wanted it to be true, his logical mind, schooled in the precise sciences, fought against it, telling him that it could only be at best a coincidence, a happenstance.

"Why did you ask if I would let you go?" he asked, leaning down toward her.

"Ask?" She opened her eyes then.

"Why did you say I had promised to let you go?"

"I heard you." Her eyebrows drew together above puzzled eyes. "It was the sound of your voice that woke me."

"So you *can* look inside me, after all." Something eased inside him, suddenly making it simple to accept her gift. At least for the moment. "I did not speak those words. Except in my mind."

"You did not speak them aloud?"

"No." He frowned. "Why do you doubt yourself? I saw no doubt that first evening."

"There is always doubt," she hedged, lowering her eyes.

She was evading him. He could feel her pulling away and, silently, he called out her name.

Chiara heard Luca call her name as clearly as she had heard the promise he had made and her gaze flew up to his.

They both stilled, one as surprised as the other. For a long moment, they just looked at each other, as the distance between them was bridged and they both felt the link.

"Can you tell me why you tried to escape?" he asked. "Why did you fight me so desperately?"

"You frightened me." She held on to the link, even as the ugly memory began to intrude on it. "You looked at me and I felt evil and cruelty and—"

Suddenly the memory surged toward her, terrifyingly clear, and the link between them slipped out of her grasp. Her eyelids grew heavy.

"Shh. You don't need to talk now."

But she needed to understand. The only explanation could be that she was mistaken, she thought. Her eyes were deceiving her. The memory etched into her mind was wrong. He could not be the man she had dragged away from Donata's body. For surely if he were, she would not feel anything but hatred for this man.

And what she felt now had nothing to do with hatred. Her heart missed a beat and began to race. Nothing at all.

And, she reminded herself, she had heard the voice inside her, telling her that he was innocent.

Her gaze was so intense that Luca fought the desire to squirm beneath it. He waited for her eyes to grow unfocused, but they stayed clear, their color a sunlit sea bright.

"You were not looking at me with your sight now, were you?" he asked when her eyes were completely focused again.

"No. I was trying to understand."

"Understand what?"

She shook her head, not willing to say more. Would she ever trust him completely? she wondered. Would she ever trust herself again?

"It's all right," he said, wanting to ease her mind. "I'm not going to press you."

Luca rose because he wanted to go back on his promise the moment the words were out of his mouth. There were still many questions. And the temptation to touch her was strong; he could already feel the texture of her skin against his fingers.

"I will send Zanetta to you. She will bring you whatever you need."

"Thank you. And thank you for protecting me against your brother."

"I'm sorry you had to hear that."

"I've heard worse." She thought of the last words she had heard from her father's mouth. "Much worse."

"I'm sorry," he repeated. "Rest now." He turned and walked toward the door before he gave in to the temptation.

Chiara lay there, her body drained, her mind numb. Even the effort to close her eyes seemed too great.

For a moment he'd looked as if he were going to touch her. And, God help her, she had wanted him to. She had wanted him to show her that she was truly alive.

As he was leaving, Luca looked back at her. "This door will remain unlocked and you are free. Free to go, and to come back if you so wish."

"Come back?" She tipped her head to the side to look at him.

"I need not tell you that it is a harsh world that is full of Manellis and Giuliettas and worse. As long as you are here, you are under my protection. If you want to go anywhere, you can have a guard to protect you."

And who will protect me from you? The thought drifted through her mind, but she did not voice it.

"If you want anything, you need only ask. Will you do one thing for me in return, Chiara?"

There was a longing in his voice, a need she was powerless against and one that echoed her own. She met his eyes.

"I don't want to find one day that you have disappeared. If you decide to go, will you tell me?"

"Why?" Her lips curved in a suspicion of a smile. "So that you can stop me?"

"Stop you? No." He shook his head. "I have caused you pain enough." He lifted his hands and looked down on them. "Forced you enough."

"There are other means besides force." The words slipped out before she could hold them back.

His blood heated and he took a step toward her even as he cursed himself for a savage. "Chiara, what are you say—"

"Please." She lifted her hand, but it fell back onto the coverlet. "Don't."

The exhausted gesture stopped him as the softly spoken words might not have. He stood there for a long time and watched her. When he was certain that she slept, he quietly let himself out of the room.

It cost him, but he did not lock the door behind him.

It took more self-control than Luca thought he had, but he stayed away from Chiara's room until the servants told him that she was strong enough to rise from her bed.

When he entered her room, he found her hunched over the table.

"You are feeling better, I'm told," he said as he approached her. "I'm glad to hear it."

Chiara started at the sound of his voice and tried to cover the small figures that she had made of kneaded bread. In her hurry, she knocked one of them off the table and it rolled to a stop in front of Luca's buckled shoes.

He picked it up and examined it. "If I didn't know better, I would have said that this is a chess figure."

"You *don't* know better," she said, and defiantly pushed the figures she had already made to the center of the table. "I may still be half an invalid, but I have to find something to do, if I am not to go mad."

He looked down at the figure in his hand that was a crude if unmistakable likeness of a knight. "You could have asked."

"So that you could scoff at me like you just did?" she demanded.

"Can I help it, if you are so full of surprises that it makes my head spin?" He smiled and lifted one shoulder in a shrug.

Chiara struggled not to be caught in the charm of the smile that softened the chiseled angles of his face.

He sat down across from her and rested his chin in the palm of his hand. "So, tell me, what else can I have brought for your amusement, Chiara?"

"Does it please you to mock me?" She leaned back and crossed her arms tightly over her chest.

"Mock you? I have never been more serious in my life."

She looked at him in silence, her eyes narrowed. "All right. If you are serious, I would like a chess set, cards and books."

"Books?" The incredulously spoken word was out before he could control it.

"I see. Because I am a Gypsy, I must be illiterate." Her voice was heavy with sarcasm. "And if I am not, then that surely means that I have risen beyond my proper station in life.''

"Did I say that?''

"You didn't have to.''

"Don't put words in my mouth.'' Anger heating his eyes, he leaned across the table.

"I don't have to put words in your mouth—'' Chiara gripped the edge of the table "—when they are written all over your face.''

Suddenly Luca began to laugh.

Fury and humiliation drove color into her still-pale cheeks. Chiara pushed back from the table and started to rise, but Luca was quicker. His hand shot out and gripped hers so that she had to struggle not to lose her balance and sprawl across the table.

"Stay, please.''

"So that you can amuse yourself at my expense?''

"I wasn't laughing at you.'' Her eyes were narrowed and disbelieving and his grip gentled, but not enough to allow her to escape. "I was laughing at myself.''

She said nothing but her dark eyebrows rose over eyes that looked at him with such elegant derision that there was no doubt left in his mind that she had not lied when she had said that her father was a Venetian patrician. Perhaps, he thought, he would make some inquiries on his own. Perhaps he could somehow find out who had fathered this magnificent creature.

"I was laughing because I was glad that you felt well enough to hiss and scratch at me like an irritated cat, although it was far simpler when you lay in your bed too weak to move.''

His eyes had gentled along with his touch. "Will you sit?"

She lowered herself back down into the chair.

"I will be right back." Luca rose and went next door to his rooms.

In a few minutes he returned carrying a heavy chessboard inlaid with ivory and ebony. Opening a drawer beneath it, he took out exquisitely carved figures of alabaster and dark green jade and set them up so that the alabaster figures were on her side.

"Would you like to begin?" he inquired, as courteously as if they had never exchanged anything but the most polite drawing room conversation.

"Are you testing my skill?" she demanded, trying to look indifferent, although the eagerness to play was already making her eyes dance.

"I am inviting you to play a game with me." He grinned. "So that you can test *my* skill."

Unable to resist, Chiara grinned back.

"I think we have to call this a draw," Luca said an hour later.

Chiara frowned down at the chessboard. She had wanted badly to win, but she supposed she could settle for a draw.

"I suppose we do." She raised her eyes to his face.

"I look forward to the next game we play." A smile touched his mouth. "We are well matched." He allowed a suspicion of innuendo to color his voice and was pleased when the spark in her eyes told him that she had understood it.

When Rico entered and deposited a stack of books on the table, Chiara had eyes for nothing else.

Luca plucked the deck of cards from the top of the pile and placed them in front of Chiara. "Cards and—" he slid the backs of his fingers down the leather bindings "—books. Boccaccio, Aretino, Dante, poetry by Michelangelo and Petrarch. I trust you will find something there that is to your taste."

Chiara looked at the books hungrily. "Thank you." She touched the rich wine-colored leather of the top volume with the same awe a nun might reserve for a holy relic. "That's very kind of you."

"Kind? No." His chair scraped over the marble floor as he pushed back from the table. "In fact, I am being quite selfish." He shrugged. "I will give you anything if you will stay."

"Anything?"

"Anything, if it is within my power to give it to you."

"Don't ask me to stay," she whispered, pulling back.

"Why not?" he whispered back. "Are you afraid you will? You could have left the moment you rose from your bed." He paused. "Or did something keep you?"

"I have my reasons." And she did, she thought. She needed to know the truth. She had to know what had caused those conflicting visions. She had to know just who he was. If he was indeed not the man who had violated Donata, she could admit those secret feelings that were burgeoning in her heart, like tiny flowers blooming in the crevices of a rocky cliff. Were the visions but a test to force her to decide not with her sight, but with her heart, if she could truly trust this man?

"And I, too, have my reasons." Pushing the

chessboard aside, he slid his hands across the table to cover hers. "Will you stay until we have explored them?"

"Don't!" She tried to pull her hands away, but his tightened, just enough to hold her.

"Afraid?" he challenged softly.

She opened her mouth to deny it, but the words died unspoken on her tongue. She *was* afraid—of herself and what she was beginning to feel for him.

"Look inside me, Chiara. What do you see?"

"Don't, Luca," she cried, and flung his hands aside.

"You can't avoid it forever."

"I can leave. You said I am free to leave."

"Yes, you are. But you won't." He smiled. "Because you are not a coward."

He rose swiftly, before she could say anything, and left the room.

Chapter Thirteen

Chiara sat at the window that looked down at the canal, but her mind was not on the busy boat traffic of barges overflowing with colorful wares, and gondolas, and the larger *burchielli* full of masked revelers.

She was procrastinating, she thought. For days she had sat at this window and longed for freedom. But now her door had been unlocked for almost three weeks and she still sat at the window, looking at the world outside, pretending to be an invalid.

She had come to Venice to find her father. Now that she was free, she thought guiltily, she still had made no attempt to do so. In fact, she admitted, she had barely spared him a thought but for a brief moment that first evening, when she had looked into the heart of that woman wearing men's clothing.

But ever since that night, her world had become circumscribed by Luca. She let her gaze drift around the room, where she had spent so many hours in his company. Here everything reminded her of him. She felt her heart open and fill with yearning.

"No." The protest came out on a moan and she

buried her face in her hands. How could she feel this for him? She ought to feel contempt and hatred. He was the man who had raped her sister. Or had he?

Where did the truth lie? Was it in her mind, her memory where he was the man of evil, of darkness? Was it in her heart, her visions, where he was the man of innocence, of light?

And there was something else. She raised her head. Something had been teasing her mind ever since the day that she had awakened from her week-long faint. She knew it was important, but, no matter how hard she had tried, she had not been able to remember it. It was always there, a constant irritation, like a pebble in a shoe, but every time she tried to reach for it, it slipped away from her grasp.

She would get dressed, she thought. Perhaps that would somehow jog her memory. Sliding off the window seat, she stood. Her head spun a little from the movement and she trod carefully as she made her way across the room and lifted the lid of a clothes chest.

Those were the clothes she had been wearing the day she had fallen down the stairs, she realized. Quickly she shed robe and nightgown and put on shift, underskirt and blouse. As she lifted the skirt out of the chest, her shabby purse slipped from among the folds and fell on the floor with a sound more solid than was warranted by the few coins it contained.

She picked it up, weighing it in her hand. It felt much heavier than she remembered and she loosened the strings and emptied the contents into her palm.

There were the few silver lire she had earned in the piazza the first day she had come to Venice.

There was the gold coin the woman masquerading as a man had given her. She frowned. And there was a heavy gold ring that had not been there before.

She picked it up, curled her fingers around it and the memory came flooding back.

Fear. Terror. Panic. The memory was sharp and clear, but she saw it from a distance, almost as if she had been an observer instead of experiencing it.

She saw herself standing at the chest of drawers in Luca's chamber, her hands quick and desperate, searching for something of his to make a spell that would free her of him. She saw her hand reach toward the bright-colored bowl. She saw her fingers close around this ring.

And—her mind stumbled—she saw this very same ring on the hand of evil outstretched toward her.

The ring still tucked in her fist, she sank down on the chest. This was what had been teasing her mind, she realized. Her mind spun as she tried to sort out the meaning.

The ring could not be in two places at once, she reasoned. That meant there had to be two. And if there were two rings, did that mean that there were two men—with the same face? A man with a heart of light and one with a heart of darkness.

Her mind found it difficult to fathom that there could be two people with precisely the same features, but she found that her heart was willing to accept this without question, for it meshed so perfectly with the emotions that lived within it.

Suddenly freed of its bonds, her heart filled with joy. Could this be the answer? she asked herself. The answer to her conflicting visions? Had her heart known the truth when it had insisted that Luca was not an evil man?

She squeezed her eyes shut. Now, finally, she could admit just how much she had wanted Luca to be innocent.

At the knock on the adjoining door, she turned toward it, a luminous smile curving her mouth, lighting her eyes.

The radiant expression on Chiara's face stopped Luca in his tracks. An ache within him rose as he realized that he would give a fortune to have the look on her face be for him.

He approached her slowly, afraid that his presence would turn her expression to the distrust and hatred he had seen there so often.

"You are feeling better, I see."

"Yes." She met his eyes, which had softened with an emotion she had never seen in them before. If he had been another man, she might have believed it to be longing.

Flustered, agitated, not just by the discovery she had just made, but by the newly admitted feelings within her and the look in Luca's eyes, she curled her fingers still more tightly around the ring, unsure of what to do or say.

"Were you—" he paused, swallowing the accusation that rose to his lips "—going out?"

She shook her head. "I decided it was time to stop being an invalid." Suddenly the questions bubbled up inside her. "Luca—" she began. But before she could continue, he lowered himself onto the chest next to her.

"Chiara." He felt something move within him,

not realizing that it was the pain and loneliness of years falling away from his heart. Unable to resist, he touched her cheek with his fingertips. "Do you know that this is the first time you have said my name?"

She shook her head.

For the first time in as long as he could remember, Luca felt a carefree exuberance and he laughed.

"That needs to be celebrated. Will you come with me?"

"Come with you?" Chiara sent him a bewildered look. "Where?"

"Anywhere." His hands curved around her shoulders. "A promenade around the piazza. No, you're not strong enough yet. The theater. Or a ride in a gondola. Yes, that's it." He laughed again. "Would you like that?"

"I don't know." Her head was spinning from her discovery, her feelings, Luca's sudden boyish ebullience. "No one's ever asked me that before."

"Then I'll have to remember to ask you that more often." Because it was too tempting to pull her closer, Luca rose. "Shall I send you someone to help you finish dressing?"

She shook her head.

"Then I'll be back in a little while." He turned to go.

Suddenly she was conscious of the ring that was biting into her palm. "Wait."

"What is it?"

"I—I need to talk to you."

"So serious?" He spoke lightly, but the fact that her radiant smile of a few moments ago was gone took some of the pleasure out of the moment.

"Yes, I need to ask you—"

"Later." He interrupted her, finding that he had no desire to hear what she wanted to ask him with that somber look in her eyes. "Let us enjoy the hour before the sun goes down."

It was an unseasonably warm evening and the air was almost balmy as Tommaso's even strokes carried the gondola down the Grand Canal.

The curtains of the *felze* were drawn back, today's mild breeze a sharp contrast to the cold wind Chiara had felt upon her face the last time she had sat in this very spot.

"Don't."

She turned so that she faced Luca fully. "Don't what?"

"Don't think about the night I brought you to the Ca' Zeani."

"How did you know that was what I was thinking?" Her dark eyebrows rose in surprise. "Do you have the sight now?"

"I don't need the sight to read what is in your eyes."

"It's past." She shrugged.

"Is it? Have you forgiven me for coming this close—" he held up thumb and forefinger a fraction of an inch apart "—to forcing you to my bed? For putting bruises on your skin?"

"You've already apologized for that."

"That's not an answer to my question."

"Why do you care at all if you have the forgiveness of a woman you bought as a slave?"

"You were never my slave and you know it," he

said. "You know well what would have happened by now had I considered you my slave."

"That's not an answer to *my* question, either."

"Why are we sparring like this? I brought you here to enjoy the air that will perhaps put some color back into your face." He stroked the backs of his fingers down her cheek.

Before she could answer, a *burchiello* with a richly set table under the red canopy skirted alongside their gondola and a tipsy male voice hailed them.

"*Olà, Signor Maschera!* Hey, Sir Mask!" a man dressed in the turbaned costume of a Moor called out. "We have good wine and food to share if you will share the wealth at your side."

A chorus of crude remarks seconding the invitation rose from the costumed and masked men lolling around the table and Chiara felt the heat rise into her face. Instinctively she shifted closer to Luca, glad that her face was at least partly hidden by the black half mask he had insisted she wear.

Luca slid his arm around Chiara and gave her shoulder a reassuring squeeze. "I suggest you learn better manners, *signori*," he said more mildly than he might have, had he been alone.

One of the men in the other boat stood and lurched forward a few steps. "It is you who should learn. Does not the Church teach us to share with our fellow man?" He laughed lewdly. "*We* all share, don't we, my friends?"

"Do not try to touch what is mine. Not unless you want the time left you on earth to be painful—and brief." Luca bared his teeth in a cold smile. "*Avanti,* Tommaso."

Tommaso speeded up his strokes and the gondola slid away quickly from the slower, heavier boat.

"That is what I meant the other day, Chiara. Do you know what would have happened if you had been alone when you met up with this pack of dogs? Do you?" He tipped up her chin so that he could look directly into her eyes. "Do you understand that they would not have taken no for an answer?"

Reminded of all the unanswered questions, Chiara jerked her face away from his touch. "I understand better than you know."

They fell silent, the void filled by the steady sound of Tommaso's oar against the water. Filled by shouts and laughter and snatches of song from the other boats that echoed over the canal.

But soon Chiara forgot the tension that had sprung up between them, and the buildings rimming the canal caught her fancy. She had only had a glimpse of the palaces on either side of the Grand Canal when the barge that had brought her from Padua had deposited her on the piazza. But now she found herself falling under the spell of the airy, ornamental stonework with its vaguely Oriental air.

The soft light of early evening flattered the colors that had been faded to pastels. The winds that swept in from the sea and the salt had turned brick red to dusty rose, amber to pale yellow, umber to tan. The marble alone seemed to have escaped the elements, its surface only growing translucent so that it shimmered like opals or pearls.

The first few shadows hid the bricks that were beginning to crumble beneath the green waterline. They masked the wooden gates and doorways that were disintegrating under the onslaught of the greedy sea.

"Do you want to go on to San Marco?" Luca asked, pointing to the left. "There will be music at Florian's and we can have coffee there."

Chiara followed the direction of his hand, where the *campanile,* the bell tower, peeked over the buildings and the lacelike loggia of the Doge's palace welcomed new arrivals on the jetty in front of it. But before she could answer, her gaze was drawn away from it.

Turning to the right, she found herself looking at a palazzo, its facade ornamented with medallions of blue, rimmed in gold.

"Paradini," she whispered, not realizing that she spoke aloud.

Luca jolted. "How do you know that that is the Ca' Paradini?"

But Chiara did not answer, did not even hear him, lost as she was in the sudden onslaught of images of her father.

"Chiara." Luca turned her to face him. Familiar now with the blankness of her eyes when the sight was upon her, he waited for her gaze to focus on him again.

"Do you know the name Paradini?" Chiara whispered, still reeling from the images.

"Of course. It is one of the names in the Golden Book, where every patrician family is recorded." He tipped his chin toward the building behind her. "And that was their palazzo you were looking at."

Chiara looked over her shoulder and concentrated on the building, asking for a picture of the inhabitants. But all that came to her was the fleeting image of a slender masked figure. The figure wore skintight silk breeches beneath the wide cloak, but she knew that it was a woman who wore them. Beyond that, all she could see was room upon room, empty but for ghosts.

Finally she turned back to Luca. "Do the Paradinis still live there?"

He wanted to ask her questions, but that could wait, he thought, feeling her urgency. "No Paradinis born with that name," he answered.

"I don't understand."

"It's a sad story, like so many others in Venice." His gaze skimmed over the building as he recalled what he knew about the Paradinis. "The one brother who was allowed to marry died without siring children. There were many brothers and some married, I think, but one by one they died. And they had no sons." He shrugged. "This has happened to many Venetian families and someday, the same thing will happen to the Zeanis."

Chiara felt the excitement of a few moments ago turn to ashes. "You mean there are no more male Paradinis in Venice?"

Even as she asked the question, she was sure that it could not be true. Surely, she would know if her father were dead. She tried to call up his image, but all she could see now was his grim face framed in the doorway, a moment before he had closed his door upon them.

Surely fate could not be so cruel as to deny her revenge on the man who had thrown his wife in all but name and the daughters he had sired into the streets of Rome like so much refuse.

"I don't know for certain, but I suspect that there are probably more than enough poor Paradinis living in the quarter of San Barnaba. Every rich family has poor relatives there. They are called *barnabotti* and everyone despises them, even they themselves."

"Why do they live apart?" She frowned. "Have they committed crimes?"

"No. Their crime is their poverty."

"But how can people cast aside their own blood?" she asked, beginning to understand why her father had found it easy to discard them as he had.

"That is the custom," he said, his matter-of-fact tone hiding how deeply he despised this practice. "They are given lodging and sometimes a little money, but they may hold no office, may not inherit money nor property, although they must wear silks because, despite everything, they are patricians."

Was her father among these poor patricians now? she asked herself. If he was, she hoped he was suffering. And if he wasn't, she would make him suffer.

"The only one living in the Ca' Paradini now is Laura Paradini, the richest and most eccentric woman in Venice." He stopped, frowning. "It occurs to me that it was she who was your first client that evening at Giulietta's. You recognized her for a woman although she was wearing men's clothing."

Chiara remembered the woman into whose hard, cold heart she had looked. Her heart, where—her pulse began to pound again with excitement—she had felt the presence of her father.

Luca watched Chiara, her eyes dazed, lean back and rest her head against the carved back of the seat. He remembered little about the Paradinis, but he remembered that all of the Paradini brothers had had eyes of the most startling blue.

Softly he instructed Tommaso to turn around and seek out the quieter canals, where they would be away from the boatfuls of revelers preparing for yet another night of pleasure.

He watched Chiara as she lay there, her eyes full of secrets. Then her lashes lowered and he felt a little of the tension flow out of her. The sun became a memory, spreading only a pinkish glow in the sky, and the evening shadows darkened into night.

At his signal, Tommaso again changed direction.

When he had reached his destination, he touched her shoulder lightly, surprised when she opened her eyes immediately.

"You did not sleep?"

"No, but I rested well." She smiled. "Thank you."

She sat up and looked around her, not recognizing the narrow dank-smelling canal, where there were no torches to light one's way. "Where are we?"

"I must leave you here. Tommaso will bring you back."

Her eyes darted back and forth and she gripped his arm with both hands. "Don't go."

"It's all right. Tommaso will make certain you are safe." He let his hand stroke over hers. "No harm will come to you."

"Harm?" The word echoed inside her, setting off ripples like a stone that is thrown into a lake.

She stilled and her vision blurred, as her mind filled with images that her sight brought her.

"Hear me, Luca."

Even in the darkness he could see her eyes grow unfocused and glassy.

"I bring you warning. Beware," Chiara whispered, lifting her hands as if to ward off the evil.

"The masked man you meet in the shadows is a destroyer."

Luca thought of their plans and almost smiled at the aptness of her words. Yes, he mused, the masked man was a destroyer. But then, so was he. They had to be. Both of them.

"Some things need to be destroyed so that other things can flourish," he said.

"And who will flourish when you are destroyed?"

"Are you saying that he wishes to destroy me?" He laughed sharply. "I am his finely honed sword. Why should he destroy his weapon?"

"He brings danger and harm. To you and others." She tried to see his face beneath the sinister mask of black and gold, but the image of the mask paled and she saw only Luca's face.

Her vision cleared. She met Luca's eyes and saw that he did not believe her.

He did not want to hear her warning, she thought. And perhaps he was right to doubt her. After all, she doubted herself, didn't she?

She no longer knew if what her sight showed her was true. Perhaps her gift was gone now. Perhaps she had gone a little mad. Perhaps she was being punished for the anger and hatred that had lived in her heart for so long.

"Do what you must." She shifted away from him. "I will not warn you again."

Chapter Fourteen

The moment Luca stepped into his chamber, his manservant was at his side to take the cloak, domino and mask from him.

"Go to your bed, Rico." Luca tugged off the dark ribbon that had tied back his hair and shook it free so that it fell to his shoulders. "It's late."

"Should I not help you disrobe, Don Luca? Bring some refreshment?" He shifted the clothing he held to his other arm. "Perhaps some of that cheese you've always liked?"

"I don't want anything and I can manage to undress myself." His own ungracious tone grated on his ears and he turned and gave Rico's shoulder a friendly squeeze. "I'll be all right. Go now."

The old servant watched his master's gaze shift to the door of the next chamber.

"She is in her chamber. I heard Zanetta speak to her perhaps an hour ago."

Luca looked at his manservant, his eyebrows raised.

"I—I thought, I would pay some attention to what the young woman is doing. I know you have some interest in her whereabouts." His last words were spoken almost defiantly, but then the old retainer looked down at his feet, uncomfortable under his master's cool, sharp gaze.

"That phrasing is worthy of a diplomat." Luca laughed shortly. "She is free to go if she wishes to. You do remember that I told you that, don't you?"

"Yes, Don Luca." Rico raised his gaze to Luca's chest. "I just saw you looking at the door and I thought to—to…"

"Ease my mind?"

Rico made a wordless gesture of assent.

"Is it so obvious that I'm making a fool of myself?"

Rico hunched his shoulders in a kind of shrug and allowed himself a glance at his master's face.

Luca laughed again. "Go to bed, Rico."

When the servant had gone, Luca filled a goblet with wine. Ignoring the door that beckoned and tempted, he crossed the shadowy room and went to stand at the window. The dark canal, silvered by a moon that was almost full, was spread out below, like a sleeping woman waiting for her lover.

He wouldn't think of her, he told himself even as the image rose strongly within him. He wouldn't think of the woman who lay sleeping in the next room.

So instead, he thought of the warning Chiara had given him. It had been going around and around in his mind for the past hours, like an animal pacing the circumference of a cage.

Yes, he knew that this conspiracy could be a trap. He'd known that from the very first time the masked man had spoken to him, his words cloaked by the turbulent gaiety around them on the Piazza San Marco. But why would anyone go to such elaborate lengths to harm him? There were enough dark corners in Venice—and cheap assassins to make use of them.

And he had to believe in something. After years of seeing the Venetian navy, and with it Venice's honor, disintegrate like a piece of old parchment, this was hope. The last and only hope.

So, despite Chiara's warning, he had not hesitated to heed the summons to meet on yet another shadowy *campo*.

The plans were coming together. At least that was what the masked man told them. Each time they met, he had yet another idea. Yet another cache of weapons to be hidden. Yet another place to be prepared, where men would be concealed until it was time to move.

He chafed a little that the masked man was making all the plans, all the arrangements. The men he had recruited were little more than runners whom he sent off on errands that needed no particular courage or intelligence. And he himself had not been assigned a single task.

"What do you need us for anyway?" Luca had finally asked him tonight when the others had disappeared into the night, leaving him and the masked man alone. "You are making all the plans. You are making the connections to the ones who will help us." He gestured impatiently. "You would have done as well with a band of paid ruffians."

"I didn't want ruffians. I wanted men who believed." He laughed. "Or don't you believe anymore?"

"I'm trying to, but it's not easy." He'd looked at the man, his hands itching to tear off his mask so that he could once, just once, look at his face. "And it's not easy to wait and do nothing."

"Your day will come." He clapped his hand down on Luca's shoulder. "Until then I will slip in and out of the shadows and prepare." His hand mimicked the motion of a snake. "I am anonymous. The man without a face. This is my task. When the day comes for us to move, it will be your turn."

"So I just wait." The words were as bitter as ashes. "I wait and do nothing."

"Does it pain you that this was not your idea, Luca Zeani? That you are not giving the orders?"

The masked man's words, spoken with a mocking lilt, pressed against his wounded pride with the precision of a surgeon's instrument probing torn flesh.

"I would be a liar if I said that I did not wish I had had the vision to initiate this, but—" he shrugged "—I am well used to following orders and it does not trouble me to follow wise ones. But you have given me none."

"And you will not get any." He put his arm companionably around Luca's shoulders. "I will prepare the way. The others will do the work of drones. But when the day finally comes, it is *you* who will be the leader." He laughed softly. "All eyes will be on you and I will melt back into the shadows where I have lived for so long."

That soft, slightly mocking laugh had stirred a long-ago memory. Matteo, he realized. The laugh reminded him of his dead brother.

Matteo, whom he had loved and hated, and who had been his dark mirror, living all the violence and cruelty that lay hidden beneath his own mask. Matteo, whose blood was on his hands, as surely as if he had plunged his own dagger into his heart.

He had been the one, after all, to turn his brother over to the constables. He had watched them lead him away in chains. And he had wept when the messenger had come to tell him that his brother had died on some road in the mountains for the few coins in his pocket.

"Do not be too impatient, my friend. When the day of the rebellion comes, the pleasures that life has to offer will no longer be yours." The man squeezed his shoulder. "Enjoy them now," he whispered slyly. "Enjoy that pretty piece you keep in your apartments."

"What do you know about this woman?" he had demanded, surprised by the sudden fury that flashed through him at the thought that this man dared speak of Chiara. He felt violated by the man's mocking tone, his derisive words. He had been spied upon in his own home. "You have no business digging into my private life."

"It is my business to know everything about everyone. I am the master of secrets and shadows, masks and mirrors." He lifted his hand in a salute. "Good night, my friend."

With a soft laugh, the masked man had leaped down into his gondola and left Luca standing there on the *campo* where the bright moonlight made the shadows only more pronounced.

Luca stared out of the window as he drank deeply of the wine, but the bitter taste remained in his mouth.

Was he so mean, so petty, he asked himself, that

he begrudged the masked man the preparations for the rebellion? Why did he feel as if he were being used solely for the satisfaction of another? He felt an icy presentiment creep up his spine at the thought of the rebellion and wondered if he had become as timid as the old men who ruled Venice.

It was Chiara who had planted the seeds of doubt in his mind. She had made him look for dangers that were not there. It was she who made him so edgy that he could not bear the thought of another man touching her, be it only with words.

He emptied the goblet and returned to the table to refill it.

When he heard Chiara cry out, the goblet slipped from his fingers and shattered.

The nightmare pressed against Chiara like a smothering pillow.

The images floated closer, became clearer. Two figures. Dark. Masked. She stared at them, paralyzed into motionlessness. She wanted to run, to hide, but she found that she could not. Instead, she fell onto her knees, staring at them with wide, terrified eyes as they drew nearer.

They came closer and closer still. Finally the terror, yawning like a black pit inside her, pushed her to move. On hands and knees, she crawled away slowly.

The man in the black-and-gold mask was there, so close that if he reached out his hand he would be able to touch her. And next to him stood a second figure, the beaked mask a ghostly white in the murky darkness. Luca. She could see him cloaked in light just as the man in the black-and-gold mask was cloaked in darkness.

Then the stench of evil was everywhere. She pressed her hand against her face, but still it filled her nostrils, her mouth, like thick, black smoke, choking her.

As she watched, the two figures moved to stand closer together, so that their shoulders touched. Their cloaks, the one of light and the one of darkness, flowed together like two rivers, mingling and melding until she could no longer tell which was which.

As one, they raised their hands and drew away their masks. Horror and panic washed through her as she looked from one to the other. She lifted her hands to press them against her eyes, but they fell away, feeble and useless.

Horrified, she looked from one face to the other, unable to deny that both faces carried Luca's features.

She could no longer tell who was the evil one. Or was it both? Which man spewed these vile, poisonous fumes that were choking her?

Again she called on her sight. She cried out to her guiding spirit. But the terror was so great that all she could see were the figures coming closer, both with Luca's beautiful face.

Simultaneously they both reached out for her. With the last of her strength, she twisted back out of their reach.

As she slammed into the carved headboard of the bed, she came awake with a cry.

"Chiara! Are you all right?" Luca slid across the last stretch of marble floor, grasping a poster of the bed to keep his balance.

With a sound like that of a frightened animal, Chiara crossed her hands palm outward in front of her eyes. The images that had filled the nightmare continued to fill her head so that she was not sure if she had woken or still slept.

"Were you dreaming?" Luca asked softly. Releasing the poster of the bed, he sat down on the edge of the mattress.

As she felt the bed dip beneath his weight, Chiara's hands fell to her sides and dug into the bedclothes. She wanted to flee, but all she could do was press herself against the headboard. The carving gouged her head and her back, and gradually the physical pain brought reality with it.

It had been a dream, she realized. A terrible dream. Some of the tension drained out of her, but enough remained that she had to close her eyes so that she would not need to look at Luca's face. The face that had been *twofold* in her dream.

The nightmare still held her in its grip, and her whole existence seemed limited to it, obscuring both her insights of just a few hours ago and the knowledge that had been growing in her heart these past weeks.

She felt his weight lift from the bed and a small sigh of relief shivered through her lips. But then a moment later the bed dipped again and her eyes flew open.

"Here." Luca held out a cup of wine. "Drink this."

Slowly she lifted her hands and took the cup from

him, careful not to brush his fingers. She took a cautious sip and then another.

"Do you want to tell me about it?" he asked softly. It was the nightmare, he told himself again, but still it hurt that she was looking at him as if he were a monster.

She shook her head.

"Shall I hold you?"

"No!" She rolled her head from side to side against the headboard so violently that wine splashed over the rim of the cup. "No."

"Chiara, I have touched you roughly. But have I not shown you that I will touch you roughly no more? Will you not let me hold you when a dream makes you tremble in the night?" He reached out to touch her, wanting to soothe, but she pressed herself still farther against the headboard.

"Don't touch me!"

Luca flinched as if she had struck him. Pain welled up like blood from flesh sliced by the tip of a dagger, surprising him with its intensity. When anger followed, he welcomed it because he knew well that its heat could cauterize even the worst wounds.

"I have never been a patient man, Chiara. You learned that the first evening of our acquaintance. But I have tried to be patient with you. By God, more patient than I have ever been with a woman." His voice was mild and those who knew him well would have recognized that as a dangerous sign.

"I have tried to be gentle. Gentler perhaps than it is my nature to be," he continued as he stood. "I do not think that I would willingly bear it again to have you look at me as if I were Lucifer himself. It may be wiser if you leave this house before I make myself guilty of what you already accuse me.''

The light of the single candle that burned at her bedside was dim, but she could see his eyes and they carried intense pain.

As she watched him turn away and move toward the door, she dipped inside herself and tried to see. Light or darkness? But her sight had been struck with blindness and showed her nothing.

Beyond all reason, something inside her moved. His need spoke to her need, as if one were the echo of the other.

''Luca.''

He stopped, his hand on the ornate door handle of polished bronze, but did not turn around.

''Don't go.''

His hand tightened on the door handle. ''I am not in the mood for games.''

''I am not playing games.''

''No?'' He turned around then, but remained where he was. ''If it is not a game, my dear, then it is certainly an excellent imitation.''

Chiara could barely see his face in the dark. ''I'm afraid.'' Even as she spoke, she wondered that the words slipped off her tongue so easily. Never in her life had she opened herself this way to another.

''Of me?''

''Of you. Of myself. Of the confusion in my mind.'' She lowered her head into her hands. ''Everything used to be so clear. I knew my path. I knew what I had to do.'' She pulled in an unsteady breath. ''Now nothing is clear.''

That wasn't quite true, she thought. It was clear that there was something between them that was deep and real, far beyond her fears, her visions. Something she was afraid to look at more closely.

Luca looked across the room and felt his heart fill. For the first time in his life, he understood true tenderness could exist beside desire that was as sharp as a well-honed sword. Slowly he crossed the floor to stand at the side of Chiara's bed.

"Why did you ask me to stay then, if you are afraid of me?"

"I don't know." Her face still buried in her hands, she shook her head.

"I don't believe you, Chiara." Not wanting to threaten her with his physical presence, he crouched at the side of the bed.

"Tell me," he said when long minutes had passed and she still had not answered. "Look at me and tell me why you asked me to stay."

Slowly she raised her head and met his eyes. "There was something in your eyes that touched me." She swallowed and, when she continued, her voice was barely audible. "Something that echoed inside me because I felt it, too."

"Why then did you look at me as if I were evil incarnate?" he probed, needing more.

Slowly the dream was dimming and she felt easier, lighter as if a poison were draining out of her system. And as it dimmed, she recalled what the terrible reality of the dream had eclipsed. She recalled her discovery of the two rings that afternoon. And she recalled that she had not asked him the questions that had been burning in her mind.

"What do you want, Chiara?" He rose and sat down on the edge of the mattress.

"I don't kn—" The lie died on her lips as she gazed into his eyes.

She saw desire there and a need that was mirrored within herself. And she saw tenderness.

And just as the nightmare had swallowed up everything else just moments ago, so now the need, his and hers, made all else slip away.

"Hold me," she whispered.

He lifted his hand to cup her cheek. "Are you still afraid?"

"Yes."

Her admission touched him, coupled as it was with how her eyes held steady on his. He slid his fingers into her hair. "Don't be afraid, *piccola*, little one," he said softly.

His fingers pressing against the back of her neck, he brought her closer. His gaze drifted down to her mouth. He lowered his head, her taste already spreading on his tongue. Then he felt her tremble.

He nestled her face against his chest, drawing her closer so that she was pressed against him. His fingers rubbed the back of her neck and his hand moved up and down her back in light, easy strokes. Gradually he felt the trembling stop and the tension leave her body so that it was pliant as it fitted itself to his.

"Better?" he murmured.

"Yes."

The warmth of her breath traveled through the lace of his shirt, spreading against his skin like a caress. Arousal was so keen, so instant that his breath caught in his throat. Suddenly, like a frayed rope that snaps when it is pulled too tightly, the unfulfilled desire of the past weeks surged through him and he felt his control give way.

Quickly he laid her back against the pillows.

"Can you sleep now?"

"No." She raised herself onto her elbows. "I don't want to."

"Drink the rest of the wine and sleep." He rose. "You still need rest."

"No." Her voice rose. "If I sleep, then I will dream again. I don't want to dream." She dug her fingers into the bedclothes as wisps of the nightmare came back to haunt her. "Don't go yet."

"I am only a man, Chiara. A man at the end of his tether." His hands clenched into fists at his sides. "If I stay, I will make love to you."

His words struck sparks within her, like flint striking rock. If he filled her body with his, she wondered suddenly, would it fill the void, the terrible emptiness within her? Would it ease the loneliness that she had lived with all her life? She almost reached for him.

Luca now understood that if he made love to her, he would need neither force nor seduction. Because he also understood that what he wanted from her was not surrender, nor acquiescence, he strode away quickly, without looking back.

"Luca."

For the second time that evening, he stopped, his hand on the door handle. "What is it now?" he demanded, impatience coloring his voice.

"You never answered my questions last night."

"You never asked them."

Afraid of the answers she would hear, her heart pounded and she drew a quick breath in an attempt to quiet it. "Is there another man with your face?"

"What?" The word tore out of him as he spun around to face her.

She shrank back from the wild look on his face, but she continued. "I see a man with your face. A man of great evil."

"In your visions?"

"Yes, and I saw him—"

He silenced her with a choppy gesture. "I had a brother. A twin brother. We were as alike in face and body as it is possible for two people to be." He swallowed audibly. "He is dead."

"No!" she cried, remembering the man on whose finger she had seen the gold ring, the duplicate of which still lay in her purse. "That's not poss—"

"My brother is dead," he repeated, as the pain welled up inside him. Then he stepped across the threshold of his chamber and closed the door behind him.

For a long time Chiara remained very still, his words echoing in her mind. If what he said was so, where did the truth lie then?

In your heart.

Yes, she thought. She would have to seek the truth there—and accept it.

But what then? she asked herself.

Closing her eyes, she let the tears come.

Chapter Fifteen

Her eyes gritty from tears, Chiara awoke from the restless sleep she had finally succumbed to when the sky was already paling with the dawn.

She had searched her heart. She did not understand, but she *knew* that Luca was innocent. That alone she might have accepted, but she had found even more in her heart. She had found—

No! She sat up in bed and drove her fingers through her tangled curls. If she put a name to it, it would make it true. There was a magic in names, in words that made real what had been but an illusion.

She had to leave, she thought. She had to escape, for now that she had accepted Luca's innocence, she would surrender. And then she would become just like her mother, who had sacrificed her life to a man's pleasure. And she would never be more for Luca than his mistress, even should he desire otherwise. She knew all too well the Venetian law that decreed a patrician could not marry beneath him.

Her measured movements hiding the undercurrents of panic, she chose the simplest and least colorful of the outfits that the dressmaker had made for her. She gathered up her hair and bound it severely at the nape of her neck. As she picked up her purse, its weight reminded her of the ring it contained.

She emptied the contents of the purse onto a table and placed the coins back into it. She then tied it around her waist and tucked it into the band of her skirt.

As she made her preparations, the memory of that one vision crept into her consciousness, teasing, tormenting. She remembered clearly how she had seen herself, her black hair in vivid contrast to the coverlet of scarlet silk, her mouth curving in a sensual smile of welcome.

This was why she was leaving, she reminded herself. If she stayed, she would surrender to him as the vision had shown her. She would surrender to him not by force but by desire. She knew that, as she had known it from the moment she had seen the vision.

You have seen the future and what you have seen will be. You can see the future, but you cannot change it.

So clearly did she hear the sound of her inner voice that her head snapped upward.

Your mother, too, saw what would be, but she knew she could not change it. Even if she could have undone it, she would not have done so.

"No," Chiara whispered. "I'm not like her."

No, you are not. You are strong where she was weak and you will master what life sends your way. But you cannot escape it.

"No!" She pressed her hands against her temples. "If I stay, perhaps it will be true. But I do not choose to stay. I choose to leave and so I will change my future."

You will see. You will see. Then the voice faded away and there was only silence.

Shaken at the message, she closed her eyes. Why did this inner voice that had shown her the way and comforted her in times of need and desperation now try to block the path she had chosen for herself? Why did it tell her that she had no choice but to accept what could ultimately destroy her?

When she opened her eyes, she saw that the sky had lightened. Its dove gray color now had a pinkish glow, its pearly light already brightening the facades of the buildings across the canal.

Defying her inner voice and her own vision, she lifted her chin. She would have a good day for her journey, she told herself.

Gathering her cloak around her, she moved forward, intent on her goal. As her gaze brushed the door that connected her chamber to Luca's, she remembered how he had asked her not to leave without telling him. She tried not to remember the expression that had been in his eyes.

A note. She would leave him a note. He could not ask more of her.

She sat down and began to write, but she had not gotten beyond the first few words when her vision began to swim. The words she had written became no more than an incoherent jumble of black lines and all she could see was the image of Luca's face.

She willed the image away, but it was too powerful. Raising her hand to her forehead, she dug into her memory for the incantation. Then, remembering that she needed something of his for the charm, she picked up the ring. Haltingly she spoke the magic words and waited for the image to dissipate. But it remained. Trapped in the vision, she began to tremble.

Luca jolted out of the exhausted sleep he had slipped into just before dawn. Certain that he had heard Chiara's voice calling his name, he vaulted out of his bed. Unmindful of his nakedness, unmindful of the cold marble tiles beneath his feet, he dashed out of his bedchamber.

Slowing down to avoid the shards of blue glass from the goblet he had dropped last night, he realized that there were no sounds coming from her room. Feeling foolish, he returned to the bedchamber and slipped on a wide robe of dark blue silk.

Restless, he wandered to the window to look out at the sky that had the translucent color of pale pink pearls. He started, again thinking to have heard Chiara's voice. Too edgy to remain in his room, he turned and strode toward her chamber.

She was sitting at the table, the back of her hand pressed against her forehead, her mouth tight as if she were in pain. Concerned, words of comfort already forming on his tongue, he started toward her. He had almost reached her when he realized that she was fully dressed, a cloak slung over her shoulders.

Within the space of a breath, the disquiet he had felt became rage that blazed like a fire burning out of control. Just barely, he curbed the roar that rose in his throat, curbed the frenzied desire to rush forward, break his promises and again lock the door. Drawing in one long, slow breath, he forced himself to relax his hands, which had curled into fists at his sides.

When he was certain that he could speak calmly,

he crossed the room to stand in front of the table where Chiara sat.

"Are you going somewhere?"

Chiara started, dropping the quill she still held, spattering ink over the paper in front of her.

The image where she had been caught dissolved. And yet she found that nothing had changed. All she saw was Luca.

"I asked if you were going somewhere."

His face was all sharp lines and angles, the generous mouth thin and severe. But she saw past the cold fury to the fatigue and the hurt, and found herself with the absurd wish of wanting to erase the shadows that lived in his eyes and bruised the skin beneath them.

"Yes," she said softly, "in fact, I was."

"I thought you weren't going to leave without telling me."

"I never promised you that." She spoke quietly, but a touch of defiance colored her voice.

"Damn you." The fury was seeping back, mingling with the hurt he did not, could not acknowledge, to form a new, explosive emotion. "Hasn't anything changed?"

It was almost hidden behind the anger, but Chiara could see the hurt that bled like an open wound. A wellspring of pain sprang up within her in answer.

"The only thing that has changed is that I have come to see that you were right."

His eyes narrowed. "What are you talking about?"

"Last night you said that it would be wiser if I left this house. When I awoke this morning, I knew that you were right.'' She spoke quickly, lightly, hoping to discharge the tension that crackled in the room like summer lightning.

Instead he rounded the corner of the table so quickly that his movements were a blur.

''How can you say that?'' he shouted as he grabbed her. ''How can you sit there as calmly as if we were discussing an evening's entertainment at the theater and say that?''

A shiver of fear rose at his rough touch.

''Answer me!'' he demanded.

''I can say that because it's true.'' Needing to calm herself, she pulled in a deep breath. ''It will be better if I leave.''

''Better for whom?''

''Certainly for me. And perhaps for you, as well.''

His mouth twisted into a sneer. ''You have my undying gratitude for your care.'' His hands tightened. ''Perhaps I should warn you that I do not deal well with ridicule.''

''I mean no ridicule, Luca,'' she said softly. ''I am causing you trouble. With your elder brother Alvise, who wants me gone. With your plans, which I have undermined. I have sown doubt in your mind and perhaps that will harm you more than any danger I might have seen.'' She paused. ''If you think about it calmly, you will see that it is best that I go.''

''No,'' he shouted. He told himself that it was absurd to feel threatened by her quiet determination. It was in his power to keep her as long as he wished. ''I won't let you go.''

She felt the pull of the passion within him and a flurry of panic rose. ''You promised,'' she said, forcing herself not to struggle against his hands.

"It was a moment of madness."

"Luca." She put her hand against his heart. "Does that make it any less of a promise?"

It was that gesture more than anything else that weakened him. If she had tried to push him away, he could have held her captive. If she had fought him hard enough, he might even have forced her. But her soft words and that gentle touch defeated him.

"No, I suppose not." Suddenly conscious of how his fingers were digging into her shoulders, his grip gentled. "I've probably marked your skin again." His fingers began to stroke, soothing the hurt he himself had caused.

"Chiara." His hands drifted upward to frame her face. "Don't go. I need you." The words slipped out, surprising both of them.

"Don't say that." She felt her heart leap within her chest.

"Why not, when it's true?"

"No." She shook her head. "You may want me, but you don't need me. You don't need me," she repeated, wanting to convince herself as much as she wanted to convince him.

"What do you know of my needs?" His voice rose again. "Look inside me with your sight, Chiara. If you dare to look, you will see."

"That is not the point, Luca."

"What is the point? Your needs, perhaps?" He saw something flicker in her eyes and fixed his sights on it with the unerring instinct of a warrior who has found his enemy's weakness. "Yes, Chiara, what of your needs?"

She tensed, suddenly afraid that his sharp gaze

would find her weak points. "My needs are not at issue here."

"They were last night."

"Last night is past."

Her eyes were steady as she spoke, but he felt the slight tremble that went through her.

"Is it? Can you look into my eyes and tell me that you feel nothing?"

"What I do or do not feel is not at issue here, either." This time it was her voice that rose. Because the touch of his fingers on her skin was sweet, she pulled back and turned away.

"The only thing at issue is that I wish to leave and you promised me that I could do so anytime I wished." She paused. "Or did you only do it because you thought I was dying and you didn't think it would be a promise you would have to keep?"

He could keep her captive. He knew that. But he understood that if he did, she would never forgive him. And he would never forgive himself.

"No." Luca lifted his hands and rubbed them over his face in a gesture that spoke of both exhaustion and defeat. "I meant it."

He could not see her face, but he heard her deep sigh of relief and it sliced into him as a dagger slices into flesh. This time, he acknowledged the hurt.

"Will you tell me why, at least?"

"Because if I stay—" She bit her lip. What could she say? she asked herself. If I stay, then I will give myself to you? If I stay, then I will welcome you into my body, into my heart and it will destroy me?

But half of that was already true, she admitted, suddenly too tired and weak to fight both him and her own feelings. Perhaps she had not welcomed him into her heart, but he had found his way there nevertheless. A deep sadness flooded her.

"If I stay," she began again, "it will not bring happiness to either one of us." The words sounded weak after the emotional storm of the past minutes.

"But why?" he demanded, anger still coloring his voice. "Can you not give me an explanation?"

She shook her head. "Not one you can understand."

The weariness, the sadness in her voice had what remained of his anger draining away. He closed the distance between them and laid his hands on her shoulders. This time he did not hold her, but only touched her gently, his thumbs pressing lightly against the base of her neck.

"All right, Chiara," he said softly. "Go, if you must."

Chiara knew how empty words could be, but now she felt Luca's true intention behind them, so that the words releasing her had all the power of a charm.

Before she knew what was happening, before she could shore up her defenses, she felt the determination that had braced her throughout their confrontation dissipate like a puff of smoke.

Luca felt something within her give. Instinctively he lowered his head and pressed his mouth against the side of her neck.

Chiara shifted beneath his touch then went still, her body hungry for pleasure, her soul hungry for gentleness. Somewhere in the back of her mind, she heard the echo of her inner voice reminding her that she could not change her fate. And she knew she was lost.

Her taste, her fragrance went to Luca's head like

strong wine. He might have been able to withstand his own desire, but there was no way that he could withstand the way she seemed to soften under his hands, like wax against a flame.

His mouth drifted upward to taste the spot just below her ear. The way her breath caught before she exhaled in a sigh almost undid him.

Chiara could feel herself softening, weakening. Even as her needs pushed her to reach for the pleasure, fear fought through the sensual haze that seemed to permeate her like a drug and found its way to her tongue.

"Stop."

She heard herself say the word, but she felt herself shiver with pleasure at the sensation of his mouth and tongue against her skin and knew that it was useless. How could any man believe a word that her body so obviously denied? How could any man believe anything spoken in that foreign, breathy voice that was itself an invitation?

Everything that had passed between them faded away as Luca trailed his mouth over her skin. He had felt her tremble. He had heard the soft sound she had made. So it was easy to ignore the token protest that had sounded far more like a moan of pleasure than a plea.

His hands slipped forward to undo her cloak. One tug and it was gone, pooling on the floor between them. As he traced the rim of her ear with his tongue, he let his hands drift downward to cup her breasts. He felt the crests rise toward his questing fingers, and his mouth curved against her ear.

Even as the pleasure from what his mouth, his tongue, his clever fingers were doing to her shot through her to lodge at the juncture of her thighs, Chiara gathered the last sorry remains of her strength.

"Please, stop." She heard her own broken whisper and hated it, but she knew she had no choice but to beg. If she did not beg, if he did not stop, he would turn her own body against her.

This time, her voice penetrated some still-lucid part of his mind. Luca lifted his head away and turned her around to face him.

"You really mean that, don't you?"

"Yes." Understanding that, for the moment, at least, the danger was past, Chiara almost sagged with relief.

"Why?" he demanded, his voice more puzzled than angry. "You trembled with pleasure. Your body flowed into my touch." Slowly, deliberately, he trailed his hands up from her shoulders, over her neck to cup her face and watched her eyes darken with arousal. "Even now, your eyes give you away."

"Please, don't."

"There is nothing shameful in what takes place between a man and a woman." His mouth curved into a charming grin. "Not when both of them want it as badly as we do." He feathered his thumb over her mouth. "Don't deny it."

"I'm not denying it." She stayed very still, knowing that every movement would have his fingers caressing her skin. "But I'm asking you to stop."

"I don't understand you."

"I'm asking you not to make me betray myself by seducing my body."

"Seduction?" he challenged. "Your body is as ready as mine." His hands went to her hips and pulled her so close that his aroused flesh pressed against her belly.

Because she felt too good, too right, pressed so close against him, he let her go. Because he could not continue to look at her and not reach for her again, he turned away, spearing his fingers through his hair.

"Never in my life have I spent so much time talking with a woman." A self-deprecating amusement warred with irritation in his voice.

Now that she was safe—for the moment at least— Chiara allowed herself a smile.

"And never have you been less bored, I wager."

"Believe me, that is scant comfort at the moment." He slanted her a brief look over his shoulder. "If you are leaving, do it now, quickly."

Chiara bent and picked up the cloak that lay at her feet.

Tensing at the rustle of fabric, Luca fought the urge to whirl around and hold her back. He slid his hands into the pockets of the robe to hide the fact that he had curled them into fists. Because he needed to look at her one last time, he turned around.

Her fingers caught in the soft woolen fabric, Chiara met his eyes. She did not call on her sight, but it came upon her unbidden. Again, as she had so often before, she saw him cloaked in light. And she saw within him an intricate weave of needs and desires that she knew mirrored what lived within her.

"Stay. I need you."

She heard the words clearly, although her eyes told her that he had not spoken.

Her heart opened a little wider, releasing her own needs, her own emotions that she had hidden so carefully. They drifted out like seeds borne by a breeze, only to return to take root and fill her. Yes, Chiara admitted. He had something she needed. She pressed her hands, still tangled in the cloak, against her middle.

Although she wanted to close her eyes, she kept them steadily on his and looked at everything he had embodied for her. The hatred. The evil. The danger. The fear.

The first two were gone. And what of the others? Yes, she admitted. There was still danger. There was still fear. But she knew that her need for whatever it was that he had to give her was far greater than either one of them.

Luca knew the moment she made the decision to stay. The brilliant blue of her eyes softened, darkened to the color of the sea at sundown. He felt something move inside him that had nothing to do with the desire he had felt for her from the beginning or the strange need that he couldn't quite define.

"Shall I make you more promises?"

"Only if you want to." She felt her mouth curve, surprised at how easily the smile rose to her lips. "And only if you mean them."

"What do you want from me?"

"For you to accept me as I am."

"Have I not done that already?" he demanded.

"You've accepted me today, but what about tomorrow or the day after? Will I have to fight you again?"

"I don't know. Perhaps you should ask yourself if you will have to fight *yourself* again. If you have accepted *yourself* as you are, and for what *you* truly want." He paused. "Have you?"

His baldly spoken words hit her like a blow to the stomach, reminding her all too clearly of those painful feelings she had not wanted to look at. She was staying, not because she was being held captive, but because she had made the decision to do so.

Luca saw her flinch as if he had struck her. Her eyes filled with tears so that they looked like twin pools of clear, blue water. The tears spilled down her cheeks, and he found himself hurting more than he had thought it possible for a woman to make him hurt.

"Chiara, someday soon we will be lovers. Not because you have surrendered to my strength, nor because I have seduced you, but because you want to lie with me as much as I do with you." He spoke the words quietly, without arrogance, as much for himself as for her. "Because from the first moment, we were meant to be together." He paused. "Know this, Chiara, that I have never said this to another woman."

He looked at her for a long moment, then he turned and left the room.

Chiara stood still, barely breathing, long after the door had closed behind him.

Your fate. She heard the faraway echo of the voice. *It is your fate.*

She fell to her knees where she stood, buried her face in the folds of the cloak she still held and wept.

Chapter Sixteen

She had dried her tears quickly, Chiara thought. Too quickly. Her attention wandered from the chess game she and Luca had been engrossed in for the past hour.

Luca had made it easy for her in the past weeks, treating her like a guest. Yes, he still touched her, kissed her with that heart-stopping skill, but he did it so subtly, so exquisitely that she could almost forget that nothing had changed. He was not courting her. Or if he was, then only with the goal of luring her into his bed.

She had allowed herself to slip into the languor of this sweet Venetian life that was as insidious as quicksand, she realized. The three months she had spent in the Ca' Zeani had disappeared like sand in an hourglass. She was forgetting her duty to her sister. She was forgetting her duty to find her father.

Well, she thought, as she reached for her queen and made her move, that was going to change.

"I must go to Padua," she said, her words cutting sharply into the mellow silence.

"Padua?" Luca looked up from the chessboard. "Why?"

Keeping her eyes on the board, she fingered the alabaster knight she had just taken. "There is something I need to do there."

He reached out and ran his finger over her knuckles. "More secrets?" he asked lightly.

Chiara looked up sharply, but she saw no mockery in his eyes. Suddenly she found that she was tired of carrying all her burdens alone. "My sister is there."

Luca leaned back, the chess game forgotten. This was the first time that Chiara had spoken about her family beyond the fact that her father was a Venetian patrician. Until this moment he had not realized how much it would mean to him to have her share something of herself.

"So you come from Padua?" he questioned cautiously, half expecting her to refuse to answer. "There is a Gypsy camp there, is there not?"

She shook her head. "No, I was born in Rome."

"And you traveled with the Gypsies?"

"No." Her mouth thinned. "My mother became the mistress of a *gadjo*," she said bitterly, all too aware that the same fate would be hers. "She could not return to her people, not even after he discarded her like a used rag."

"And he is the man you have come to Venice to find?"

"Yes." She thought of the palazzo with the blue medallions and the woman who lived there. The woman who had something to do with her father. She wondered why she felt this reluctance to pursue the only clue she had, and why her sight had not helped her.

"Why did you not bring your sister with you to Venice?"

"She—" she hesitated. "She is not well," she hedged. "I need to make certain that she is treated kindly by the family I paid to care for her."

She shivered, suddenly uncomfortable talking about Donata with Luca, whose face was the likeness of the man's whom she had pulled off Donata's ravished body. "It is your move," she said, tipping her chin toward the chessboard.

"Will you let me take you to Padua?"

She shook her head. "It is better if I go alone."

"Chiara, be reasonable. There are too many men abroad looking for easy sport."

"Indeed." Her gaze brushed over him and shifted away.

"All right. I will have my *burchiello* prepared and you can go as you please," he growled and stood. "You will hardly refuse that. Or will you?"

She made a gesture of grudging acceptance, then glanced up at him. "And our game?"

"Our game is over." He leaned over the board and gave his queen a nudge. "Checkmate, my dear."

She gasped, realizing that he had bested her. "You tricked me."

"No, I played more cleverly than you." He tapped his finger against the knight he had sacrificed, blinding her to his strategy. "All's fair in love and war and what is chess but a civilized battle?" As he slowly lifted her hand to his mouth, he sent her a smile.

Her heart leaped at the touch of his lips against her skin and, unable to resist, she smiled back.

But her smile died as she watched him stride out of the room. He was winning on both fronts, she thought, and the feelings that had flowered in her heart had made her too weak to thwart him.

Zanetta lifted her head from her sewing and sneaked a peek at Chiara, who was staring out of the window. For a moment she allowed herself to wonder if she had that sulky look on her sultry face because Don Luca was not sharing her bed. And she knew *that* for certain, for she checked the bed for telltale signs every morning.

Down in the servants' quarters they had learned not to talk about Don Luca and the Gypsy if Signora Emilia was near, for she had good ears and a quick backhand. But the moment she was out of earshot, speculation about Don Luca and the woman who had been living in his apartments for weeks now was rife. And then she, Zanetta preened a little, was the center of attention, for it was her duty to wait on the Gypsy now or to accompany her, should she wish to go abroad in the city.

"Zanetta?"

The servant girl ducked her head, afraid that she had been caught staring, but she saw that Chiara was still looking beyond the window.

"What do you know about Signora Laura Paradini?"

"She is very rich and—" the girl giggled a little "—she does things that shock even Venetian patricians."

Zanetta leaned forward, eager to show off her knowledge. "Half the noblewomen in Venice are forced to enter convents because the custom is that only one brother in a family may take a wife. But she has buried three husbands. Three. And—" her voice lowered "—they say she has had so many lovers that she keeps a list to remember them all. They call it Laura's Golden Book."

Chiara thought of what she had seen when she had looked into the lives of Giulietta's guests and wondered why Laura Paradini's behavior could shock. Perhaps because she was honest about it.

"And she married two brothers," Zanetta continued. "The last two Paradini brothers."

"What did you say?" Chiara gripped the girl's arm so strongly that her eyes widened with fright.

Zanetta repeated what she had said.

"Their names. What were their names?"

"Antonio and Marco."

"Marco?"

Zanetta nodded. "Sh-she was almost forty when Marco Paradini came rushing back to Venice when his brother died. Antonio was barely in his grave when Marco married his widow."

Marco Paradini. Chiara closed her eyes, feeling as though someone had driven his fist into her stomach. No, she cried silently. He couldn't be dead. It had to be someone else by that name. He couldn't escape her justice so easily.

"Is something wrong?"

"Wrong?" Chiara forced herself to speak. "No, nothing's wrong."

"You've gone so pale. Should I get you something?"

Chiara shook her head. Rising, she began to pace, needing to move in time with her racing thoughts.

Was this why she had been so reluctant to start looking for her father? Because at some level she had known that he was dead? No, she thought again. He couldn't be. But if he was? She stopped in the middle of the room. Then what?

Pressing her fingers against her temples, she called on her sight to tell her if the man she had loved and hated all her life was truly dead. But this was too important, too personal and her gift for seeing beyond the world that one could touch had slipped away from her again. All she could see was that last image of his face.

Perhaps there were two men with the same name. Needing that one last slim hope, she held on to it. She had fed off the thought of revenge for three long years. It had been that thought that had sustained her as she had watched her mother die. As she had watched her sister slip into madness. She could not let it go now.

"I am going out." She headed for the chest where the cloaks were stored.

Zanetta slid off the window seat and followed her. "May I accompany you?"

"No, I will go alone."

"But—"

"I will go alone, Zanetta."

"But Rico said—" The girl began to cry.

Chiara closed the clasp on her cloak and turned toward Zanetta. "Remind Rico that Don Luca said that I could come and go as I pleased."

"Then you will come back?" Zanetta swiped the tears away with the back of her hand.

"Yes," Chiara said, "I will come back." *God help me,* she thought, *I will come back.*

The streets were half-deserted at this early hour. Instead of crowds of masked merrymakers, there were servants hastening to the market. Instead of musicians and clowns and acrobats, there was a thin stream of long-robed senators, portfolios of papers under their arms, making their way to a council meeting at the Doge's palace.

The only reminder that this was carnival time in Venice was the occasional pale reveler, stumbling home from some debauch or a night at the *casino*.

There seemed to be more pedestrians abroad once she reached the vicinity of the Paradini palazzo and at first Chiara thought that it was only because of the proximity of the Piazza San Marco. But when she found the side entrance of the Ca' Paradini in a narrow alleyway, she saw that many of the people she had encountered on the way now stood bunched up against the doorway.

Now that she was here, her impatience nearly sent her up to the door demanding entry, but curious, she decided to wait and see what was going on here. She took her place at the back of the small crowd and observed the motley group.

An old woman with a pail of late-blooming flowers leaned tiredly against the gray Istrian stone of the building. A man in a grease-stained coat held a large basket full of tiny, squirming puppies. Another man had an assortment of birdcages full of tiny songbirds. A young woman with a heavily painted face fanned herself with a sheaf of sheet music. A thin-faced man with a withered arm stood apart from the others as he waited. Chiara saw that he was wearing a coat of good quality that was almost transparent at seams and elbows and the front of his shirt held the remnants of what must have once been fine lace.

"Make way."

Chiara turned at the shout that was followed by the tinkle of a handheld bell.

"Make way for the *signora*'s hairdresser."

A tall, gangly boy dressed in a dark, serviceable coat marched down the alley shaking a wooden-handled bell at the line of people crowded near the entrance. They muttered and cursed, but allowed themselves to be pushed farther against the building.

A man wearing a narrow-waisted coat of canary yellow brocade rounded the corner into the alley. In one hand he held a powdered wig that he carried in front of him with as much majesty as a priest might carry a chalice. In the other he had a lace-edged handkerchief that he pressed against his nose. As he passed by Chiara, she wrinkled her nose at the heavy scent of a sweet perfume that did not quite mask the underlying smell of the rancid lard used as a pomade to hold the fashionable powder. The rear of this small procession was brought up by a boy carrying a large basket full of combs, brushes, curling irons and hairpins.

The door opened and a footman in black livery with silver trim gestured the hairdresser and his helpers inside. Then he looked down his long nose at the crowd.

"You riffraff have to wait," he said with obvious relish, and slammed the door shut.

The minutes passed and the crowd was joined by others. A pinch-faced merchant with several bolts of brocade and satin. An elderly abbé wearing a cassock that was shiny with age. A young man wearing stylish clothes and an air of arrogance.

The young man strolled to the head of the line, then back, examining everyone who waited. When he stopped next to Chiara, she turned away, but he remained standing there.

"What do you have to sell, *bella?*" he asked. "Confide in me and I shall tell you how to sell it better to her." He tipped his head toward the palazzo.

"Go away," Chiara said. "I have nothing to sell." To show her disinterest, she demonstratively looked at the froth of lace at his neck instead of at his face. "And nothing to say to you."

"Ah, *bella,* you wound me." The young man touched his fingers to his breastbone as if she had struck him. "Let me guess. You've run away from home with your lover and need money."

"Leave me alone."

"Or have you been abandoned?" He reached out and tipped her face upward.

"Take your hands off me." Chiara slapped his hand away, meeting his eyes for the first time.

"No," he said. Not seeming to take offense, he sent her a charming smile. "No man in his right mind would abandon a woman with that face."

Chiara stared at the young man's brilliant blue eyes and felt a jolt of recognition although she was certain that she had never seen him before. She dipped inside herself to look, but she found that she was too edgy to focus.

The image of her father rose and she looked away from the young man's face to the building that carried the Paradini name. The face she saw was younger than she remembered—unlined, the mouth not thin and sour, but curved in a smile.

"So tell me, why are you here?"

The young man's voice had the image dissipating.

"You might as well talk to me, *bella.*" He hooked his thumbs into the waistband of his skintight breeches of pale blue silk and leaned back gracefully against the gray stone. "It will be a while before they let us in. These days she needs longer to repair the ravages of the night."

Curious, Chiara looked at him more closely. "You sound like you know her well."

He shrugged. "Better than I would like to."

"Why are you here?" she asked, her curiosity getting the better of her. "Why are these other people here?"

"They all have something to sell her. A puppy, flowers, a song. Because she is addicted to power, she enjoys having this parade every morning. It gives her pleasure to know that every one of them is desperate for a few *zecchini* that she can give them or deny them."

"And why are you here? You don't look desperate for a few *zecchini.*" She gauged him. "Besides, you look as if you would rather spit in her eye than take her money."

"Well, well. Not just beautiful but clever." He tapped a finger against her temple. "I just come around when I have nothing better to do and enjoy the show."

"And I think you're lying." She, too, leaned back against the building and as she did, her cloak fell open to reveal her flounced skirt.

"Ah, a Gypsy. Did you read my mind?"

"I didn't have to. All I had to do was read your face."

He frowned briefly, then shrugged her words off. "Have you come to tell Laura's fortune? That's an easy task." He laughed, but the sound had an edge to it. "If you tell her that the night will find her sharing her bed with at least one man, you are certain to be right."

Before she could answer, the door opened and the footman appeared again. "All right, you trash there, inside with you. But the minute you annoy the *signora*, you will be out on your ass. Remember that."

Pushing and shoving, the crowd moved through the narrow doorway. When Chiara and the young man reached the door, the footman blocked their entry with his arm.

"Not you," he said, glaring at the young man.

"Who's going to stop me." He sneered. "You?" Before the footman could say anything, he brought the side of his hand down sharply on the lackey's arm. Then he picked him up by the lapels of his coat and dispatched him against the wall.

Without giving the man a further glance, he straightened the lace at his wrists and gestured to Chiara to follow him.

They passed through a series of corridors and then climbed a narrow staircase of stone, made uneven by centuries of tired servants' feet. They passed through a phalanx of footmen into a hall-like room, but before Chiara had a chance to look around, the double doors to another room opened and the crowd spilled into Laura Paradini's chamber.

Laura Paradini, wearing a dusky rose dressing gown of satin and lace, lounged in the middle of the room on a daybed.

The hairdresser was still flitting around her, adding

the finishing touches to her hair. Three elegantly dressed men sat near her, all obviously vying for her attention that was on none of them.

The crowd of supplicants grouped itself a respectful distance away from her and when she waved a languid hand at one of them, they stepped forward and offered their wares. Within a few moments, she either waved them away again or instructed the footman who stood nearby to give them a few coins from the fat leather purse he held.

The heavily painted girl had just begun to sing when Laura's gaze landed on the young man who still stood near Chiara.

"Why is he in here?" Laura's full, rich voice silenced the singer. "I gave instructions not to let him in again. Have him removed."

Her face was cold, imperious, but Chiara felt flickers of pain radiate from her faintly, as if coming from far away, long ago. Wanting to see more, she focused. Just as an image began to emerge from the mist, someone jostled her, jolting her out of the vision.

Chiara saw that two footmen had approached the young man. But he only smiled and, shaking off their hands, took a step toward the daybed.

Again Chiara caught traces of emotion—stronger this time. She looked from Laura to the young man, unsure which direction they were coming from.

Laura thrust the delicate porcelain cup she had been holding at one of her elegant cavaliers, rose and walked toward the young man until they stood face-to-face.

Her father. Chiara felt his presence so strongly that

she glanced over her shoulder, almost believing that he would be standing there.

"Why do you come here?" Laura's voice trembled a little before she controlled it.

"To remind you. You have such a notoriously poor memory, *signora*."

"You are wrong, Renzo. I have forgotten nothing." She reached out and touched him, but he brushed her hand off as casually as one would brush away an annoying insect.

Raw from the emotions that bounced off these two people so strongly that they almost seemed her own, Chiara tried to step back. But she found that her father's presence kept her in place as if it were a chain linking her to them. She tried to fight her way past them, to find her way to her sight, but the emotion that flashed around her like lightning blocked her way. She threw up a wall to protect herself, but it crumbled like a house of cards.

Crossing her hands palm outward in front of her, she murmured an incantation in Romany, only half-aware that she spoke aloud.

Slowly she felt herself calm as the shield of light she wrapped around herself protected her from the worst of the emotions like a soothing balm. Still her father's presence remained strong.

She opened her eyes and found both Laura and Renzo staring at her.

"Well," Laura said. "If it isn't the Gypsy. What are you doing here?" Her eyes, the color of deep, rich chocolate, narrowed. "Are you with him?"

Chiara gave a shake of her head.

"What do you want?"

"I have come to ask you about your husband."

Laura laughed lightly. "Which one?"

"Marco Paradini." She was so focused on Laura that she did not see Renzo look at her sharply.

"What about him?"

"Is it true that he is dead?"

"Yes, but shouldn't you see that?" A corner of her full mouth tilted upward toward the heart-shaped beauty patch on her cheek. "You saw well enough last time."

"I do not see everything. And my sight is not always biddable." Her chin went up, but because she had to know, she moved forward.

"*Signora,* I have to know. Was he the son of Giacomo, born on the first day of February 1713?"

"I believe that was the day of his birth. Yes."

Chiara felt as if an unseen hand had jerked the rug she was standing on from under her feet. Unable to speak, she simply stood there.

"Of course. How could I have missed it?" Laura's eyes narrowed and she took a step closer. "You have his eyes."

"No," Chiara whispered. "He can't be dead."

"Do you need money?" Laura motioned for the footman with the purse to step closer and took it from him, the coins jingling.

"Money?" Her eyes focused on Laura's face and then slid down to the purse.

"Here." Laura held out the fat purse. "Take this."

"I don't want your money." Chiara took a step back. "I wanted revenge for what he did to my mother, to my sister. Don't you understand? He took so much from me and now—" her eyes filled with tears and overflowed before she could control them "—now he has taken that, as well."

"You had your revenge without knowing it," Laura said.

Chiara shook her head.

"If you can truly see, if you are not a fraud, you would know that he suffered."

"Nothing can compare with how my mother, my sister suffered." Whirling around, she ran from the room.

Blinded by tears, Chiara leaned against the rough stone of the building. If she had had the strength, she would have howled with disappointed rage, but she could do nothing but let the tears streak down her face.

"Are you all right?"

Chiara recognized the young man's voice, felt his light touch on her shoulder but could not muster the strength to respond.

"Here, let me help you."

Before she could protest, he had picked her up and carried her to a low wall that served as a base for the high cast-iron fence that surrounded a small, exquisite garden. Putting her down on the stone ledge, he crouched in front of her and chafed her icy hands.

Chiara leaned back against the fence, her eyes closed. For three years she had lived and breathed revenge. She had wanted revenge as badly as a person dying of thirst wants a drink of water. And now she had seen that revenge dissipate like smoke.

Suddenly it occurred to her that the only reason she and Donata had been on the road, on the outskirts of a Tuscan hill town two years ago, was because *she* had been on the way to Venice and her revenge.

She almost moaned aloud. She would not think of that. She couldn't. If she did, she would go mad.

Wanting to escape from the memory and the guilt, she opened her eyes. But there was no real escape, for the minute she looked at the young man crouched in front of her, she felt the presence of her father.

"No!" She covered her face with her hands, but the presence remained.

"What is it?"

Her hands fell back into her lap. "I'm going mad," she whispered. "Who are you?"

"Lorenzo Sanmarco. People call me Renzo."

"Why do I feel my father's presence when I look at you?"

"Because I, too, am Marco Paradini's son. His son and—" he tipped his head toward the palazzo "—hers."

"I don't understand."

"It's a long story."

She was confused and so tired, but through it all she felt his pain and knew that it was as great as hers. Her heart softened and she reached for his hands.

"Tell me."

Before he could say a word, he was being dragged away and shoved up against the fence.

Chiara looked up and saw Luca's furious face inches away from Renzo's.

"Damn you," Luca shouted. "Just what do you think you're doing?"

Chapter Seventeen

"Stop it!" Chiara jumped up and grabbed Luca's arm. "What are you doing?"

Luca felt Chiara's hand on his arm. But the rage that had risen within him like a black cloud at the sight of how she had reached for the young man's hands, her face soft with tenderness, clouded his senses and made it easy for him to ignore her attempts to pull him away. Nor did the sound of lace and brocade tearing deter him as he slammed the man yet again against the iron bars of the fence.

"I should kill you for putting your filthy hands on her!" Wanting to hear the satisfying sound of the man's head hitting the fence again, his muscles bunched, but before he could follow through with the movement, he found himself staggering back and gasping for breath from the solid punch to his middle.

Dragging in a breath, he started forward again, his eyes glittering with the desire to draw blood, but he found his way blocked as Chiara stepped directly into his path and gripped his shoulders.

As he reluctantly looked away from his target,

some of his anger found its way into his voice. "Get out of my way, Chiara."

"No." Her hands on his shoulders tightened. "Luca, listen to me."

"I tell you again, get out of my way," he snarled. His eyes shifted for a moment to make certain that his quarry was not about to flee. When his gaze returned to Chiara's face, he found something within him softening. "I don't want to hurt you, Chiara. Step aside."

Chiara could feel the violence vibrating within him. Desperate, she released her grip on his shoulders and before he could take advantage of his freedom and move away, she framed his face with her hands.

"Luca, please, I beg you," she said, stepping closer so that her body was pressed against his. "He is my brother."

He stilled as the meaning of her words slowly sank in. "Your brother?"

Chiara nodded, letting her hands fall back down to his shoulders as relief swept through her.

Luca frowned, glancing to the young man, who was straightening the torn lace at his throat, and then back to Chiara. There was no obvious similarity in their features, but, he realized they both had eyes of the same fabulous sea blue color.

Dismayed, Chiara watched all warmth leach out of Luca's eyes. Shrugging her hands off his shoulders, he took a step back from her.

"How does he come to be your brother? This man, who lives by his wits and his skill at cards and in the bedchamber just like Giacomo Casanova."

Renzo sent him an insolent smile and bowed. "Lorenzo Sanmarco at your service."

Chiara glanced at him briefly over her shoulder. "Marco Paradini was his father." She paused. "And mine."

"I thought you didn't know your father's name?" It gave Luca a dark, ugly satisfaction to watch her lower her eyelids and he laughed unpleasantly. "And here you had me convinced that you were a woman without lies."

He lifted her chin with thumb and forefinger so that she was forced to meet his eyes. "If you had confided in me, *signorina,* I could have told you all about your father that very first evening."

"I was afraid of you. I was afraid you would somehow use that against me."

"Believe me, the question of who is or is not your father has nothing to do with—" he paused, his mouth twisting in a derisive smile "—the reason why you have been my guest."

Renzo stepped closer. "May I suggest that we repair to a café and continue this conversation in a more civilized manner?" He grinned. "Unless, of course, it appeals to you to be the spectacle for those greedy for amusement." He gestured toward the small crowd that had gathered round to watch their altercation.

Luca glanced around and his dark look had part of the crowd scattering.

"I have nothing to converse with you about, *signore,* civilized or otherwise. Come, Chiara." He took her arm. "I will take you home."

"But I *do* have something to converse with him about." She squirmed out of his grip.

"Chiara——" He reached for her again.

"Should I remind you again of the promise you made me?"

Luca sighed and his hand dropped away from her arm.

Renzo chuckled to himself as he watched them. Although he had managed to keep his heart free of all but the lightest of infatuations, he easily recognized a man enamored beyond help.

"We shall have coffee at Florian's and talk. Then I shall return her to your doorstep." His mouth twitched in a mischievous smile. "If the Ca' Zeani is where she wishes to go."

"You know who I am?" Luca's eyebrows rose.

"How could I not know one of our heroes, who keeps Venice safe so that people like me can flourish," he said, his smile taking on an ironic cast.

Chiara saw Luca's mouth tighten again, felt the new flare of anger within him and touched his arm lightly. "Don't."

Luca took a deep breath and felt some of his control return. He looked at Chiara.

"You will return to the Ca' Zeani?" he asked softly, urgently, appalled at how much just the possibility that she might not come back pained him. "Won't you?" He lifted his fingertips to her cheek.

"Yes." Her heart gave a skip and she had to forcibly remind herself that neither the urgent words nor the gentle touch meant anything but that he still desired her. Her lips curved in a sad smile. "I will return."

Turning away, she hooked her hand through the arm Renzo proffered her and let him guide her through the crowd toward the Piazza San Marco.

Without realizing that he did so, Luca raised his hand and rubbed it over the insistent ache in his chest as he followed them with his eyes. He stared after them long after they had turned the corner.

The afternoon sun was slanting its rays into the window when Chiara closed the door to her chamber and leaned back against it. She was exhausted, empty, as if the emotional seesaw of the past hours had wrung out every last drop of her blood.

It was over, she thought, as her eyes began to fill beneath her closed eyelids. What she had lived for these past three years was over. She had watched her mother die a miserable, painful death. She had taken on the hardships of the long road from Rome to Venice. She had done the most menial, demeaning work. She had lied and begged and stolen. She had sacrificed poor Donata on the altar of her revenge.

And for what?

He was dead. Her father was dead. And because she had hesitated, because she had avoided looking for him all these weeks, she had lost her heart to a man who wanted only her body.

"You have been well amused, I trust."

At the sound of Luca's voice her eyes flew open and overflowed. She tried to fight back the tears, but, now that the dam was broken, they kept coming, as if she had a bottomless well within her.

"Well?" he demanded, from where he slouched at the table.

"Yes, well amused. Thank you," she said through her tears.

Her tear-choked voice cut sharply through the haze from the wine he had been drinking all afternoon.

Luca sat up sharply and set down his goblet with a thump.

"Chiara?"

She remained silent and still and he rose quickly and strode to where she stood.

He could not have described the whirlwind of emotions that rose within him at the sight of the tears that flowed down her face.

"What has he done to you?" He gathered her against him, his mind suddenly as sharp as a well-honed dagger. "Damn him, I will kill the bastard." Drawing her hair back, he swiped his fingers helplessly across her cheeks. "Shh, *piccolina,* don't cry."

Chiara drew breath to protest his assumption that Renzo had somehow harmed her, but before she could form the words, his fingers were awkwardly wiping the tears from her face as he whispered words of comfort, words that she had gone without for so long.

Suddenly sobs broke free, gushing like a shower of hot rock from a volcano. Shaking with their intensity, unable to control them, she surrendered herself to the paroxysm of weeping.

Picking her up, Luca carried her to one of the chairs that stood in front of the fire. Cradling her like a child, he sat down with her in his arms, helpless to do anything but wait for the tears to run their course.

Slowly the sobs quieted, less because they had eased the pain than because they had exhausted her. For a long time, she lay against him, so still that she barely seemed to be breathing. The light was beginning to dim when she stirred against him.

"Can you tell me what happened?"

"It was all for nothing," she whispered.

"What?" he asked, not understanding her meaning.

"I came to Venice for revenge, but he is dead."

"Ah." He combed back the curls that had tumbled into her face. "Marco Paradini?" His voice was gentle, his earlier anger that she had kept secrets from him forgotten.

She nodded, her eyes filling again.

"And your mother?"

"Was his mistress." She felt his fingers comb through her hair again and the caress spurred her to share her pain.

"She sacrificed everything for him, but when she had grown old before her time, he tossed all three of us out on the street." Unaware that she did so, she snuggled her head against Luca's fingers.

"I can still see her, kneeling in the filth of the street, begging him to at least have a care for the children she had borne him." She drew a long, shuddering breath. "But he said he had done enough already, caring for a slut's brats, whose paternity was uncertain." For the first time she had said the words aloud to another human being and she was surprised to find that they eased her.

"A week later my mother had fallen ill and I returned to the house where we had lived, hoping for help. But he was gone. A servant told me that he had gone home to Venice. I swore then that I would find him. And I have." She made a sound that might have been a bitter laugh. "But it is difficult to take revenge on a dead man."

"And this is why you wept?"

She nodded.

"And Sanmarco? He didn't hurt you?" Cupping her face, he tilted it up to his.

"Why should he hurt me?" Her eyes were puzzled.

"Why do men hurt women?"

For a moment she was silent as she absorbed his meaning. "He's my brother. My half brother. He has a good heart and he was wronged, too. Perhaps worse than I was. At least I had a mother who loved me."

Luca's arms were warm and strong around her. His fingers were still gently stroking her hair. It would be easy, she thought, to surrender what she had already surrendered in her heart. But the reminder of the woman her mother had been was strong.

She gathered up what remained of her strength, shifted out of his embrace and stood.

"I have to go."

"Go?" Luca stood also, restraining himself from reaching for her again. "Go where?"

"Away. I came to Venice to find my father. Now that I know he is dead, there is nothing for me here." Her breath caught at the pain her own words caused her. "I will go to Padua and get my sister and then we will go—" She stopped.

"Where will you go?" He forced himself to speak calmly, although the storm was already rising within him.

"Somewhere, anywhere." She shrugged, the gesture aimed as much at the terrible ache that was growing within her as at him. "Gypsies are born to wander, after all." Swaying a little, she steadied herself against the back of the armchair.

"May I suggest that you rest before you wander anywhere." He thrust his clenched hands into his pockets because he wanted to shake her and remind her of the dangers that lurked beyond his protection. He wanted to lock the door so that he could keep her with him forever. He wanted to comfort her. And, God help him, he wanted to make love to her.

As she moved away from the chair, her step faltered.

With a muttered curse, Luca was at her side, sweeping her up into his arms.

Chiara looked up at Luca as he carried her to the bed. His face was taut with what she recognized as desire. For the first time, she acknowledged how seductive it was to be wanted so passionately. And, as she let her eyes rest upon his face, she truly acknowledged for the first time what was in her heart. What had been growing there since that very first evening, no matter how fiercely she had fought it.

And for the first time she wondered if this was what it had been like for her mother. If she had surrendered to her lover's passion and to the love in her own heart. If she had believed that it would be enough. She caught the wisp of an image of a couple entwined in an embrace and knew that it was so.

His arms around her were strong but as gentle as they had ever been. As he laid her down on the bed, Chiara found that she was tired of fighting herself. Tired of fighting Luca for what she wanted to give him. She let go and felt herself surrender.

Luca felt her body grow pliant as he placed her on the soft mattress. But it was more than that. He felt something within her yield and knew that now he could take her.

But with that yielding he could feel the strength, the power drain out of her. And although his body was already pulsing with desire, he knew that he wouldn't take her like this.

Now that she was surrendering, he found that it was not her surrender he wanted. He didn't want the proud girl who had stood up to him for so long to yield. There would be triumph there perhaps, but no joy.

"Sleep now," he whispered, and brushed his lips lightly over hers. "Sleep."

She would not even have that. Well, perhaps it was better so, Chiara thought as the pain began to wind through her. Silently she turned her face into the pillow.

Tommaso, Luca's gondolier, brought Chiara to the dock near San Marco where the *burchiello* awaited her.

The pain, strong and deep, had still been with her when she had woken, but the gods of sleep had given her a gift in the long, dreamless night. That fatal wish for surrender seemed to have been lifted from her. But Luca had stayed away from her chamber this morning, so she had not had the opportunity to test if this was truly so.

A simple barge, open but for a small shelter of ragged canvas, had brought her to Venice. It was nothing like the boat that now bobbed gently at the dock. Luca's *burchiello* had a large cabin made of gleaming wood that was decorated with marquetry work. Instead of rough plank benches, there were chairs bright with gilt and crimson velvet should the passengers wish to take the air during their journey.

Tommaso handed the bundle containing her

clothes to a servant, while a second man stood ready to help her down.

Chiara bent forward and put her hand on the man's arm when she heard Luca's voice calling her name.

Straightening, she turned and saw him. He leaned against a building, his dark cloak a stark contrast to the white marble behind him, his deceptively casual stance at odds with the tension on his unmasked face.

Their eyes met and held. Again she heard him speak her name although she knew his lips had not moved.

Her heart filled and overflowed, but there was no taint of weakness now. Slowly, but with no hesitation, she walked to where he stood, stopped an arm's length away.

Then she held out her hand and smiled. "Come with me," she said softly.

This was what had been missing last night, Luca thought. This strength, this power. Emotion flashed through him like lightning. He recognized the desire, the joy, the need. If he had had the courage to look more closely, he would have recognized the love.

He put his hand in hers and lifted their laced fingers to his mouth.

Then, hand in hand, they walked to the boat.

Chapter Eighteen

The salty breeze against their faces, they stood at the prow of the *burchiello* as it was towed to Fusina, where the choppy waters of the lagoon mingled with the glassy water of the Brenta Canal.

Chiara watched the servants uncoil the heavy ropes with the ease of long practice, then toss them up on the flat, sandy banks where the mules, who would pull the boat, stood, patiently waiting for the ropes to be attached to their harnesses. The drivers flicked their whips in unison and the boat slid into the narrow, shallow canal.

The sky was a hazy blue that edged into white, and a thin morning mist lay over the vineyards that spread, brown and empty, on both sides of the canal. They had still been green and heavy with fruit when she had last passed by all those weeks ago. Fruit that was perhaps already fermenting into the full-bodied red wine she had drunk in Luca's house.

They had not spoken as they had crossed the lagoon. Nor had they touched as they stood side by side. But now Luca felt her light shiver.

"Are you cold?"

"A little."

He started to ask her if she was afraid, but he bit back the words.

"A little of that, too," she said, the words tumbling out of her mouth before she could stop them.

"Are you looking into my mind, Chiara?"

"Not really." She turned to face him. "Sometimes I can hear your thoughts as if you had spoken them."

"Then listen." He bent down to her and touched his forehead to hers.

"*Non hai paura.* Don't be afraid," she said softly, her breath catching a little as she thought to hear an endearment.

"Go on." He lifted his head and smiled.

"*Carissima,*" she whispered, her eyes on his. "Dearest."

"*Sì.*" He bent down and brushed his mouth over hers. "*Carissima.*" He felt something move through him as he spoke the endearment, aware that, for the first time in his life, it was not an empty word. For a long moment, he looked at her. "Come inside, where it is warm." Twining his fingers with hers, he drew her toward the cabin.

It was indeed warm inside from the iron braziers where hot coals glowed, spreading heat and the sweet scent of incense. The walls were covered with yellow silk that reflected the light of the oil lamps, making it seem as if sunlight were streaming through the cabin.

There was something faintly Oriental about the ambience, an impression accentuated by the fact that the only furniture was two long, low tables that gleamed with mosaics of lapis lazuli and jasper and coral, framed by some dark, exotic wood. Wide, soft cushions covered with ivory velvet were strewn with silk pillows the color of sapphires and emeralds and amethysts.

Chiara let her gaze sweep around the room. When it reached the far corner of the cabin, she went still. Ivory cushions widened to form a bed, with a coverlet of crimson silk.

For a moment, panic had her heart racing as she recognized the spot. This was the image her sight had shown her. The image that was her fate.

But, she reminded herself, she had not surrendered in a moment of weakness. She had not been seduced by words or wine or caresses. Nor had she been forced. No. She had made the decision consciously. And since she had chosen the beginning, she told herself bravely, she could choose the end.

Her hands were almost steady as she reached for the clasp of her cloak.

Moving forward, she sat down on a cushion and crossed her ankles under her wide Gypsy skirt.

Luca followed her and, although his inclination and the excitement that was already moving through his blood would have demanded that he take Chiara into his arms, he did not. Instead, he threw off his cloak, revealing none of his usual brocades and lace, but instead only a simple shirt of fine linen and dark breeches.

Chiara looked at the trays of food, the carafes of wine that stood on the low tables.

"It seems like a great deal for one person." She sent him a cool look that was full of questions. "Or were you planning to accompany me whether I issued an invitation or not?''

He lowered himself to the cushion beside her and, stalling for time, reached for a bunch of plump purple grapes before he lay back against a pile of bright silk pillows.

''I like to think that I would have let you go.'' He shrugged. ''But you never know what you are going to do until you do it.'' He looked up at her. ''Do you?''

The honesty of his answer pleased her, but she felt driven to ask more questions.

''That night when I almost escaped from your palazzo, you told me that you would not have let me go. What has changed that you would have released me now?''

''Why do you bother to ask?'' He slanted an impatient look up at her. ''You seem to know my mind better than I do myself.''

''I've told you before that I do not limit my life to what my gift shows me.'' She did not try to keep the annoyance from her tone. ''I would be a poor excuse for a human being if I did so.''

''So you said.'' Tossing aside the grapes that he had barely touched, he sat up, tension tightening his muscles.

''Chiara.''

''What?'' She jolted a little, although his voice was very soft.

''Make an exception.''

''What do you mean?''

''Look inside me and know that you have nothing to fear.''

''No.'' She shook her head violently. She knew he

desired her. She knew that in some strange way he needed her. But what if she looked and found not even the smallest spark of feeling to echo what lived in her heart?

"No," she repeated. "I do not want to look."

"When you lay unconscious, I promised that I would never again put you in a cage. And—" lowering himself to an elbow, he reached out and drew his knuckles down her arm "—I won't. No matter how much I might want to."

His words released something within her, quieting the nerves. It was her choice, she reminded herself. If she kept it that way, she would remain free.

"Will you tell me what you want, Chiara?"

She turned so that she faced him.

"Will you show me?" He lifted his hand toward her, but he let it fall back. He would not touch her now. He wanted—no, he needed her to take the next step.

His dark eyes held no guile. There was desire there, but its turbulence was softened, gentled by tenderness. And because she knew better than most that this was a man of sharp edges, because she knew how many passions lived within this man, she knew she could not ask for more.

Her eyes on his, she stood and held out her hand.

Luca's heart leaped and began to race. Lacing his fingers with hers, he rose. When she moved toward the far corner of the cabin, he moved with her.

"Why?" he asked softly as they stood next to the cushion with its covering of crimson silk. "Why now?"

Chiara turned toward him, her movement bringing

her to within a hand's breadth of his body. Lifting her hand, she touched her fingers to his mouth.

"No more questions, Luca." How could she explain to him that this was her fate and she had accepted it? She could not change it, any more than she could change whether or not the sun rose tomorrow morning. Nor did she want to.

Luca would have questioned further, despite her words, but there was something in her eyes that stopped him. There was a sadness there, a distance and he felt a spurt of panic. Suddenly he understood.

She was giving herself to him today, but when they arrived in Padua, she intended to walk away from him. The pain that the thought brought was terrible in its sharpness and his breath caught in his throat.

No, he thought. She could not leave him, when he needed her so badly.

He would make love to her, he thought. He would bind her to him with his body and the pleasure he could give her, and she would be his forever.

She lifted her fingers away from his mouth, but he caught her hand and brought it back to his lips.

Slowly he kissed his way the length of each finger, then rested his mouth in the center of her palm. Lightly he touched the tip of his tongue to her skin, then traced a line down to her wrist where her pulse was already pounding.

"Will you let me love you, Chiara?"

His lips moved against her skin as he spoke, sending heated messages throughout her body, and she almost moaned with the sheer pleasure of it.

He placed her hand against his heart.

"Can you feel it beating?" he whispered.

She nodded, finding herself unable to speak.

"For you, Chiara." He drew her closer, until she was pressed against his body. That quick, sharp pleasure of body against body pushed his arousal higher even as it steadied him. This he was familiar with, this feeling of a woman's body against his. Still, he understood that it would be different. Perhaps on some level he had known it from the very beginning, when he had desired her even before he had touched her for the first time.

"Chiara, *amore*." The words rose from his heart, although he was barely aware that he spoke them. Giving in to the temptation, he took her mouth.

The desire for the words to come from his heart and not be merely a part of the accomplished lover's repertoire had her stiffening. She closed her eyes against the ache that wove through her.

Luca felt her tense and drew back. "It's all right," he whispered, and let his hands drift soothingly down her sides to lie at her waist. "Will you open your eyes and look at me?"

Chiara willed the ache away. Later, she thought. But when she opened her eyes, a shadow of the ache was still in them.

He lifted his hands to her hair, which she had tamed into a knot at the back of her neck, and began to remove the pins, one by one. When he had tossed them aside, he combed his fingers through her hair, releasing it to spring back to its natural, wild curls.

Its flowery fragrance drifted toward him, seducing a man already seduced. His hands twisted in the black strands as arousal rose so relentlessly that he found himself unprepared for its violence.

A small, soft sound pulled him back from the madness and, thinking that he had hurt her, his grip loosened. But he could not bear to relinquish the silky curls, and his fingers tunneled deeper and cupped her head.

"Do you have a Gypsy spell, Chiara, that will cool my need for you?" Even as he spoke, his body made a lie of his words as his hips shifted forward, imprinting his desire upon her. "I have hurt you enough." He brushed his mouth over hers briefly, afraid to take more. "I don't want to hurt you again."

Touched, she raised her hands to his face. "You won't hurt me today, Luca. Not in any way that counts." She smiled an oddly serene smile. "Now it's my turn."

Her hands went to the dark ribbon that held his hair back and untied it with a tug. Then she combed her fingers through his hair, thinking that the strands looked like pale gold in the lamplight.

Again Luca felt the arousal rush through him like a wave breaking against the beach. He bent forward, but this time he did not possess her mouth. Instead he began to make love to it with teasing touches and caresses.

But when her lips parted against his, he could not resist the mute invitation and his tongue slipped into her mouth and began to taste.

Chiara surrendered to the kiss, opening her lips for his invasion as, in a little while, she would open her body. Her senses began to swim, as if she had drunk too much wine, and her fingers tightened in his hair as she fought for purchase.

The tug of her fingers in his hair had his arousal growing feverish.

"Chiara." His breath was choppy. "I know I should make love to you slowly." He leaned forward to sow a row of hungry kisses along her jawline. "But I can't wait." His hands moved down, tracing the line of her back, then sliding between them to touch her breasts.

She stilled as his hands covered her breasts. When they shifted, just a little, so that the thumbs lay against the tips, her breath stumbled. When his thumbs began to stroke back and forth over the crests that rose to meet his touch, she moaned his name.

"*Sì, amore,*" he murmured approvingly against her mouth. "Let me love you."

Again the words that she wanted to be words of love so badly had the pain rising within her, but it was fainter this time, obscured by the pleasure that his touch was unleashing.

Of its own volition her body shifted closer, pressing against his aroused flesh. This was real. There was no lie here.

The press of her soft belly against his swollen body had fresh arousal surging through his blood. He unlaced her blouse and, his fingers quick, urgent, loosened it and pulled it down to expose her shoulders.

In the lamplight, her skin was the golden color of a ripe peach. He lowered his head to taste, sliding the tip of his tongue over the curve of her shoulder, but that one taste made him greedy for more. He tugged open the ribbons of her chemise and, hooking his fingers into both her blouse and the thin silk underneath, pulled them down, effectively imprisoning her arms.

The sight of her luxurious breasts, their tips of

dark rose already hard and ripe like berries, whipped up the tempest in his blood. Wary of the fire that was consuming him, he picked her up and laid her down on the cushion.

Chiara's eyes almost closed from the pleasure as he began to caress her breasts, but she kept them open and on Luca's face as his hands stroked her, teasing the crests with his fingertips. His nostrils were fluttering with passion just barely held in check and, she realized, his hands trembled.

Aroused as much by his expert caresses as by his needs, she melted under his hands as his palms cupped her. When his fingers tightened on her hardened nipples, she arched up toward him with a muted cry.

Luca went still at her cry. She was the picture of wanton abandonment as she bent back beneath his hands, which were dark against her golden skin. He stared down at her, knowing that with a single movement he could tear her clothes asunder and bury himself in the blessed relief of her body. He was a breath away from doing just that when, in a desperate quest for control, he lowered his head and pressed his face against the skin that quivered from the pounding of her heart.

His hands were driving her to the edge of madness. Just as Chiara thought there could be no greater pleasure, his clever fingers closed on the tips of her breasts. The pleasure shot down like a heated arrow to the apex of her thighs and, in counterpoint, she arched up against it.

He stilled above her and she saw his face harden with the rapacious hunger of the male animal who has long not had his fill. He would take her now, she thought, with all the passion, all the violence that lived within him. A quiver of fear danced over her skin.

But then something changed, so quickly and subtly that she could not have described it, and he buried his face between her breasts.

Chiara could feel his hot, uneven breath against her skin. She could feel the trembling of his muscles as he fought for control. It was for her, she realized. He had done it for her.

Her heart filled and opened and she knew that if she had not already loved him, she would have loved him now.

Luca lay still, every muscle taut as he struggled against himself. The desire did not ebb, but the heart-beat that raced against his face somehow blunted its voracious, selfish edge. Raising his head, he looked into her eyes.

They were as blue as the sea and as deep. Then she smiled at him, a calm smile that contrasted sharply with the currents of desire that were pulsing through the room. Something moved within him and he had the oddest sensation that he had come home.

"I want to see you," he said, his voice hoarse with passion held in check. "I want to touch you."

There was no fear in her now. There was only desire. Desire to experience again the lavish pleasure that she already knew his hands could give. Desire to give of herself and slake the thirst that burned within him.

"Yes," she whispered, her eyes on his. "Yes."

Chapter Nineteen

Luca undressed her slowly, taking more care than he had ever taken with any woman, although he was not aware of it at the moment. He was aware of nothing beyond Chiara's beauty, her fragrance, her taste.

When she was naked, he allowed his gaze to wander over her. She was slender, but her breasts were full and her hips lush as if her body had been created just for love—for making love and for carrying its fruit. For a moment, one thought teased the fringes of his consciousness—how her body would look swollen with the child he had planted inside her. But before he could wonder at the image, the desire and need took over and he began to touch her.

Again his fingers teased her breasts, but this time they only blazed the trail for his mouth.

The taste of her skin was dark and rich like the sweet wine made from the last grapes of the season and it rose to his head until his senses began to swim.

Had he ever wanted like this? Needed like this?

His mouth was doing incredible things to her breasts. That was Chiara's last coherent thought as the sensations he sparked there were echoed in the ache that built between her thighs. In a mute plea, her hips arched upward.

His mouth was still roving her breasts, finding yet another spot to caress, to taste, but he felt the movement of her hips. Raising his head, he saw that her eyes had fallen closed.

"Love," he murmured, "look at me."

The pleasure was like a drug and her eyelids were heavy, but she obeyed. As her eyes met his, he stroked his hand toward her center until his fingers tangled in the black curls at the apex of her thighs.

"Open for me."

Her thighs trembled once and then fell open, as a fortress opens its gate to the conqueror. Slowly his fingers moved downward to brush over her slick flesh.

Chiara cried out at the relief of that first touch against her body, but the relief lasted only a moment before it became provocation.

"Luca, please." She gripped his arm.

"What is it?"

"Please," she begged, not knowing what she begged for.

"What do you want?" he whispered. "This?" He traced tiny circles over her sensitive flesh with a single finger. "Or this?" Slowly he slid his finger further down and slipped it inside her.

Again she cried out, the arch of her hips pushing him deeper.

The way she tightened around his finger almost sent him over the edge. His arousal was beyond pain, but now he knew that he had to possess her or go mad.

Pulling away from her, he discarded his clothes

with a speed that spoke of desperation. Yet when his clothing was gone, he did not turn back to Chiara immediately.

For weeks, from the first time he had laid eyes on her across the crowded room, he had waited for this moment. Now that this moment was here, he found that he was afraid. He had seen hatred in her eyes. When the desires he had roused in her were slaked, would she look at him with hatred for taking what she had given him? He didn't think that he would be able to bear that.

Chiara felt the link with Luca. She could not read his thoughts—there were too many of them and they were too confused, like a tangled ball of thread of many colors. But she understood that he needed something from her—a touch, a sign. She lifted her hand and laid it lightly against his back.

He jolted at her touch. Then he looked over his shoulder, not sure what he would see.

Her mouth was tilted upward in a gentle smile that was reflected in her eyes like sunlight upon the sea. Turning around, he covered her body with his.

The slide of skin against skin had them both sighing in a duet of need. But while Chiara floated in that nebulous, achy world of incipient pleasure, Luca was plunged headfirst into the urgent, desperate need to mate.

His hands unsteady, he fitted his body to hers. The way her head fell back in surrender, the damp heat that welcomed him almost robbed him of the last of his control. But, his muscles trembling, he forced himself to tarry at her gate.

"Chiara," he whispered. "Look at me."

The heated pleasure of his body against hers was

flowing through her like wine in her blood. She heard Luca's voice, but it seemed to come from far away as she drifted.

"Look at me," he repeated. "I want your eyes on mine when I take you for the first time."

His voice, raw with passion barely restrained, blazed through her like a row of flames. She opened her eyes and saw him, poised above her. The conqueror in the moment of his triumph. And yet, there was no triumph in his eyes, but something softer.

"Yes," she whispered, and, knowing instinctively what both of them needed, lifted her hands and placed them firmly on his hips. Then her mouth curved in a smile that was both invitation and welcome.

This was what he had been waiting for, he realized. This sign that she was not surrendering to him, but that she was meeting him in the act of love as an equal. *This* was the woman he had wanted. *This*— he understood it now—was the woman he had fallen in love with.

For a moment he was still, stunned, but then the fire in his loins compelled him to finish what he had begun.

Their eyes held as he entered her slowly so that the barrier of her innocence was not harshly broken, but pushed aside. When he was fully sheathed, he lowered himself to her and took her mouth as he had just taken her body.

He filled her. There had been no pain, she thought wonderingly. Or if there had been, she had not noticed, perhaps because she had been so taken with the changeable expressions in his eyes. Now he lay still within her as his mouth made love to hers.

But she needed something more, and her arms twined around him, pressing him closer and closer still.

Her arms were strong as she embraced him. And the embrace was echoed below, where their bodies were locked together. Again the urgency he had been holding at bay took over.

"Chiara, forgive me." He dragged in a ragged breath. "I can wait no more."

She shifted so that he lay fully within the cradle of her thighs. "Neither can I."

He began to move then. At first he moved slowly, but the delights of her silken body quickly spurred him. The rhythm grew faster and then faster still.

Aware of just how close he was to the edge, Luca tried to slow the tempo as he slid his hand between them. For a moment he succeeded, but then Chiara moaned as he touched her and arched upward. The reins broke and he knew that his body was beyond control.

Chiara felt the edgy excitement build within her. From her center, where their bodies were joined, it flowed outward in concentric circles of sensation. The pleasure grew and when she thought it could grow no more, his body pushed her to some further level of delight.

When his hand slid between their bodies to stroke her, she heard herself moan as her body arched upward to capture still more of his touch.

His movements within her grew stronger, faster, and she felt herself rise with him until they both spun toward some dark, secret whirlpool of pleasure.

Then, the whirlpool reached, they fell as one and let the last pleasure take them.

* * *

They lay together, their limbs entwined, their bodies still intimately joined, their breath just beginning to calm.

Slowly Chiara surfaced from the aftermath of pleasure. She heard the sound of the water lapping against the boat. She smelled the fragrance of the sweet incense and the scent of their lovemaking. This was what the vision had shown her, she thought. The vision had shown her that she would welcome Luca into her body. What the vision had not shown her, she thought, was how deeply, how truly she would come to love him.

And yet she knew that this was all she would have with him. She knew that at the end of this day, she had to walk away from him because if she did not, it would destroy her.

Now, for this day, she was his lover. Today, they were equals. But to become his mistress, a woman to be hidden and kept for secret pleasures, would destroy her.

But would it destroy her any less to leave him? Tears pricked at her eyes and she closed them.

Slowly Luca surfaced from the aftermath of pleasure. He felt Chiara's heart beating against his. He smelled the fragrance of her skin and the scent they had made together. He had known that they would be lovers. What he had not known, he mused, was that he would love her.

Love. He had loved before, he thought, but everything he had felt was but a pale shadow compared to what he felt for Chiara. His heart full, the words on his lips, he tilted her face up to his.

And saw the tears seeping under her eyelids.

''Chiara? Why the tears, *carissima?*''

She gave no answer, but only shook her head.

"Look at me. Tell me." He gave her a little shake. "*Ti prego.* I beg you."

Chiara opened her eyes and, although more tears spilled down her cheeks, she managed to smile. "Why does a woman cry when she has been well loved?"

"Don't lie to me, Chiara. Not now, not when—"

The faint echo of the words he was about to say sounded within her and she started, her heart leaping in panic. These words were a charm, a spell and she knew that they would bind her to him forever. Desperate, she silenced him with her mouth.

Luca felt his body begin to reawaken and, cupping Chiara's face, he pulled back from the kiss.

"Not now, my love."

"Luca—"

Slowly he withdrew from her body. "Later."

Her eyes were wide and he stroked his hand over her cheek. "Why are you afraid now, Chiara? Why now when I—"

She silenced him again, this time laying her fingers on his lips. "Not now, my love."

The contrast of her smile and the fear in her eyes stilled the arguments he would have made. Rising, he opened a chest and covered himself with a robe of wine red silk. Then he took out a robe of azure and brought it to where Chiara still lay.

"This is the same color as your eyes."

When she had pulled the robe over her head, he held out his hand.

"Come now, let us eat. Or do you have something against that as well?"

She rose and, leaving one hand in his, put the other

on his chest. "Luca, there are so many things you don't understand."

He frowned. "Perhaps I understand better than you think. Come now," he urged.

They fed each other tidbits of cheese and smoked venison and paper-thin slices of ham from San Daniele. They drank wine from a goblet of cobalt blue glass. They kissed and touched and did not speak the words that were in their hearts.

When Luca made love to her again, he felt her edgy fear that did not leave her, not even in passion. He wanted to share the feelings that had bloomed in his heart with her, but he did not. Instead he cradled her until she slept.

When he felt the boat bump against the dock, he went outside and surveyed the area. A small group of people haggled with a bargeman. A clutch of booths where provisions were sold huddled around the dock. Itinerant peddlers spread their wares on the ground.

"Find me a carriage," he said to his boatmen. "And a driver."

"*Sì, Don Luca,*" the elder one answered. "Do we return to the city tonight?"

"I have not decided yet. But make ready."

When he returned to the cabin, he found that Chiara had already risen and was tying the tapes of her skirt.

"You're up." Disappointed, he reached out for her. "And I wanted to wake you myself."

But Chiara evaded him and backed away. She had only pretended to sleep, afraid of the power of the feelings that were sweeping through her.

"Please, Luca." She looked down at the floor. "Let me go now as you promised."

Luca felt the pain slash through him. Perhaps it would indeed be better if he let her go, he thought. To keep a woman who could hurt him with such ease was madness. And yet he knew that without her, he would be but half a man.

"I thought to accompany you a ways yet," he said stiffly.

"No, Luca, please." She pressed her hands against her heart, which beat madly. Run, she told herself. Run. This time he will not stop you. He promised to let you go. And yet she remained still, as if her shoes were nailed to the floor.

It was silent in the cabin, so silent that they could hear each other's breathing.

"Chiara," he said softly, "look in my eyes and tell me that you feel nothing. Tell me that we are lovers in body only. If you can do that, I swear I will let you go."

She could not do it, she thought. But she had to. If she stayed now, she would be sentencing herself to repeat her mother's fate.

Slowly she raised her head and met his eyes.

He did not speak. He only looked at her. But she heard the words as clearly as if he had. Suddenly she moaned, the sound rising from deep within her. Covering her ears with her hands, she sank down to her knees, bowing her head until she was almost curled into a ball.

The sound she made—like a mortally wounded animal—sliced into Luca like a dagger. He moved toward her but stopped in the middle of a step. Would he cause her still more suffering if he touched her? If he tried to comfort her?

But the feelings within him spurred him on. He knelt in front of her and pried her hands away from her ears, gently, mindful of how many times he had marked her skin with a rough touch.

"You've already heard the words in my heart." He brushed a kiss over one palm and then the other. "Will you look into my eyes when I speak them?"

As he had told her so often, he was not a patient man. But this time, he schooled himself to patience, his only touch his fingers that lightly circled her wrists.

She was lost, Chiara thought. She was well and truly lost. Although no words had yet been spoken, she had heard them nevertheless. The charm was said. The spell was done. And even as she despaired, part of her rejoiced.

For the second time, she raised her head to meet his eyes.

He released a breath he had not realized he had been holding. Letting her wrists go, he slid his hands upward until they were palm to palm.

And so they knelt and spoke the words that sealed their fate.

Chapter Twenty

As their carriage rattled into the yard, the farmer's wife dumped the chicken feed that had been in her apron onto the ground and clapped her hands in welcome.

"Oh, *signorina*," she cried, and she ran alongside the carriage as it rolled to a stop, "we were beginning to worry."

"Is something wrong with Donata?" Chiara jumped down unaided and grabbed her arms.

"Oh, no." The woman beamed. "She's doing fine." A shadow came into her eyes. "She still hasn't spoken a word though. Not a word."

"And she is well?"

"*Sì, sì.*" The woman nodded, her gaze shifting beyond Chiara's shoulder to where Luca stood. Then she looked at Chiara with a sly grin. "And so, it seems, are you."

"Where is she?"

"Inside, by the window. She sits there every day for hours and hours. Come." With a respectful glance in Luca's direction, she took Chiara's arm and led her toward the house of grayish brown fieldstone.

Donata was indeed sitting at the small window that looked out onto the fields, barren now but for the stubble of the harvested cornstalks.

Chiara approached slowly so that she wouldn't frighten her. Kneeling down, she covered her sister's hands with hers.

"Donata, *piccolina,* little one." Raising one hand, she cupped her sister's cheek, turning her head so that they faced each other. "Are you well, dearest?"

Holding her breath, Chiara waited for a sign of recognition, a sign that she had understood, but Donata looked at her with eyes that were empty of all expression. Then she turned back toward the window.

Chiara felt all hope die. This was how Donata had been for almost two years, but somehow she had hoped that now, in this quiet place, her sister's condition would improve. But there had been no improvement and she had turned away from her as if she were a stranger.

Tears rose and she lowered her head into Donata's lap. This was her punishment, she thought.

When she felt a hand on her hair, she jerked her head upward. But Donata was sitting as still as she had before, her hands folded in her lap. It was Luca, she realized, who had stroked over her hair.

"No," she whispered urgently, sitting back on her heels. "You shouldn't be here. Your presence could trouble her. Please."

"Why?" Luca asked softly. "What is wrong with her?"

"Please go. Later." She gestured him away.

Suddenly Donata turned her head, tilting it to one

side as if she were listening to something. Then she lifted her face toward Luca.

Chiara's breath caught in her throat as, for the first time since she had slipped into madness, Donata's eyes lost some of their blankness. Stunned, afraid to move, she watched her sister's mouth curve into a sweet smile.

Could it be that Donata recognized his face? she asked herself suddenly. Recognized it and yet knew that he had not been the one to harm her? Had Donata in her madness recognized Luca's innocence more readily than she had?

Softly she spoke to her sister in Romany. But there was no answer. Instead the eyes grew blank again, as if a curtain had descended. Then she turned her head back toward the window.

Finally Luca came and lifted Chiara up. "Come now, *cara*. You can do no more here."

Her heart heavy, she allowed herself to be led away. But her mind would not let that moment go.

The farmer's wife looked up from her task of rolling out thin leaves of pasta dough and dusted her hands off on her apron. "Would you like something to drink, *signorina?* You look pale."

Chiara shook her head and reached for the purse at her waist.

Luca stopped her hand. "We could take her with us."

"Us?" Her eyes flew up to his. "Where?"

"Back to the city."

They had not spoken of this, but he assumed that she would be returning to Venice with him, she thought bitterly. But, she sighed, they had spoken of other things. And they both knew that she was his for as long as he cared to keep her.

"She would be well cared for."

"No." She was afraid, she acknowledged. What if Luca's presence brought Donata out of her madness only to make her remember what had happened? Would she be worse off then than now when she lived in the safety of a void? "The *signora* will look after her."

Luca stayed her hand as she reached again for her purse, and placed a handful of coins on the table—enough that the girl would be looked after well and not enough to make them too greedy.

"Why did you do that?" she demanded when they were back in the farmyard. "Donata is my responsibility."

"And you are mine."

"Ah, yes." She covered her face with her hands. It was already beginning, she thought.

"What is it?" Luca gripped her shoulders. "What's wrong with my doing this for her? For you?"

"I thought we would have one day as lovers." She lowered her hands. "As equals. But I am already nothing but your mistress."

"You have a poor opinion of what I feel for you." Again he marveled at how deeply her words could cut him. "You still cannot truly see what is inside me, can you?"

Chiara looked up at him and saw the hurt in his eyes. Felt it. "Forgive me. I do not mean to blame you for the decision I have made." She sighed. "I will learn to live with it." But even as she said the words, she did not believe them.

* * *

When they returned to the *burchiello*, it was almost dark. Torches had already been fastened to the prow of the boat and more torches were given to the drivers who would guide the mules.

"We will dock at the villa near Dolo," Luca said to the boatmen. "See if you can find someone who will ride ahead so they are prepared."

"It is too late to return to the city tonight," he said to Chiara as they entered the cabin. "I have a small villa on the canal and we will stay there."

Chiara nodded but said nothing.

The braziers had been refilled with glowing coals and incense. The oil lamps had been lit and the food and wine replenished. But Chiara paid the surroundings no mind as she wrapped herself in her cloak and curled up on the cushions.

Her mind kept returning to the moment when Donata's eyes had lost their blankness and she had looked at Luca and smiled. She had known. Despite her madness, she had somehow known. And if that was so, there could only be one answer, she thought. The brother, whom Luca believed dead, had to be alive.

She thought back to all that had happened. Her visions of Luca in the light with that mysterious hint of evil behind him. The evil man with Luca's face that day she had fallen down the stairs. And now this.

Sitting up, she looked at Luca who was brooding into a goblet of wine.

"Will you tell me about your brother?" she asked. "The brother you say is dead."

Luca slanted her a grim look. "I do not speak about Matteo."

"Please." She slid closer to him and put a hand on his arm. "Speak of him to me. It is important."

"Why?"

Chiara sighed. "I believe your brother lives."

"My brother is dead." He turned away, but a moment later he shifted forward and shouted, "Damnation, what does my brother have to do with anything?"

"Do you remember how I looked at you with hatred in my eyes that first evening?"

"How could I forget?" He lifted the goblet and drank deeply. "My blood still runs cold when I think of it."

"Two years ago Donata and I traveled with a group of Gypsies. We were camped outside a hill town in southern Tuscany and I had gone into the town with some others to beg and tell fortunes." The memory was suddenly so clear that she turned away, unable to look at his face.

"When I returned to our wagon, I found—" her words faltered as the memory gripped her. She pulled in a long, deep breath. "I found a man raping my sister. I dragged him off her and slashed him with my dagger, but it was too late." She forced herself to look back at Luca. "That man had your face and form."

Luca stared at her, silent, stunned, his mind spinning with the possibilities opened by her words.

"Did you hear me?" she screamed, his silence grating on her nerves. Grabbing his arm, she shook him. "He had your face."

Suddenly the memory of that night, coupled with everything that had happened since, overwhelmed her and she began to sob—huge sobs that seemed to rise up out of her like waves.

Luca reached to take her into his arms, but she rolled away, crying uncontrollably.

He let her go, thinking that he had already forced her too many times, and buried his head in his hands.

My God, he thought. If what she said was true, what must she have felt when he had bought her from Manelli? What must she have felt when he had caged her, kissed her, threatened her with seduction that would have been little different from rape?

And, he asked himself, what had she felt this afternoon when he had made love to her? Had the image of her sister's rape been with her then?

Luca did not know how long he sat like this, the thoughts tormenting his mind like whips. Suddenly he realized that her sobbing had stopped, that the cabin was silent. He raised his head and found her looking at him.

Chiara wept until she could weep no more. In some strange way, she realized, she felt cleansed, relieved, as if a heavy weight that had burdened her had been lifted from her heart. And yet she knew that nothing had changed.

She sat up and looked to where Luca sat, his head in his hands. Pain radiated from him like heat from a fire and she almost reached over to touch him. But then she remembered that it had been she who had stirred up all this pain within him and thought he might not welcome her touch. He raised his head and looked at her.

"If you still want to hear it," he said dully, "I will speak of Matteo now."

She nodded and he began the story of their lives

that had been intertwined from birth like two vines, one bearing fruit that was sweet and one with fruit stunted and bitter.

"And so it went all our lives and yet I always loved him more than I hated him. But Matteo's hatred for me only seemed to grow." He paused. "Then I fell in love. Her name was Antonia."

He fell silent. Chiara did not push him, but only waited quietly for him to continue.

"Matteo was born with this hatred, this madness, inside him. But it grew worse." He shook his head. "One day he entered Antonia's house pretending to be me. He raped her, then he cut her throat. When I arrived, his hands were red with her blood." He lifted his eyes to hers. "I wanted revenge so badly I could taste it on my tongue." He paused. "I almost killed him then with my own hands."

"But you did not," she said softly, understanding perfectly just how great the need for revenge could be.

"No. Instead I turned him over to the constables to be led away in chains. And at his trial I spoke against him, although Alvise begged me to be silent, for what is the honor of the Zeanis against the life of the daughter of a merchant." He laughed harshly.

"He was imprisoned in the *Pozzi*, the Cisterns, as the dungeons beneath the Doge's palace are called. Somehow he managed to bribe a jailer and escape." He poured more wine into his goblet, his hands trembling with the memories. "Two years later a man came. He said he had stumbled upon Matteo, dying after being set upon by robbers on some road in the Appenines. He said that with his last breath Matteo had asked him to come and tell me that I was free of him now.'' The memory of the bitter guilt he had felt was thick on his tongue and he quickly drank down the wine to drown it.

''When that man came—'' his voice was low and hollow ''—I felt as if I *had* killed Matteo with my own hands. And I can tell you this. The taste of revenge is not a sweet one.'' Again he buried his head in his hands.

His pain was so great now that she could no longer bear to not touch him. She shifted closer and put a tentative hand on his shoulder.

Luca jolted as if she had burned him and she jerked her hand back.

He lifted his head and stared at her, his eyes dull with despair.

''How can you touch me?'' His voice was a hoarse whisper. ''How could you bear to lie with me after what I did to you?''

Chiara shook her head and frowned, not understanding his meaning. ''What you did to me weeks ago has not changed between this morning and this moment. You were not gentle, that is true.'' She rubbed her wrist where the marks made by his hands had been. ''But even that first evening you showed me kindness.''

''When I think of what you must have felt to have me touch you when you thought I was the man who had raped your sister—'' he rubbed his hands over his face ''—I shudder.''

''That is what was so strange, you see.'' Her voice grew dreamy. ''My eyes told me you were the one, but with my sight I saw you cloaked in light. I thought I was going mad.'' She laughed softly. ''Or perhaps being punished because even then you stirred me.''

Luca felt the tight knot in his stomach ease a little. ''Stirred you?''

''Do you not remember?''

''No. I remember most precisely.'' He smiled ruefully. ''*Dio*, Chiara, I have rarely asked forgiveness of anyone. But I ask it of you now.'' He would have wanted to reach for her, to touch her, but he did not dare.

She shifted closer and, sliding her arm around his shoulders, pulled him into her embrace.

The weight of guilt, shame and horror slipped away as he allowed himself to sink against her, his face pressed against her breasts.

Cradling him against her, she lay back against the soft cushions. As she stroked his pale hair, her heart filled with love. It would be worth it, she thought. It would be worth both the pain and the shame to love someone this deeply.

As she held him, his story and hers sifted through her mind. What odd paths did fate send you on, to bring you to the place you were intended to be, she mused. That was why she had not stayed hidden in the darkness that night when she had escaped from her room. She remembered the feelings that had risen within her so strongly that she had had no choice but to accept them, even then.

Suddenly her heart leaped. She remembered the evil that had spread from the masked figure who had been in the gondola with Luca. It was the same evil she had felt when the man with Luca's face had reached out to touch her.

If they were one, if Luca's brother truly lived, then

this was the man who had drawn Luca into the secret net that endangered his life.

She closed her eyes. But would Luca believe her? She still was not sure that he completely believed that his brother still lived. What would he say if she told him this now?

Luca felt Chiara's heart leap beneath his cheek and despite the turmoil of the past hour, he felt his body quicken.

As he raised his head in search of her mouth, he felt the boat bump against the dock.

Liveried servants holding torches were waiting for them as they disembarked.

Arm in arm they walked along a graveled path that led to a wrought iron fence behind which lay a small, pretty building painted a light blue color. To the right of the house, she could see the garden, its paths edged by slender poplar trees.

"I bought this villa years ago because I wanted something that belonged to me alone, not to all the Zeanis. Foolish and vain perhaps, but—" He shrugged.

At the doors of the villa, the majordomo, his shoulders stooped, bowed deeply at their approach.

"We were not expecting you back so soon, Don Luca."

Luca smiled at the old man's forgetfulness. Poor Paolo, he thought. He had already been an old man when his father had still been alive. He would have to see that someone else was hired to do any actual work.

The spacious entry of the villa was cool, but it was not the temperature that made Chiara shiver.

"Do you wish to dine, Don Luca?" the old retainer asked.

"Have something brought to my chambers, Paolo." He gave the old man a friendly pat on the shoulder. "Have you been well? Do you still keep those fish I always liked in the pond?"

"I thought you had forgotten, Don Luca." The servant beamed. "You did not mention them before."

Luca gave him another pat and steered Chiara toward his chamber.

The old man hurried forward to light their way. He threw open the double doors with their gilt molding and bowed again as Luca and Chiara passed him.

Chiara stepped over the threshold and stopped so suddenly that she almost lost her balance.

The pervasive stench of evil—evil she recognized all too well—drove the nausea into her throat.

"No," she whispered. "I cannot."

"What is it, Chiara?" Luca asked, concerned at her sudden pallor. "What's wrong?"

"Take me away from here." She shook her head wildly. "Take me away."

He had heard and seen too much today. He picked Chiara up in his arms, horrified to find her trembling.

"Light the way to one of the guest apartments, Paolo."

The old man scurried forward to obey.

Luca sat in an armchair, Chiara still curled in his lap. A fire had been lit, the bed made, the servants dismissed. She had long stopped trembling and now she was so still that he thought she might have fallen asleep.

How was she going to explain it to him? Chiara asked herself. She had already told him much today and asked him to believe it. How was she going to make him believe all that she had yet to tell him?

"Luca?"

"I thought you were asleep."

He waited for her to speak, but when she did not, he stroked a hand over her hair. "Can you tell me what happened? What was wrong before?"

"There is so much I haven't told you."

He tilted her face up to his. "Then tell me now."

She looked long into his eyes. Perhaps he was ready, she thought. Perhaps he would believe.

"The day I fell down the stairs I saw him. The man with your face."

He stiffened. "Where?"

"In your apartments. He opened the door and looked at me. Spoke to me. Reached for me." Her voice dropped to an almost inaudible whisper. "And I felt the evil." She began to tremble again. "Then suddenly he was gone. When I saw you on the stairs, I thought he had come back. That's why I fought you as I did."

He shook his head. "I'm trying to understand, to believe you, but this is—" He gestured helplessly.

"I know." She spread a hand on his chest. "But I finally understood that there were two men with the same face.

"I stole this from your room." She dug into her purse and showed him the ring. "To make a spell. To free myself of you. The man of evil was wearing the same ring. Much later I finally understood that if there were two rings, there had to be two men.

"And the evil I felt that day is the same evil I felt

when I stepped into your chamber just now.'' Shifting so that their faces were level, she gripped the front of his shirt. "He was here. Do you understand, Luca? He was here. And he means you harm.'' She closed her eyes for a moment, gathering strength. "Do you believe me?''

For a long time Luca looked into her eyes. He was a rational man and yet— Suddenly he remembered old Paolo's words and realized their meaning. And he understood that Chiara spoke the truth.

"Yes,'' he said. "Yes, I do.'' He laughed shortly. "And I see that Matteo has played yet another trick on me.''

"And yet there is more.''

"No more.'' He pulled her closer. "Not tonight.''

"But it is important. It—''

"Please, Chiara, I have heard too much today.''

Rising with her in his arms, he set her down at one side of the wide, canopied bed.

"I need to sleep,'' he said as he passed a hand over his face. "Perhaps things will be clearer in the light.'' He feathered his knuckles over her cheek. "Good night.''

Chiara undressed, aware of Luca's every move. But he seemed to pay her no mind and she wondered if what she had told him had made him despise her.

It was a long time before she slept.

Chapter Twenty-One

Chiara awoke at first light with a start, all that had happened the day before flooding over her. But that first little burst of panic was immediately quieted by the solid warmth of Luca's body at her back.

So he had turned to her in the night. A smile full of woman's secrets curved her mouth. Perhaps she was only his mistress, she thought, but he needed her enough to turn to her in the night. Whatever tomorrow might bring, she still had today. She shifted back, cuddling more firmly against him.

Luca awoke slowly, his mind dull with the memory of all Chiara had told him last night. But that was quickly wiped from his mind as he became aware of the press of Chiara's body against his.

"Good morning." He nuzzled her hair aside and tasted his way up her neck to her ear.

The touch of his lips and tongue along the rim of her ear had a luscious ache blossoming between her thighs. The ache that she remembered from the day before. She pressed her thighs together, the movement shifting her derriere against Luca's already aroused sex.

He groaned, his teeth closing lightly on the fleshy part of her ear.

Chiara felt the ache intensify. "Luca?" she whispered.

"Yes, love?"

Again she felt the little catch in her heart at the endearment spoken so easily.

"What is it?" he coaxed. His arm, which was slung around her waist, loosened and his hand shifted upward to cup her breast.

With a moan, she arched upward to meet him, her movement freeing his erection so that it slipped between her thighs.

They both stilled. Luca, because he was afraid that he had frightened her. Chiara because the slide of his body against her dampening flesh had the ache spiraling still higher.

Slowly Luca pulled back, but, unwilling to let him go, Chiara tightened around him.

"Chiara," Luca whispered. "Tell me that you are not frightened."

"Does it feel as if I'm frightened?" She pushed back against him until he was again cradled fully between her thighs.

Luca's laugh ended on a moan of pleasure. "No, but last night I—" He remembered wondering if thoughts of her sister's rape had somehow insinuated themselves into their lovemaking. "Later," he whispered. "I will tell you about it later." Now he wanted no intrusions.

He slid the shift that had already ridden up to her waist still farther.

"Raise your arms, *cara.*"

She obeyed and he lifted the shift away.

Chiara started to turn to face him, but he slid both arms around her. He was unwilling to give up the warm nest her thighs had made for his arousal, and desperate for the feel of her skin against his. He pressed an openmouthed kiss into the curve between neck and shoulder.

The slide of skin against skin inflamed her, made her want. Needing to touch him, she curled her hands around his.

Again Luca traced that path up to her ear with his mouth.

"Show me," he whispered.

She shivered at the caress of his breath on her ear. "Show you what?"

"Show me what you want. Show me where you want me to touch you."

His seductive whisper feathered over her skin as if he were already caressing her.

"Go ahead," he urged. "Show me."

Heat suffused her, but the temptation was too great. Obeying, she slowly moved their joined hands toward her breasts.

"Like this?" He covered her breasts with his hands. "Or like this?" Slowly, deliberately, he flicked his thumbs over the already aroused crests.

"Yes." Her mind already clouding with passion, she breathed the word on a sigh.

"And then?"

She hesitated, but the need that had bloomed within her made it easy to be bold. Their hands still linked, she lowered them toward her center.

The first teasing touch had her stilling, but only for a moment. Then she began to move, ever quicker, ever more urgently, rocking against his caressing fingers, against his aroused flesh as he pushed her inexorably toward the peak.

He was driving her mad, she thought, for surely it was madness to be ablaze with needs so lavish that they drove her to such wantonness. And yet she was unable to stop as he drove her higher and higher still.

Needing more, she reached to touch his hand, to urge him on, but instead her fingers brushed his sex. He groaned, but when she would have jerked her hand away, he brought it back.

"Again. Please."

Again she touched him, reveling in her own pleasure, reveling in her power to give it.

All too aware of his own limits, Luca suddenly pulled back. But before she could protest, he turned onto his back and lifted Chiara to lie above him.

She could not stop moving, her unschooled body ravenous yet unsure how to feed the hunger.

Reaching up, Luca hooked his hands behind her knees so that she straddled him. When he lifted her and fitted her body to his, he barely controlled the urge to arch his spine and fill her. Then his hands skimmed upward to cup her hips, but only for a moment before he lowered them to lie at his sides.

Chiara looked down at Luca and understood that he was surrendering to her the power to take, the power to give. Bending forward, she framed his face with her hands. Then, her mouth on his, her eyes on his, she slid down and took him inside her.

Later, much later, they lay, their limbs still intertwined, weak with pleasure taken, pleasure given.

He wanted to give her promises, Luca realized with a start of surprise. All his life he had found the custom forbidding him to marry because another brother had been chosen to perpetuate the Zeani name, a gift that guaranteed his freedom. But now, for the first time in his life, he found that he wanted to bind himself to a woman. To Chiara.

But what could he offer her, he thought, when he did not know what lay in store for him? In a few weeks or days he could be dead or in the dungeons above or below the Doge's palace.

All the things Chiara had told him yesterday came tumbling through his mind like leaves driven by the wind. If it was true that Matteo lived, if Chiara had truly seen Matteo in his rooms, if Matteo had been here at the villa pretending to be him…his thoughts stumbled as he remembered how the mocking laugh of the man in the black-and-gold mask had reminded him of his brother. If the masked man and Matteo were one, then— He shook his head. No, he thought. That was too much. It could not be.

Chiara lay, her cheek against Luca's chest, listening to his heartbeat, which was only now slowing after the passion they had shared. She felt him shift and raised her head to look at him. He was staring up at the canopy of the bed and she knew that he was far away.

"Are you certain, Chiara?"

She did not consciously link with him, but the link was there nevertheless.

"Yes." She nodded, needing no further explanation. It was a tangled web of thoughts within him, but she knew that she could not help him. She could only warn and hope that he heeded her warning.

"Luca." She shifted and gripped his shoulders.

"Remember what I told you about the man in the black-and-gold mask. He is a destroyer."

He sat up and tunneled his fingers through his hair, his movement dislodging her hands. Perhaps she was right, he thought. Perhaps Matteo lived. Perhaps the man in the mask and Matteo were one.

But even if that were so, he could not believe that Matteo would purposely do him harm. There was too much love between them for that. No matter what old rivalries, old hatreds lay between them, the love they had shared would weigh more.

They stood side by side, hand in hand as the *burchiello* was towed across the lagoon toward the city, which was wreathed in fog. As they approached the dock, the shapes and colors of San Marco and the Doge's palace were barely visible and the figures on land snaked in and out of the mist like ghosts.

Already, Chiara thought, she could feel him slipping away from her.

Tommaso approached them as they stepped off the boat, unable to hide his grin, and Chiara quickly lowered her gaze. This is what she would need to become accustomed to, she thought—the knowing smiles, the whispers.

She turned to take her bundle from one of the boatmen and when she turned back, she saw that Luca had been pulled aside by a cloaked figure wearing a white beaked mask.

Before she could focus on the man, Luca returned to where she stood.

"Tommaso will take you back to the Ca' Zeani."

He leaned down toward her, but his mouth barely

brushed her cheek and she saw that his eyes were shining with excitement.

"Luca—"

"We will speak later, *cara*."

One more touch and he was gone, his step buoyant with eagerness.

Chiara watched him disappear into the mist with dread in her heart. He had listened to her, she thought, but he had not heard her.

She did not know how long she stood there staring after him. When Tommaso touched her arm, she jumped.

"Do not worry, *signorina*. He will not betray you." He shook his head. "I have never seen him look at a woman as he looks at you."

He grinned at her, but, she realized with surprise, there was no contempt there, but approval.

"I have known Don Luca many years, but even that first evening—" He clapped his wide, rough hand against his heart and raised his eyes heavenward. "Come now." Taking her bundle from her, he put his hand on her elbow to guide her toward his gondola. "I will keep you safe for him."

Luca hurried at the side of the man who had been sent for him. Chiara's warnings were not forgotten, but the excitement pushed them to the very edges of his awareness. He was a man, after all, and he could not let a woman's words make a coward of him.

"What are the plans?" he demanded. "Does it begin soon?"

"I know nothing," the man said. "I was only sent to fetch you." He turned his head so that he could look at Luca through the eye openings of the mask.

"He was not pleased to learn that you had left the city."

"I am not his servant." Luca felt a flash of irritation. "Does he expect us to wait upon his pleasure if he tells us nothing?"

"We are less than his servants," the man said. His voice trembled a little and he ducked his chin into the collar of his cloak. "We are his tools to use or to discard."

A *traghetto,* one of the ferry gondolas, took them across the canal. They walked quickly through the warren of alleys behind the church of St. Barnaba until Luca's companion guided them into a courtyard. He knocked, three short raps, on a ramshackle door.

The door opened and Luca stepped inside, hardly noticing that his companion had melted away into the mist and that he was now alone.

The dank room smelled of mold and fear. As his eyes slowly grew accustomed to the dim light, he saw that the only other person in the room was the man in the black-and-gold mask.

"Where were you?"

Luca concentrated on the voice, but it was muffled behind the mask and he could not be sure. "My life is my own." He made no attempt to keep the annoyance out of his voice. "I answer to no one."

The masked man was silent for a long moment before he spoke again. "Have you changed your mind?" He fingered the dagger at his waist. He did not want to use it, but he would if he had to. "Are you no longer with us?"

"I am here am I not?" Luca demanded. "Besides,

if you know me as well as you say you do, you know that I am a man of my word.''

"Good. It pleases me to hear that, Luca Zeani." He put his gloved hand on Luca's arm. "It begins tomorrow at dusk. Each man already has his orders."

"And mine?"

"We meet at the end of the Riva dei Schiavoni, you and I."

"And then?"

"All is prepared. Within two hours the Doge's palace will be ours."

"Why do you need me?" Luca flared, his disappointment turning to anger. "I have done nothing."

"I have told you. Your task will come tomorrow." He paused. "And thereafter." He laughed softly.

The sound of the masked man's laugh had a shiver coursing down Luca's spine. He had discounted it before, but now—

"Who are you?" he whispered.

"I've told you. I am the man who will make you famous in the annals of Venetian history."

"Damn it, who are you?" Luca shouted and, lunging forward, gripped the black-and-gold mask and ripped it away.

It was with mixed feelings that Chiara watched the metal gate of the Ca' Zeani open. Now she was truly stepping into the cage of her own free will, she thought as the gondola slipped into the dim entry.

Luca felt something for her. She knew that. But how deep were his feelings? How lasting? That she did not know. But she knew that her feelings were as deep, as lasting as the sea. And wasn't that what counted in the end? She repeated those words to herself as she mounted the slippery steps.

The old retainer, who guarded the entry, stood at the door and, as she neared, he raised an arm to block her way.

"You cannot enter."

"What do you mean?" Tommaso moved past her and pushed the old man aside. "Don Luca bade me bring the *signorina* here."

"I have my orders from Don Alvise and the *signora.*"

"Are you mad, old man? Don Luca will have your head."

"I give the orders here." Alvise's somber voice sounded from just beyond the doorway. "And her presence here has offended me and my wife long enough."

"Yes, enough." Emilia's shrill voice joined his. "Indeed, I have had a priest come to bless with holy water the chamber desecrated by the Gypsy witch."

Chiara flinched as if she had been struck. She had seen a Gypsy woman once who had been accused of witchcraft and questioned. She had seen the scars and burns that the woman would carry all her life. She would not allow her child's soul to be subjected to this.

She pressed her hands against her middle as the sudden knowledge spread through her. Although the thought brought an edge of panic, the joy was greater. They had made a child between them. A child of love. Whatever happened, she would always know that this child had been made with love.

"No," Tommaso blustered, "Don Luca will not allow the *signorina* to be treated such."

Chiara put her hand on his arm and tugged him back. "Let us go, Tommaso."

"But—"

She drew herself up very straight. "I will not stoop to a tussle on a doorstep."

"How dare you?" Emilia hissed. "You Gypsy bastard."

"Yes, I am a Gypsy and illegitimate," she said softly, but there was nothing submissive about her tone. "But my mother was the daughter of a chieftain. My father was Marco Paradini." Her head high, she looked first at Emilia, then at Alvise. "There are princes with lineage less noble."

She turned around and carefully made her way down the steps.

As the gondola glided back out onto the canal, Chiara felt the world around her darken to a murky blur. The image rose of Luca and the other man with his face, entwined in battle and she felt the danger as one feels the nearing of a thunderstorm.

When she surfaced from the vision, she saw that Tommaso was looking at her with devotion and respect.

"Where do you wish me to take you, *signorina?*"

"We must look for Don Luca, Tommaso. Can you think where we might find him? Where do you take him when he goes out in the evenings?"

"I do not think—"

She reached up to where he stood on the stern of the gondola and gripped his ankle. "We must find him. We must."

Tommaso nodded and began to row toward San Barnaba.

* * *

The mask of black and gold splintered in Luca's hands and he stared into the man's face, feeling as if someone had driven a fist into his middle.

"Matteo." His whisper was barely audible.

"Yes," Matteo said defiantly, even as he fought back the panic.

"She was right. She told me you were not dead." Luca fought for air as his throat seemed to close. If she was right in this, was she right in the other?

"Who? Your little Gypsy wh—"

"Do not insult her." Luca raised a fisted hand.

He should have killed her, Matteo thought bitterly. He should have taken his knife and slit her pretty throat.

"So that is the way of it." Matteo's smile was sly. "You have found someone to love more than you loved poor Antonia."

The sudden flash of panic turned Luca's blood to ice. Chiara. He had to keep Chiara safe. He moved his shoulders as if to shrug away his brother's words. "Why have you come back after all these years? After making us believe you were dead?"

Matteo saw the fear in his brother's eyes and almost smiled. It would be so easy, because his only thought would be to protect his little whore. Almost too easy.

"To pay you back."

"Revenge, Matteo?" He made a tired gesture. "Believe me, the guilt that has gnawed at me is revenge enough. Even for you."

"Revenge? No, Luca." Relaxed now, he leaned against the rickety table that held the single candle that lit the room.

"I have not had an easy life these seven years. But I have learned much and become a man far different from the man I was." Stepping forward, Matteo held out his hand and smiled. "I have come to repay you, not to take revenge."

As Luca stared at his brother's sweet smile, all of Chiara's warnings slipped from his mind. This moment all hatred was forgotten and all he remembered was the love.

He stepped forward and clasped Matteo's hand.

Chapter Twenty-Two

"Luca!" Chiara scrambled out of the gondola unaided and dashed across the small square.

Surprised, Luca paused for a split second, then began to run toward her.

"What is it?" He gripped her shoulders, almost lifting her off the ground. "What's wrong? What has happened?"

Chiara's hands went to his waist to steady herself. "Are you all right?" The words rushed out on one urgent breath because she could sense the other man's evil that swirled around Luca like a faint but persistent smell.

"What are you doing here?" His hands tightened. "Answer me."

"Looking for you." Dread filled her heart as she saw how his eyes shone. These were the eyes of a man who had witnessed a miracle. Hope withered and died as she understood that there was nothing she could say that would make him see the truth.

"Why?"

Tommaso had reached them and, when Chiara did

not answer, he spoke. "Your brother and his wife turned the *signorina* away from the doorstep."

"They did what?" His eyes narrowed. "Damn them, I will not stand for this."

She swayed as the image came to her abruptly, without warning. The reflection of shimmering torchlight on water. Luca surrounded by men whose hands bristled with weapons. The other one fading away into the shadows, a laugh on his lips.

Luca saw her eyes grow blank, but only for a moment. Then she was looking at him again.

"No," Chiara said softly. "Don't fight them."

The gentle sadness in her tone caught his attention far more than temper would have. "What did they say to you to make you like this?"

"They?" She shook her head, remembering the image she had seen. It would be soon, she thought. Too soon. "It does not signify."

"Come. I will take you back. They will not defy me."

"No." Her voice rose as she grew suddenly desperate. She knew she could not turn him from his path. No matter what he felt for her, no matter how great the power she had over him was, she had no power to turn him away from this. She would not waste time with useless quarrels. "My brother has given me the key to his lodgings. Let us go there instead."

Luca frowned. "There are enough other places we could go if you do not wish to return to the Ca' Zeani."

"Please." How could she explain to him that when he had gone to his fate, she needed to be with someone who would not despise her?

"All right." He nodded, but his expression made it clear that he was not pleased. "We will do as you wish."

The house on the Rio dei Greci was small and far more respectable than Luca would have expected from a man whose livelihood was gambling and women.

A plump, merry-eyed woman opened the door for them and led the way up the narrow staircase whose wooden steps were scuffed but scrupulously clean.

"The *signorina* is not the first to claim to be Signor Renzo's sister." She chuckled as she knocked on the door. "But the first one I've believed. You have the same eyes." She knocked again. "You have company, Signor Renzo."

"Go away, Maddalena." The voice was muffled. "Let me sleep."

"Your sister is here, *signore*. Your true sister."

There were sounds of movement beyond the door and within a few moments the door opened.

Incongruously dressed in a simple linen shirt and breeches of fine ivory satin, Renzo ran both hands through long, dark brown hair that was tousled around his shoulders, as he eyed his visitors.

"Have you tired of her already?" His eyebrows raised in a sardonic curve, he gauged Luca.

"Damn you—"

"Please." Conscious of the landlady, who was listening with obvious interest, Chiara put a hand on each man's arm. "Can we come in?"

Stepping back, Renzo gestured them inside. "Maddalena, my treasure, if you bring us some coffee, I will be eternally grateful."

The older woman giggled. "How can an old woman refuse such a charming rascal anything?"

"That's what I'm counting on." Renzo laughed and, closing the door, leaned back against it. "Something must be very wrong, if you enter the lodgings of a man such as me, Don Luca."

"I am here because Chiara asked that we come here."

"Please," Chiara said, looking from one to the other. "There are reasons why I do not wish to stay at the Ca' Zeani. Can I—we stay here until—" she looked at Luca "—until when, Luca?"

She knew, Luca realized with a start as he looked into her eyes that were huge and moist with unshed tears. Somehow she knew that the time was almost here.

"Until tomorrow afternoon," he said, not taking his eyes from hers.

Renzo watched them carefully with his sharp gambler's gaze. Whatever was happening here, he admitted grudgingly, they were both in pain.

"My humble abode is at your disposal, Chiara, for as long as you need it." He laughed lightly. "It is not difficult for me to find another bed to sleep in."

There was a knock and Maddalena bustled in, carrying a tray with coffee and small pastries.

"Thank you." Renzo sent his landlady a brilliant smile. "My sister and her—companion will be staying here for a while. Will you change the bed linens and make some order here?"

"Of course." Maddalena bobbed a curtsy. "I will get what I need and start right away."

The minute she was out of the room, Luca turned on Renzo. "Aren't you going to ask what's going on?'' he demanded. "She's your sister, for God's sake.''

"He's not my keeper, Luca, and neither are you,'' Chiara flared. "Besides, we are barely more than strangers.''

"And yet you insisted on coming here.''

"Perhaps because blood is thicker than water.'' Chiara shrugged. "But then you would know about that, wouldn't you?'' The tears rose to her eyes so suddenly that she had no time to blink them back.

Uncomfortable with the level of emotion in the room, Renzo went into his bedchamber and closed the door behind him.

"Chiara, you don't understand.'' Luca gathered her into his arms. "You were right that Matteo lives, but you were wrong about him.''

"I do not judge your brother solely by some image in my mind. I judge him by what I have seen.''

Luca shook his head. "He's learned, he's changed.''

"You saw Donata. Is what he did to her the action of a man on the path of good?'' she demanded fiercely, forgetting for a moment that she knew she stood no chance of convincing him.

"Perhaps you were mistaken, love. And if you were not, I tell you, he is different now.'' His eyes shone with love. "He believes in this.''

She sighed and touched a finger to his lips to silence him. Perhaps these next twenty-four hours would be all that she would have left with him. She refused to have this time spoiled by useless argument. Still she could not control the tears that kept spilling from her eyes.

Renzo emerged from the bedchamber, fashionably

dressed, cloak over his arm, his mask dangling from his fingers. *"Addio."* He sent them an ironic salute with his tricorn. "I leave my nest to the lovebirds."

"There is something I need to do tonight." Luca rose. "Would you stay with Chiara until I return?"

"Where are you going?" Chiara felt a spurt of panic and reached out to grab his sleeve. "Don't go."

"There is something I have to do." He stroked a hand down her cheek. "For you, love."

"Then stay."

"I will be back in an hour. Two at the most. I need to do this." When she still clung to him, he curved his hands around her shoulders. "Please."

This was a man who seldom asked. A man to whom gentleness did not come easy. Yet he had given her what he could. She nodded and let him go.

He was back within the hour.

"I would ask another favor of you," he said as he stood at the door with Renzo. "I have an—" he looked Renzo directly in the eyes "—engagement tomorrow afternoon at dusk. Would you keep Chiara company?"

"All right." Renzo nodded, understanding the message that passed from man to man.

"There is money there," he said softly, indicating a small satchel he had set down near the door. "Just in case."

Renzo nodded again. "She will be all right. I will see to it."

When the door had closed behind Renzo, Luca returned to sit beside Chiara where she sat curled in the corner of a sofa.

"Aren't you going to ask me where I've been?" He tried to inject a bantering tone into his voice, but her eyes were so full of sadness that his tone turned flat.

She shook her head. "I don't want to speak of anything." Throwing back the coverlet that Renzo had wrapped around her, she slid across the shabby velvet to Luca's side. "Not anything." With a gesture that spoke of desperation, she reached up to tug his head down to hers.

"Are you sure?" He resisted her attempt and instead, lifted her to his lap, settling her so that she straddled him. "Should I not tell you that I love you?"

Her eyes filled and overflowed before she could do anything to stop her tears.

"Don't cry, love." He reached up to wipe her tears away with his fingers. "Everything will be all right. Believe me."

But instead of comforting her, his words only made the tears come more swiftly.

"How could it be anything other, when I spent the past hour arranging for our marriage?"

"What?" She stilled completely, almost forgetting to breathe. A wave of joy engulfed her, but it ebbed quickly as she remembered. "You cannot. I know the laws of Venice. I heard them often enough from my father."

"Precisely, *cara*, your father. His name was in the Golden Book. So it will be possible to gain permission, in time. I have instructed an *avvocato* to do what is necessary."

She shook her head. "But what about your brother?"

"I have told Alvise. It is time that he admitted that his wife is barren. We will marry, love, and we will make children together." He put his palm on her belly. "And the Zeani name will live."

She saw the joy in his eyes and the words rose to her tongue. Perhaps then he would not go tomorrow, she thought. If she told him she knew that already his child, his son, was growing inside her, perhaps he would not go. She almost told him then. But she did not.

He would stay then, she realized. He would be safe. But she would lose him nevertheless, for he would never forgive her for keeping him from what he viewed as a matter of honor.

So she seized the moment and pressed her lips to his.

The next day was gray and misty and dusk came early. As Luca readied himself to leave, his hands were steady although nerves quivered in the pit of his stomach. This was not the first time he had readied himself for battle, Luca thought. But it was the first time that he was going into battle completely blind, with no plans, no strategy of his own. For the first time in his life, he was putting himself entirely into the hands of another. In Matteo's hands.

And for the first time, he was leaving behind a woman he loved. He found that he had underestimated how difficult it would be to do that.

They had not spoken of it, but when the moment came to say goodbye, they parted as lightly as if they would meet again in an hour. Luca only brushed his mouth over Chiara's. She touched him briefly but did not cling. It was as if that casual parting could guarantee that they would be together again and soon.

Luca ran down the narrow staircase, but he stopped before he had reached the bottom of the stairs. He had to tell her, he thought. He had to tell her one more time how much he loved her. He had to remind her one more time that he would always love her—so much that someday she would forget how harsh he had been with her in those first days.

As he turned on the stairs, he saw that she had stepped just beyond the doorway and held her arms outstretched, hands crossed, palm outward to stop him.

"Do not turn back," she said, her voice urgent. "It brings ill fortune to return once you are on the road." She lowered her hands and her mouth curved in a smile. "I have heard you."

They exchanged one more long look and then Luca was gone.

"Are you all right?" Renzo asked softly, and put his hands on her shoulders.

Instead of an answer, Chiara shoved him aside and darted back through the door. She snatched up her cloak and quickly stuck the dagger that Maddalena had acquired for her into the waistband of her skirt.

"Just what do you think you're doing?" Renzo demanded, and grabbed her arm as she ran past him. "Where are you going?"

"Let me go!" she shouted as she tried to twist out of his grip. "Let me go or come with me."

"No, you can't go after him. I won't let you."

"I must." She fought against his hands, her desperation making her strong.

Breaking away, she dashed through the open door and down the stairs. Renzo was a few steps behind her.

Chapter Twenty-Three

Luca walked quickly through the narrow streets, but he did not take the direct route, which would have brought him to the meeting place in minutes. Instead, a vague sense of unease tugging at him, he took the roundabout way that brought him east to the *arsenale,* the shipyard.

They had spoken of enlisting the aid of the *arsenalotti,* the shipyard workers, who for much of Venice's history had been firefighters, guards and a sort of militia all in one. Privately he did not believe they could be successful without them.

He slipped past the two lions who guarded the entrance. The smell of pitch was strong here and he could hear far off sounds of sawing and hammering. Hope rose at the approach of loud voices, but a group of workers pushed past him arguing about a game of dice and which *malvasia* would get their custom that evening.

Just in case, he crossed over to the double columns of the Tana, where the hemp ropes were made, but there was no sign of anyone gathering for the work they had planned for this night. A sound behind him had him stiffening and he turned to see two cloaks disappearing between the columns.

He took a few steps in their direction, thinking to investigate, but then he heard a woman's whisper. It was just a couple looking for some privacy, he thought, and with a shrug, he turned toward the quay.

Luca had been trained as a warrior from the time he was a boy, when his father had decreed that he was more suited for the Venetian navy than for the family spice business and he had never had occasion to doubt his courage. But he doubted it now as he walked among the carnival revelers, who made their way toward the piazza, eager for yet another night of pleasure.

He kept waiting for some sign of the fighting men Matteo had promised, but he saw none. The quay was no more crowded than it normally was and he found his steps slowing as doubts surfaced, obscuring the hopes he had cherished.

Chiara had put the doubts there, he thought. But no. He had felt doubts and spoken them at the conspirators' very first meeting on that dark *campo*. It was not she who had put the doubts in his head. They had been there from the beginning, but he had ignored them, because his need to *do* something had been so great. Because the masked man, because Matteo had been so persuasive.

But it was Chiara who made it difficult now to keep the promises he had made. He stopped on his way up the steps of a bridge and watched the lights winking on, on the islands of San Giorgio and the Giudecca.

Chiara had not tried to dissuade him, but he had seen the anguish in her eyes. And it was that silent anguish that had asked nothing of him that slowed his steps now. It would have been easier, he realized, if she had begged him. But she had not.

He must not think of her, he admonished himself. If he thought of her now, it would make him weak. So he took the steps of the last bridge quickly, determined not to allow her to rule him, but she was still there, an image branded on his mind.

At the crest of the bridge he stopped and looked down at the quay. A group of men was there. Some were standing still, some milling about aimlessly as revelers with jests and songs on their lips strolled past them. It was precisely the group that had met on the shabby side of Venice for the past weeks, he realized. There were no shipyard workers ready for a brawl. They had brought no fighting men, not even a few mercenaries.

What was going on? Was this a trick? he wondered. Had Matteo planned this as a huge farce to make fun of him? To humiliate him? To—for the first time he allowed the thought to form in his mind—kill him?

Luca had always done what he felt he had to, without much thought to the consequences for himself. But now, suddenly, life had become infinitely precious and he shifted back, ready to turn and retrace his steps.

Just at that moment, he saw the figure slip out of the doorway and, although today he wore the same mask they all did, something within him recognized Matteo. The figure stopped and looked up to where Luca stood at the crest of the bridge.

In his heart Luca felt something move in welcome and he walked down the steps toward his brother.

* * *

Chiara knelt in the shadow of the wide balustrade of the bridge, Renzo at her side. Just for a moment, the link with Luca was strong and she felt his doubts. Her determination to let Luca do what he must was suddenly forgotten and she quickly murmured a verse in Romany, a spell to turn him from his path. But beneath his doubts, she felt his determination and knew that her spell was powerless.

"How can you be so sure that his brother will betray him?" Renzo whispered. "You said yourself that blood is thicker than water."

"Have you ever seen evil, Renzo? True evil?" She glanced at him briefly before she returned her gaze to where Luca stood. "Not the weak imitation of evil that was our father, or the casual cruelty of your mother, but true evil born of the darkness?" She continued before he could answer. "I have." She shivered. "I have seen that evil in the eyes of Luca's brother."

Then she saw Luca move forward and she began to mount the stairs of the bridge.

As Luca walked down the bridge stairs, he watched Matteo move to stand in the circle of light from one of the lamps and for a moment strip off his glove so that the scar on his left hand was visible. Immediately the men, who waited on the quay, fell into a semicircle around Matteo like well-trained animals.

Again he felt reluctance slowing his steps, but he pushed it aside. The time for doubts was past. The time had come to act.

They clasped each other's arm in greeting.

"Where are the men you spoke of?" Luca asked,

keeping his voice low. "Do you think to take over the city with this paltry handful of men?"

"What do you think I have been doing for weeks?" Matteo poked an elbow into Luca's side as if he had just made a joke. "It is all arranged."

"What is arranged? I relish a fair fight as much as the next man, but I have no wish to be a sacrificial lamb."

"Doubts, my brother?" Matteo laughed softly. "Fears?" he added insidiously.

"Caution. I have no wish to die today." A quick smile flashed beneath his mask. "Or any day soon."

Matteo saw his brother's smile and felt the old envy gnaw at him. But he quickly reminded himself that today he had no need to be envious. Today it was *his* turn.

"Do not fear." He clapped Luca's shoulder with his gloved hand. "The men who guard the Doge's palace are ours. No one will die today." Then he motioned to the group of men to follow them and they set off down the quay.

"What are you going to do?" Renzo grasped Chiara's hand as they descended the bridge steps. "You can't mean to go with them."

"I do." Snatches of images constantly assaulted her and her voice was grim. "If there is any chance to save him, I must take it."

"You're mad. I won't let you do this." Before she could escape him, he pulled her close. "I've wanted a family all my life," he said with a quiet desperation. "I won't lose you now."

"I love him," she said quietly. "He is my fate." His arms loosened and he took a step back. "You don't have to come with me, Renzo. This is not your fight.''

The group of men began to move in the direction of the Doge's palace. When Chiara turned and slipped into place with them, Renzo was at her side.

Swiftly, silently, they strode along the quay, their determined pace at odds with those who sauntered in search of pleasure. Suddenly Chiara stumbled and went down on one knee.

Renzo immediately bent to help her up and she found herself needing to lean against him with her full weight as all the strength drained out of her.

'''E fatto,'' she murmured. ''It is done.''

''What? What is—''

Before Renzo had a chance to finish his question, the quay exploded into chaos as the palace guards in the bronze helmets and short red cloaks that they had worn for centuries stormed over the bridge toward them, their weapons drawn.

In that first moment when Luca saw the palace guards rushing down the marble steps toward them he stood perfectly still. He felt no fear, no despair, so paralyzed was he by the pain of betrayal.

''Now the score is even,'' Matteo hissed in his ear. ''And I have kept my promise to make you famous in the annals of Venetian history.'' He struck him on the back with the flat of his hand, sending him stumbling forward.

''Welcome, traitor,'' the captain of the guard said, and reached up to tear away Luca's mask.

The cool air that swept over Luca's unmasked face brought him out of the daze where Matteo's betrayal had plunged him. With a quick, subtle movement he shifted back, drew his sword and began to fight.

It was precisely the image she had seen. The flickering torches reflected in the water of the lagoon. Luca alone against the men with their weapons drawn.

Chiara saw Luca stumble forward and muffled a cry with her hand. Her eyes on him, she almost missed how the man who had shoved him forward shifted away with movements so subtle that he almost did not seem to be moving.

She slipped out of Renzo's grip. As she moved forward, she reached beneath her cloak for the dagger.

The evil wrapped itself around her throat like a rope, cutting off her breath, choking her so that she grew faint. For a moment her step faltered, but she reminded herself that she had a weapon against the evil now.

Drawing on the strength and light from the love that filled her heart, she moved directly into his path so that when he next took a graceful, sliding step, he backed straight into the point of her dagger.

"This is where it ends," she said. Keeping her dagger in contact with his body, she circled him so that they faced each other.

"Well, well, Luca's little whore comes to his defense," Matteo mocked. "What are you going to do, kill me?"

"Only if I have to."

"Don't make me laugh."

"I shed your blood once before." Hatred and the old need for revenge welled up within her. "I will not hesitate to do it again."

"What are you talking about?" he demanded roughly.

She reached up and pulled down her mask. The evil was still at her throat, even more strongly, now that her face was bared to his gaze, but she fought it, refusing to give in to it.

Gradually the evil retreated from her, taking with it the hatred that she had carried in her heart for so long, although at first she did not realize it.

"The scar on your left hand is from my knife. But that no longer matters." With a start she realized that what she said was the truth. "It no longer matters," she repeated.

"What matters now is Luca's life. Are you going to let him die because he trusted you too much?" She paused. "Loved you too much?"

"Loved me?" he spat. "Do you know what he did to me? All my life he was there. Luca. The brave one. The good son. The good brother. Everything I ever wanted he got. And when I finally took what was his for myself, he handed me over to the constables." His voice rose toward hysteria.

His eyes shone through the eyeholes of the mask like polished disks of obsidian. He was mad, Chiara realized. Had his own evil driven him to madness?

Suddenly he laughed. "Now I shall again take something of Luca's for myself." Shifting sideways, he brought the side of his hand down on Chiara's arm.

Chiara cried out in pain and although she managed to keep her grip on the knife, she knew that her advantage was lost.

* * *

Luca fought against the overwhelming odds with the strength of a man desperate to live.

The men who had come to this place with him had scattered or were watching his lonely fight with the fascination of rabbits in front of a snake.

Suddenly, above the clash of weapons, he heard a woman cry out. Chiara. His attention wavered, just for a moment. He lost his footing and found himself sprawled on the damp stones with the point of a sword at his neck.

The cry of triumph had both Chiara and Matteo looking to where Luca lay on the pavement.

"Please," Chiara whispered. "Don't let him die."

"I have been waiting for this moment for years." Matteo drew in a long, shuddering breath. "I will not give it up now."

"I beg you." She reached out and touched his arm. "Matteo. Let Luca live to see his son."

Matteo spun his head to stare at her. Something, perhaps her sea blue eyes brimming with tears, perhaps the love that filled her so completely that it surrounded her like a golden light, perhaps the fact that she had said his name so softly, so gently, touched him, penetrating the darkness that lived within him.

For a long moment he stood very still. Then, without a word, he turned to walk to where his brother lay.

"Stop." He lifted one hand palm outward. "He is innocent."

"Who are you?" the captain of the guard demanded.

Matteo reached up and took off his mask.

The captain blanched. "What? Who?" he sputtered.

"Matteo Zeani at your service." A suspicion of a smile touched his mouth as he sketched a bow.

"B-but Matteo Zeani is dead."

"It suited me to pretend so. I thought to revenge myself on my brother with this little farce, but I find that—" He paused and brushed his gaze over Luca before he looked back at the captain. "He knows nothing. I tricked him into coming here."

"I don't believe you. The inquisitors have sworn statements that—"

"That a man calling himself Luca Zeani has been planning a rebellion," Matteo finished. "That man is me." He shrugged. "It was easy to pretend to be my brother. Let him go."

The captain gave a sign to a guard who stepped back, allowing Luca to rise.

"And these men with you?" the captain demanded. "What of them?"

"Paid puppets." Matteo gestured disdainfully with one hand. "All of them."

"Matteo Zeani," the captain intoned, his voice taking on an almost festive cadence. "The inquisitors await you and your testimony."

Matteo ignored the captain as if he had not spoken. Instead he turned toward Luca.

For a moment the two brothers silently stood face-to-face. Then Matteo placed both hands on Luca's shoulders.

"All my life I wanted to be like you and I was the opposite. All my life I have loved you and I have hated you. But the hate was always greater than the love."

His mouth curved in an oddly sweet smile. "Now, for one single moment in time, I can love you more than I hate you." He gave Luca a small push and stepped back. "Go now." His gaze flickered over Luca's shoulder to where Chiara stood at the edge of the crowd. "And live for both of us."

"Matteo—" Luca began, but fell silent as his brother lifted his hand.

"If you can forgive me, do it, and if you can't—" A shadow of the old mockery flashed over Matteo's face. "If you can't, it doesn't matter. I will burn in hell with or without your forgiveness."

Then he turned and moved toward the *sbirri* who waited with their manacles and chains.

Chiara moved forward to stand at Luca's side and slipped her hand in his.

The quay emptied, quieted and even the revelers who reappeared from their hiding places were subdued.

"How did you do it?" Luca asked softly, sadly. "Did you make a spell?"

"Yes," Chiara answered, "but not the kind you mean."

Luca looked at her with questions in his eyes.

"My heart filled with love. So much love that there was no more room for hatred." She shook her head. "So much love that he felt it. And it made him remember that he loved you, too."

Luca pulled her close. "Come, love, let's go home."

Epilogue

The servants who had undressed her closed the door softly behind them. In her nightgown of linen that was fine enough to be almost sheer, Chiara sat propped up against the pillows and waited for her husband to come to her. Her husband.

Softly she spoke the word aloud into the silence of the bedchamber, still not quite believing that it was so. She had not initially believed Luca when he had told her that the authorities would recognize her as the daughter of a patrician so that she could become his wife. Even when she had seen the decree, sealed and stamped, she had not believed it. And when they had stood at the altar of the church this afternoon, it had not been real. She wondered if it would ever be truly real to her.

Tired—she tired easily these days—Chiara leaned her head back against the lace-trimmed pillows and closed her eyes. Within moments, her breathing had evened out in sleep.

Luca stepped into the bedchamber. Standing at the edge of the bed, he looked down at his wife. His wife.

Softly he spoke the word aloud into the silence of the bedchamber, still not quite believing that it was so. He had never thought he would have a wife. He had never wanted one.

But he had wanted Chiara to be his wife with such a passion that he had fought both the authorities and his elder brother with a single-mindedness that left no room for anything else. Even when the council had given him the men and ships he had asked for, there had been room for no more than a brief flash of triumph.

He wanted to spend his life with her, he had realized. He wanted to make children with her and he wanted them to be his heirs and not his bastards.

She was tired, he thought with a flurry of anxiety in his belly. Her skin was pale and there were lavender shadows beneath her eyes that never seemed to go away, no matter how much she slept.

Careful not to wake her, he slid into bed beside her.

Chiara surfaced from her light sleep the moment the bed dipped under Luca's weight. A smile already curving her mouth, she turned toward him.

"I'm sorry. I didn't mean to wake you." Although he wanted badly to touch her, he remained very still.

"I would not want to miss my wedding night." She shifted closer.

"You should sleep." He touched the bruised-looking skin beneath her eyes with a fingertip. "You're tired."

"Only a little." She caught his hand in hers and brought it to her mouth.

"Chiara—" he began, but she leaned closer and silenced him with a kiss.

His arousal was sharp and immediate. When she moved still closer so that her body was pressed against his, he stifled a moan of need. When she reached down to touch him in silent invitation, he was lost.

Schooling himself to slowness, he undid the ribbons of her nightgown, sliding the thin fabric down. When she was naked, he gazed down at her.

Her body had grown even more lush in the past months. Her breasts were heavier, her hips more pronounced. He slid his hand downward, mapping her curves. He spread his hand on her soft belly. "Do you think we will make a child tonight?"

She shook her head. "No, love." She smiled a little at his frown. "We already have." Putting her hand on top of his, she pressed it against her.

"What are you saying?" Panic and joy mingled within him.

"I'm saying that we have already made a child. The very first time you made love to me, you put a child inside me." Her lips curved in the secret little smile of pregnant women.

"How long have you known?" he demanded.

"I knew the next day."

"And you didn't tell me?" He drew back from her. "Why?"

"You did not need a further distraction."

"You should have told me." His voice sharpened. "What if things had turned out differently. I would never have known."

"If things had turned out differently and you had known," she said matter-of-factly, "you would have suffered even more." She reached out to pull him closer. "Are we going to argue about it on our wedding night?"

But he resisted her. "If you knew, how could you have put yourself in danger like that?"

She stroked her hand down the side of his face. "Because I love you."

He stared at her, humbled by her words. "Despite everything?" Catching her hand in his, he glanced down at her wrist, remembering how in his lust for her, he had bruised her skin. The guilt would be with him always, he thought.

"Luca, what is past can never be undone. You can torture yourself with it or you can let it go." She smiled. "I have."

"I love you, Chiara, and I swear to you that I will spend my life showing you how much."

"Starting now?" She smiled suggestively and pressed herself sinuously against him.

He slid his hands down her body. "Starting right now."

* * * * *

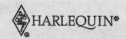

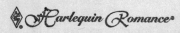

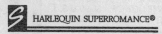

HARLEQUIN ULTIMATE GUIDES™

A series of how-to books for today's woman.

Act now to order some of these extremely
helpful guides just for you!

*Whatever the situation, Harlequin Ultimate Guides™
has all the answers!*

#80507	HOW TO TALK TO A NAKED MAN	$4.99 U.S. ☐ $5.50 CAN.☐
#80508	I CAN FIX THAT	$5.99 U.S. ☐ $6.99 CAN.☐
#80510	WHAT YOUR TRAVEL AGENT KNOWS THAT YOU DON'T	$5.99 U.S. ☐ $6.99 CAN.☐
#80511	RISING TO THE OCCASION More Than Manners: Real Life Etiquette for Today's Woman	$5.99 U.S. ☐ $6.99 CAN.☐
#80513	WHAT GREAT CHEFS KNOW THAT YOU DON'T	$5.99 U.S. ☐ $6.99 CAN.☐
#80514	WHAT SAVVY INVESTORS KNOW THAT YOU DON'T	$5.99 U.S. ☐ $6.99 CAN.☐
#80509	GET WHAT YOU WANT OUT OF LIFE—AND KEEP IT!	$5.99 U.S. ☐ $6.99 CAN.☐

(quantities may be limited on some titles)

TOTAL AMOUNT	$
POSTAGE & HANDLING	$
($1.00 for one book, 50¢ for each additional)	
APPLICABLE TAXES*	$ _____
TOTAL PAYABLE	$ _____

(check or money order—please do not send cash)

To order, complete this form and send it, along with a check or money
order for the total above, payable to Harlequin Ultimate Guides, to:
In the U.S.: 3010 Walden Avenue, P.O. Box 9047, Buffalo, NY
14269-9047; **In Canada:** P.O. Box 613, Fort Erie, Ontario, L2A 5X3.

Name: _____

Address: _____ City: _____

State/Prov.: _____ Zip/Postal Code: _____

*New York residents remit applicable sales taxes.
Canadian residents remit applicable GST and provincial taxes.

HARLEQUIN®

MEN at WORK

All work and no play?
Not these men!

July 1998
MACKENZIE'S LADY by Dallas Schulze

Undercover agent Mackenzie Donahue's
lazy smile and deep blue eyes were his best
weapons. But after rescuing—and kissing!—
damsel in distress Holly Reynolds, how could
he betray her by spying on her brother?

August 1998
MISS LIZ'S PASSION by Sherryl Woods

Todd Lewis could put up a building with ease,
but quailed at the sight of a classroom! Still,
Liz Gentry, his son's teacher, was no battle-ax,
and soon Todd started planning some
extracurricular activities of his own....

September 1998
A CLASSIC ENCOUNTER
by Emilie Richards

Doctor Chris Matthews was intelligent, sexy
and *very* good with his hands—which made
him all the more dangerous to single mom
Lizette St. Hilaire. So how long could she
resist Chris's special brand of TLC?

Available at your favorite retail outlet!

MEN AT WORK™

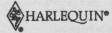 

Happy Birthday, Harlequin Historicals!

Now, after a decade of giving you the best in historical romance, LET US TAKE YOU BACK...

to a time when damsels gave their warriors something to fight for...ladies wooed dashing dukes from behind their fans...and cowgirls lassoed the hearts of rugged ranchers!

With novels from such talented authors as

Suzanne Barclay	Margaret Moore
Cheryl Reavis	Ruth Langan
Deborah Simmons	Cheryl St.John
Susan Spencer Paul	Theresa Michaels
Merline Lovelace	Gayle Wilson

Available at your favorite retail outlet.

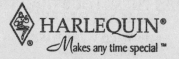

HARLEQUIN®
Makes any time special ™

Look us up on-line at: http://www.romance.net   HH10ANN

COMING NEXT MONTH FROM
HARLEQUIN HISTORICALS